The Cruise of the Jest

The Cruise of the Jest

Jon Adams

Slack Water Press
Los Gatos, California

To the Skipper and crew of the Schooner FAIRWEATHER, *1960—1965.*

Contents

CONTENTS

. . . the sea and the sky hold another world.

San Francisco

He was waiting to find out what Jack wanted him to do next. Jack told him to be on *Jest* at ten that morning. He didn't want to be early, so he was lying on his bed, listening to the radio. He was thinking that ten was an odd time. Usually when Jack wanted him to do something, it was more like six in the morning or eight in the evening, dawn or dusk. Back in the summer, the last time Jack told him to be on *Jest*, it had been eight in the evening. That was when Jack told him to sail *Jest* down to Half Moon Bay. Jack said he would be there, at the harbor in Half Moon Bay, waiting for him when he came in. But it hadn't happened that way.

He couldn't help going over that trip down to Half Moon Bay, trying to understand once more what he had done, as opposed to what Jack said he had done. The trip began with a warning. He was in the bow of *Jest*, casting off the forward mooring lines, and Jack was standing on the pier, looming above him in the weak evening light. That was a problem he still had, seeing Jack, massive and immobile, not as a man who was his father, but as a man who had learned the trick of surviving in an equatorial jungle and who was now, sixteen years later, playing that trick on him. "Remember," Jack told him, his voice filling the space between them, "pass Mile Rock to port." It wasn't actually advice, but rather a reminder of the mistake he once made on the *Astrolabe*, Jack's 56-foot ketch. He was at the helm when Jack told him to pass Mile Rock to port, and he almost ran the *Astrolabe* aground as he headed her in between the rocks and the coast. There had been a lot of yelling and confusion at the time, but the main confusion in his mind was how there could be two port sides, one for the *Astrolabe* and one for Mile Rock. And he had picked the wrong one.

So Jack telling him to "pass Mile Rock to port," as he was about to back *Jest* out of her berth in the Sausalito yacht harbor, was a warning not to do the sort of things he usually did when Jack told him to do something. He understood the warning, and at first, sailing *Jest* down to Half Moon Bay hadn't seemed so bad. He had the ebb and a light wind going out the Golden Gate, and once he left Mile Rock astern, he could see the lights of the Sunset District and, farther down the coast, those of Pacifica. He figured all he had to do was stay awake so that he didn't get run over by a freighter. But after he got about three miles off the coast, almost up to the number eight buoy of the main ship channel, the fog started to set in. He was afraid of the fog because of the freighters, but at the same time he didn't want to get too close to the coast. He was afraid of the coast, too. In the fog he was afraid of everything, so he headed farther west, outside of where he thought the shipping lane was. The next morning he couldn't see the coast, only the booms and bridge of a freighter, hull down, off the port bow. He felt a certain freedom then, away from everything, so he hove-to and went below to sleep. After he got up, late in the afternoon, he set sail again and headed in toward the coast. As the sun set behind him, he could see the light at Montara Point. He thought of trying for Half Moon Bay in the dark, if the fog didn't move in. But it did. So he headed back out to sea again. As long as he was in the fog he was afraid to leave the cockpit, so again he spent the night listening for foghorns. In the morning he hove-to again and went below to sleep. But this time when he woke up, Jack was there, sitting in the cockpit. Later he figured out that someone must have brought Jack out in a powerboat, a powerboat that didn't make much noise, but it was only much later still, before he was able to figure out how Jack knew where he was, how he found a 35-foot sailboat, hove-to off the coast of California.

"Bubba, what the hell are you doing way out here." It wasn't a question. "You're lucky I found you before you spent the rest of your life drifting around in the middle of the Pacific Ocean." He didn't really care what Jack said, because he felt that he hadn't done anything wrong or even anything particularly stupid. He hadn't wrecked the boat or anything, and he knew more or less where he was. His mistake, as he understood later, was not so much in forgetting that Jack would be watching him, for he knew Jack would be doing that, but in not realizing that Jack would be watching him so closely. He thought he could get to Half Moon Bay in his own good time. After all, Jack hadn't told him when to be there.

At first, as they headed toward the coast, Jack didn't do anything. He just sat in the hatchway, facing forward, and told him what to do, what course to steer and how to trim the sails. Then Jack turned to him, in his decisive manner, "Thousands of people have already led a better life than you'll ever lead. They have done more than you'll ever do. They have seen more than you'll ever see. And they have learned more than you'll ever learn." As Jack continued to stare at him, it became clear that he was being challenged to say something.

"They aren't me." He tried not to make it sound like a question. "I'm different. I'm unique."

"There's nothing different about being unique." Jack turned away, facing forward again, his back filling the hatchway. "Everybody's unique."

After the light at Montara Point came on, Jack asked him once in a while for the heading. They sailed into Half Moon Bay just after midnight. The fog hadn't set in this time. In the morning they started back to Sausalito. The trip was short and uneventful. There was no wind and they motored all the way. Again Jack sat in the hatchway, saying nothing. But he knew the meaning of Jack's silence. He could see it written on his back, as he sat there facing forward, the warning: "Wait until next time."

Now, waiting for ten o'clock, it was that next time, and although he knew he wasn't good at predicting what Jack would do, he thought that Jack would make him sail *Jest* up to Bodega Bay, or maybe down to Monterey, or even farther south. He knew Jack would make him sail *Jest* until he did it right, that is, until he did it the way Jack wanted him to do it. Waiting for ten o'clock meant waiting for ten o'clock and not five before or five after. When it was time, he turned the radio off and he went down the outside stairs and walked toward the Sausalito yacht harbor, pacing himself by singing the song he had just been listening to: *Don't know much about geography. Don't know much trigonometry.* Then he remembered Jack saying that what you don't know always hurts you.

His sea bag was already on *Jest*, had been there since last weekend, and he didn't take anything with him except fifty-six dollars and his Case knife. He didn't want to second-guess Jack by taking anything he wouldn't need. Any attempt to do so would be ridiculed. It was a minor variation of what he thought of as the pillow-dilemma. Once in the main cabin of the *Astrolabe*, sitting around the table with Jack and some of his guests, he made a particularly thoughtless remark. Jack told him to close the skylight, but instead of doing so, he said he wasn't cold. Jack looked at him for a moment and then took the pillow he was leaning against and threw it across the cabin at him. Although the action was sudden, he could see the pillow coming and he had enough time to duck. He also had enough time to realize that he didn't have to duck. It was only a pillow, not a fork, which Jack had used on him once, the four white points still visible on the back of his right hand. So he let the pillow hit him in the face. He thought at the time that his action was a clear statement that meant: "I see that it's only a pillow so I don't have to do anything." But Jack gave his action, or lack of it, a different meaning by saying: "What's the matter. Are you too slow, or too stupid, or both, to catch it." It's true, he hadn't thought of that possibility, but then catching the pillow was playing Jack's game, for that is what Jack would have done, though no one ever threw pillows or anything else at Jack. Afterwards, he still preferred his version, mainly because he had the suspicion that Jack hadn't thought he would let the pillow hit him. But although he felt he hadn't failed, he was still ridiculed in front of Jack's guests, because in all games Jack played, Jack made the rules.

He stopped on the main pier, before going out on the floating dock, and looked down at *Jest*. Over the past year he had stripped and painted most of her, except for the topsides, which were painted black. Now there was something different about the way she looked. Aft, behind the cockpit, was a wind-vane that hadn't been there the last time he was in the harbor, just a few days ago. He walked out to the end of the floating dock and looked under the stern. There was a shaft with a trim tab on the end of it, running from the wind-vane down into the water. He wondered why Jack thought he needed a self-steering rig, whether Jack wanted him to sail all the way to Santa Barbara, or even Long Beach or San Diego. He stepped onto *Jest*, putting all his weight on the rail, and felt the boat move heavily in the berth, then he stepped back on the dock again and looked at her trim. She was lower in the water, especially forward, obviously loaded with something.

Jack wasn't on *Jest*, not that he expected Jack to wait for him, but when he saw the envelope on the cabin table, he knew Jack wasn't coming. The envelope made him pause. It wasn't Jack's way, to leave him written instructions. It was unexpected and suggested that Jack was about to surprise him with something. The note in the envelope was short:

Sail to position 21° 19´ N, 157° 58´ W
Depart March 4, 1961

The date was today, but the latitude and longitude looked strange. He opened the chart drawer, and on top was a chart of the Pacific, a new one that he hadn't seen before. He took the chart out and put it on the table to study it. But without having to plot the position, he could see that Jack wanted him to sail *Jest* to Hawaii.

He checked the lockers and under the bunks and found food supplies everywhere he looked: beans, rice, flour, noodles, canned meat, vegetables, and fruit. Peaches, he liked canned peaches. For a moment he became suspicious and checked the bookcase. There were a lot of new books, all hardback, but with some satisfaction he found that there were no schoolbooks. It looked like he was finished with high school, at least for now. But Jack had provided him with a substitute, *The Elements of Celestial Navigation,* one hundred and twelve pages. In the locker under the chart table he found a sextant.

He knew that if he looked he would find everything he needed, including things he never would have thought of himself. But he knew he had to check the water and the fuel, just to make sure. The aft water tank was empty, not because Jack had forgotten it but because Jack had left it for him to check. As he filled the water tank, he looked across the harbor. The *Astrolabe* was in her berth but there was no one on deck. Jack was on the *Astrolabe,* waiting for him to leave, so he tried to think of somewhere to go. He could sail down to the South Bay and anchor there for a few days, and then see what happened. Or he could go up the Delta and hide in the marshland, perhaps for months. He couldn't decide, but he had to leave, he had to go somewhere and then decide what to do. He couldn't decide here, knowing that Jack was watching him. He turned on the engine, cast off the mooring lines, and started to back *Jest* out of her berth. Jack wasn't there this time to warn him about Mile Rock. Mile Rock. It made him think of Half Moon Bay. He could spend at least three or four weeks in Half Moon Bay while Jack was waiting for him to turn up in Hawaii.

Half Moon Bay

He had the wind and the tide against him, so it took him most of the afternoon to tack out the Golden Gate. And since it was still dark when he reached Half Moon Bay, he decided to heave-to and wait for morning before going into the harbor. Late in the night, while sitting in the cockpit, he thought about the logbook. This time, he decided, he would keep one. Back in June, after he and Jack returned from Half Moon Bay, Jack became angry, or perhaps just disgusted, when he learned that he hadn't kept a logbook, hadn't made even one entry in it. So Jack took the empty logbook from *Jest*, and in the following weeks, in the cabin of the *Astrolabe*, he would show it to everyone, calling it "Bubba's logbook."

Then Jack told him to write a description of his trip to Half Moon Bay, using any form he wanted. Jack gave him one week. He had spent a lot of time thinking about what to write, but he had trouble getting started; that is, he hadn't been able to start at all. The day before the week was up he had an appointment at the dentist, Dr. Yamamoto. While sitting in the waiting room, he looked at the Japanese-American newspapers on the low table in front of him, and he was reminded that he was probably one of Yamamoto's few non-Japanese patients. He picked up a copy of *Mainichi Shimbun* and inside he found an English section with a number of short poems about snow and cherry blossoms. For some reason he liked them, though he couldn't say why, and he had started to read them a second time, more slowly, when Yamamoto said "Haiku!" He jumped because he hadn't heard Yamamoto come in.

Yamamoto was very apologetic about frightening him, and perhaps because he didn't have any other patients at the moment, Yamamoto began talking about the poems. Japanese haiku has a special form, but Californian haiku is a little different; the form is not always so special. The word "form" made him suddenly very interested in the poems, and he asked Yamamoto why the poems did not rhyme. No rhyme! No rhyme in haiku: even in Californian haiku all the meaning must be packed into seventeen syllables only, which are divided into three lines of five, seven, and five syllables. He told Yamamoto that he would like to learn to write such poems. Yamamoto seemed pleased and even helped him write a few lines:

Bow in the night-fog
making the world disappear—
foghorns bring it back.

He sent the poem he wrote with Yamamoto's help to Jack with a title: "A Description of Sailing Toward Half Moon Bay: Written in a Form of My Choice." Later, on the *Astrolabe*, Jack called him "Bubba the Minimalist" and then began to ask him about what he had written.

"Where did you learn about haiku, and don't tell me in school."

"From Yamamoto."

"Yamamoto. Of course. In that case, now that you're an expert, what about using kigo?"

"Yamamoto said California haiku doesn't need one. It's enough just to talk about nature."

"In that case, talk about it some more. I want you to write twenty-five poems about sailing toward Half Moon Bay." He couldn't do it. All that came to his mind was the fog. The following week he had another appointment with the dentist and he told Yamamoto his problem. How could he write about the fog if he had already written about it? Yamamoto smiled. Shiki wrote tens of thousands of haiku in his short lifetime of thirty-six years. He told his disciples that they had only to look carefully at one scene in nature to be able to produce over twenty haiku. Yamamoto's advice seemed to open his eyes, for once it was clear to him that he could write about the same thing over and over, it became easy. Writing the poems gave him something to do in school. He could write them in his head, while pretending he was paying attention to his English teacher. In the end, he wrote many more than twenty-five, though he sent Jack only that many. Number twenty-six was a variation on his first one, a kind of tribute to Yamamoto:

Bow in the night-fog
making the world disappear—
Haiku brings it back.

In his room there was a notebook full of poems, and he had started a second notebook when Jack took him out of high school in his junior year to work on *Jest* full-time. He was too tired to write after that. But now, as he sat in the cockpit off Half Moon Bay, keeping watch, he had time to think about haiku again. It made the night pass and kept him awake.

When it started to get light, he turned on the engine to charge the battery and to have it ready; then he sailed toward the entrance of the harbor. Before the first buoy he took down the sails, motored in behind the breakwater, and anchored near another yacht, a 40-foot double-ended ketch. When everything looked as it should, he turned the engine off and then he noticed the seagulls for the first time, crying as they wheeled overhead. He left his coat on and started the stove, heating water for tea and porridge. After eating he decided to leave the washing up for later and got in his bunk, falling asleep almost immediately.

He woke suddenly in the early afternoon. Something had touched *Jest*. He climbed out of his sleeping bag and went on deck. He could see a hand on the aft rail. Someone was in a dinghy, under the stern. It was a man with a very black beard. As he looked at the man, he reminded himself that when he got old enough, never to grow a beard.

"Oh, I was admiring your self-steering rig. Is the skipper on board?"

"Yeah."

"I'd like to talk to him."

"Come aboard then."

The man handed up his bowline and climbed over the rail. "I'm Pete Petersen. That's my ketch, *Ariel*." He indicated with his thumb the double-ended ketch anchored near by.

"Hi. I'm the skipper."

"Well, Skip, that's a very impressive self-steering rig. Are you a single-hander?" Without waiting for an answer Pete went over to take a closer look at the self-steering gear. "So this is the wind-vane rig, just like Hiscock describes it." As he watched Pete squat over the self-steering gear, he tried to remind himself to check the Hiscock book Jack had left in the bookcase. He had seen it next to Bowditch's *The American Practical Navigator.* "What do you do," Pete asked, without looking up, "get your boat to hold her course and then just tighten this wing nut here? It's really simple. But I can't get *Ariel* to hold a course. She's too much weather helm. Besides, putting a rig like this on a double-ender means building some kind of boomkin aft." He already liked Pete, beard and all, mainly because he tended to answer his own questions. Besides, Pete had revealed how the self-steering gear worked. So he invited Pete to see below.

Pete was a talker, and as he talked about buying his boat in Florida and sailing it back to San Francisco, he snooped about the cabin in what appeared to be a harmless sort of way. Ignoring the dirty dishes, the unmade bunk, the scattered clothes, he studied the chart on the chart table, ran his hand once over the logbook that was still open, swung the stove gently to test its gimbals, but in the end it was the bookcase that attracted him most. "I see you have Hiscock's *Cruising Under Sail,* too. And look here, the *Snark* and Slocum. I read London first and then Slocum. London said that Slocum's cruise around the world got him to build the *Snark,* and head for the South Seas. But for me it was first this one here, *The Sea Wolf,* and then *The Cruise of the Snark* that made me crazy about the South Seas. I guess nowadays it's these books that make us want to go to sea." Pete paused and looked over at him.

"I haven't read many of them yet."

"You will if you go cruising. You'll have plenty of time with that self-steering rig, that's for sure. Anyway, why don't you come over to the *Ariel* for dinner? Anna is making beans and corn bread. There'll be plenty. Say, about nineteen hundred." In his dinghy, Pete struggled a little getting his oars in place, but before he rowed away, he looked up and said, "Bring your logbook when you come over."

He wasn't sure he wanted to go over to the *Ariel*. He knew all about beans from Jack. Jack had taught him to make beans and eat beans, mostly chili beans. But in any case, he wasn't sure he wanted to show anyone his logbook, and the first thing he did when he went below again was to close it and put it in the chart drawer. But Pete had just come up from Panama. So he had charts of the coast. Jack hadn't left him with any charts of the coast, only the North Pacific and the Hawaiian Islands. With charts of the coast he could sail down to Mexico. There must be plenty of harbors where he could stay for months without anything happening. So, he unlashed his dinghy and, with the help of the main halyard, put it over the side.

At exactly seven o'clock he arrived along side the *Ariel* with a can of peaches and his logbook. Anna was a small and slight woman who seemed observant but somehow out of place on the ketch. Again, Pete did most of the talking, and he had the suspicion that Pete also did most of the cooking. The beans were Boston, not Texan. He liked the corn bread and remembered to say so. "Listen, Skip, I'll give you the recipe if you let me read to Anna from your logbook." His logbook was on his seat next to him. There didn't seem much he could do, so he handed it to Pete. Pete's voice became slightly deeper and somehow more professional:

March 4, 1961
1700
Course 220
Log set to 0

The wake drifts leeward
toward Mile Rock and the shore—
ahead lies the sea.

2300
Hove-to
Log 32

Lights shinning to port
While hove-to off Half Moon Bay—
darkness to starboard.

March 5
0930
Half Moon Bay
Log 43

Behind the seawall
the sails furled, the deck washed down—
now writing the log.

"The Haiku Logbook," Anna said. "Is there more?"

"I've only gotten this far."

"Where're you headed, Skip? Down the coast?"

He had prepared himself for this question. He was headed for Hawaii, but he wanted to sail down the coast a bit first; however, he didn't have any charts of the coast. He tried to look at Pete the way Pete had looked at him on

Jest, when Pete had said that nowadays it was books that made people go to sea. Pete's slight smile suggested that he got the point. But Pete wanted to keep his charts, not so much because he planned to use them again, but because they were a record of their cruise. "Maybe if we had kept a logbook like yours it would be different."

The next morning Anna hailed him from her dinghy and asked permission to come aboard. As she climbed over the rail, he realized that she was much younger than he had thought, much younger than Pete. She said she and Pete were driving into San Francisco in about an hour and they wanted to know if there was anything he needed. But as she continued to talk, it became clear that she really wanted something else. Finally she came out and asked him directly why he was alone.

"Jack, that's my father, wants me to sail to Hawaii."

"But you don't want to."

"No."

"Why not?"

"I don't know. Or I do know but I can't say, I mean I can't explain it."

"So what are you going to do?"

"Stay here. . . . If I had some charts, I could sail down to Mexico."

"What would you do then?"

"I don't know. It's a long way to Mexico."

"I think you'll make it down to Mexico, Skip. And when you do, promise to send me a copy of your logbook." Like Pete, Anna called him Skip. He liked the name and decided that he would use it from then on.

The night before he had put a bowl of red beans to soak and now he needed some onions. He walked along the beach to the town of Half Moon Bay, taking his time, and so he didn't get back to the harbor until it was dark and he had to watch where he stepped. As he cut through the parking lot, with two pounds of Spanish onions in one hand and two heads of iceberg lettuce in the other, he saw, parked under a street light, a 1955 black Cadillac Coupe de Ville. Jack's car. He ducked behind the car next to him. He couldn't hear or see anyone. Bent double, he moved toward the landing. He half expected his dinghy to be gone, but it was still tied up as he had left it. He rowed out to *Jest* as fast as he could, trying to keep the fish boats between him and the shore. When he got close to *Jest*, he stopped. No one was on deck and no lights were on below. He did everything automatically, without thinking about what he was doing. He tied the dinghy aft, turned on the engine, and went forward and started hauling in the anchor. As soon as the anchor was off the bottom, he let it hang, went aft and headed *Jest* along the breakwater, toward the entrance. The anchor caught on the bottom once and he had to go forward and haul it up to the surface. While heading out the harbor, he cut the turn too close at the end of the breakwater and felt *Jest* scrape her bottom. He kept heading out to sea until he felt calm enough to think of the anchor and the dinghy. Getting the anchor and dinghy on board, especially at sea, was a chore, and he felt exhausted but better when it was done.

He didn't know what to do next, but he didn't want Jack to find him again drifting around off Half Moon Bay. He set the staysail and went aft to lash the wheel over. There in the cockpit he found something, a cardboard mailing tube. After taking it below and turning on the light, he looked at the label: San Francisco Instrument Company. Inside were charts of the California coast and the west coast of Mexico, plus a small Mexican courtesy flag. There was also a note: *Skip, You owe me a copy of your logbook when you get to where you are going. Bon Voyage, Anna.* He took out the chart of the west coast of the United States and Mexico. The chart table was too small for the entire chart, so he flattened it out on the cabin table and studied it for a few minutes. Then he set a course for Cabo San Lucas.

Ensenada

He had been a fool to panic, and while trying to get out of Half Moon Bay he had almost run *Jest* into the breakwater. He wasn't even sure if the car was Jack's, though he had never seen a 1955 black Cadillac Coupe de Ville before, except Jack's. And even if it was Jack's car, what did it mean? Was Jack trying to find him to ridicule him? Or was Jack trying to scare him out to sea again? But it was too early for Jack to be looking for him in Half Moon Bay. He should be on his way to Hawaii, and Jack should be expecting him there in three or four weeks. He didn't want to go to Hawaii. He didn't want Jack to meet him and he didn't want Jack to find him. He didn't want to be called Bubba anymore.

Once he got the boat on course and the sails trimmed, he engaged the self-steering gear. After about an hour the boat was still holding her course, so he went below to cook some beans. Later, standing in the hatchway, he saw the light at Montara Point fade. Looking forward, he saw an orange light off to port, and he remembered that he hadn't turned his navigation lights on. The light to port seemed to be growing bigger, as if a ship was bearing down on him. He jumped aft and disengaged the self-steering gear and brought *Jest* into the wind. When he looked over his shoulder, he suddenly realized that the light was just the moon, full and rising.

The wind was increasing, so he thought he had better take down the mainsail before it became too strong. He got the jib in without any problems, but the main seemed to be stuck and he had to claw it down with one hand as the boat pitched into the sea and water poured over the bow. Later, with a following sea and just the staysail up, he had to steer again. Then he remembered that he hadn't set the Walker log. He got the line and fed the spinner into *Jest's* wake. The log still read forty-three miles, as it had when he entered Half Moon Bay. Pigeon Point was almost on the beam, so he estimated that he had made about fifteen miles. He wondered what else he had forgotten, then went below and closed the valve to the engine exhaust. He started to pump the bilge, but the bilge was dry. He had a lot to think about and a lot to do. He had to study the charts. He had to read the almanac so he wouldn't be fooled by the moon again. And he had to look more thoroughly through everything to see what Jack had stored for him on *Jest*.

By morning the wind had died down enough for him to set the main and jib again and use the self-steering gear. He headed the boat away from the coast and went below to sleep. At noon he estimated that he was about ten miles off Monterey. Later in the day he began to search the boat. He found the ship's papers—which he had expected to find—but with them was his passport. Did he need a passport to go to Hawaii? Did Jack have further plans for him? A cruise to Japan perhaps? But more puzzling were the three cartons of cigarettes he found in the oilskin locker. Lucky Strikes. Jack, as he liked to claim, only smoked in the jungle, but Jack had carried cigarettes on the *Astrolabe* to give to port officials in Mexico. But what was he supposed to do with the cigarettes? Give them to port officials in Hawaii? Did Jack guess that he wouldn't sail for Hawaii and head for Mexico instead? No, if there were cigarettes for Mexico, there would also be charts for Mexico on board. Jack was always very liberal when it came to gear and supplies. Maybe Jack was letting him know that he was allowed to smoke now.

At night he headed away from the land and in the morning he headed back in again, so he could see about where he was. When he saw that the light at Arguello Point was on the beam, at about nine o'clock in the evening, he changed course to sail outside the Channel Islands. In the morning he was off Santa Rosa Island. He hadn't been sleeping enough and now it was catching up with him. He hove-to and slept until early afternoon, then sailed on. The next day he did the same thing off San Nicolas Island and again the day after that off China Point and the day after that off Los Coranados. Everything seemed to be going well, and since he was only about sixty miles from Ensenada, he decided to go in and get his clearance for Mexico. The following evening he hove-to off of San Miguel Point at the entrance of Todos Santos Bay, and in the morning he motored into Ensenada harbor and anchored next to a ketch called *Hurricane*. He had been at sea for eight days and had logged 473 miles.

As he hoisted the quarantine flag and the Mexican courtesy flag, he noticed a few other yachts in the harbor. He waited about an hour and when nobody came out to him, he decided to go in and find the Port Captain. He thought he would probably have to wait all through the siesta or even come back the next day, but his main worry was that he would be charged more than the fifty-seven dollars that he had. As it turned out, the clearance fee was only sixteen dollars, but then it seemed that the Port

Captain thought something was suspicious, probably his age or that he was alone. The Port Captain looked at him for a moment and then asked him in English if his name was really Johnston Johns.

His name was always causing him problems, especially since it wasn't only his name but Jack's as well. He had given up expecting anyone to call him Johnston. At the same time, people called him all kinds of other things: John, Johnny, and Jay—short for J. J. And some even called him Bubba, having heard Jack use it and thinking that was his name. But no one ever called him Jack. And no one had ever called him Johnston except Mrs. Pickings. Mrs. Pickings never made the last-name-first-name mistake. She knew the first time that Johnston was his first name. She was from the South, from Texas, that's how she knew. Mrs. Pickings had been his sixth grade teacher, and he remembered the day she talked not only about Texans but also about the English, the Scots, and the Irish. Then she told the class that they were to go home and ask their parents about their heritage. He wasn't quite sure he understood what "heritage" was about, and asking Jack about his heritage wasn't much help. Without hesitation, Jack told him, "You're half Texan, half Mexican, and half African." Even at that age he had learned that that was Jack's way of saying he had asked a Bubba question. The next day at school he thought he could wait and see what some of the other kids said about their heritage and just copy them, but Mrs. Pickings, for the first time, didn't proceed alphabetically. She called on him first:

"Johnston, tell the class about your heritage."

"Ma'am? .... I'm a Southerner—on my father's mother's side."

"Are you a Johnston?"

"Yes, Ma'am."

"Which one?"

"Ma'am?"

"Which Johnston are you related to, Albert Sidney Johnston or Joseph E. Johnston?" He wanted to say both, but something told him not to. "They're both great military men, but they're not related," she went on, and he thought if she got going on the topic he wouldn't have to answer. Usually she could talk all afternoon about Texas. That thought gave him an idea.

"Ma'am, the Texas one, Ma'am." From that day on it didn't matter what he did, he could do no wrong in her class. That year permanently ruined him for school.

The Port Captain said he was familiar with the name Johnston Johns. He had studied engineering at the university, of course, but he had always been interested in anthropology. Was he related to Johnston Johns, the famous anthropologist, the one with the three wives? For that would explain a number of things. Then the Port Captain smiled and said he looked a lot like the actor in the TV series "Adventures in Paradise." As the Port Captain handed him his clearance papers, he hoped that he found plenty of adventure in the South Seas.

Late that afternoon, the three Americans from the *Hurricane* came aboard with two bottles of tequila. They wanted to mix the tequila with some fruit, so Skip gave them his bilge bucket and a few of the limes he had bought at the market after leaving the Port Captain. There were two men, Jones and Whitman—they called each other by their last names—and a woman, and as far as Skip could tell, all in their twenties. At first he was happy to have them on board, to help celebrate his arrival in Mexico, as they put it, but his enthusiasm for their company gradually began to fade. When they learned that he was alone, they started to give him advice, such as where he should go and how he should get there. Then they got more specific and gave him advice about his boat, how many hours he should sleep, how often he should check his battery, and even the way he should set his sails:

"With a sloop like this," said Whitman, "you have to keep the mainsail sheeted in tighter than the headsails, to counteract a lee helm."

"Cutter."

"What's that?"

"*Jest* is a cutter, not a sloop. And she doesn't have a lee helm."

"Doesn't this cutter have a head?" The woman had opened the forward locker and was staring somewhat bewildered at bins of rigging and paint. The locker had originally been the head, but Jack had taken it out, saying that the fewer seacocks a boat had, the better.

"The head's in the forepeak. It's the bucket."

"You use a bucket in the forepeak?"

"That's gotta be the advantage of a bucket," Whitman said. "You can use it anywhere. Go on, let's see you use the bucket."

"Hear, not see."

"What's that?"

"You'll be able to hear her, but if she closes the door, you won't be able to see anything." The three of them sat there, as if spellbound, as the woman used the bucket. "When you sail alone, it doesn't seem to make so much noise."

For the most part, though, he didn't get a chance to say much because they were too busy arguing among themselves. After a while they decided that he shouldn't sail alone at all, but that instead Jones should sail with him. There was plenty of room for Jones, and anyway, *Jest* was almost as big as their ketch. Then they argued about whether Jones or Whitman should sail with him. Then one of them suggested the woman. The woman giggled through it all, and he could never figure out which of them she belonged to. Toward sunset, as they got down toward the bottom of the bucket, they found a few matches and a cigarette lighter, but by then they didn't seem to care much. He had poured two cups of their mix over the side and was drinking lime juice with water. By then he was thoroughly tired of them and he wanted them to shove off for their own boat, but when he tried to suggest that he needed to get some sleep, they simply ignored him. Since they were out of tequila, they began to rummage around in the cabin, looking for something else to drink. Without thinking about it, Skip began to do what Jack would have done in such a situation. He got out his charts and studied them. Then he turned on the engine, but they thought he was just charging his battery, so he went on deck and raised the anchor. Jack said that to be impolite to impolite people was not impolite. As he headed the boat out of the harbor, the three of them, Jones, Whitman, and the woman, tumbled on deck, shouting and swearing at him, and he thought for a moment that they were going to attack him, but then they realized that they were getting farther and farther from the shore, so they jumped into their dinghy, forgetting to untie it. Skip took out his knife, cut their bowline, and they were gone. As he went forward to raise his sails, he thought that putting to sea was a convenient way of solving at least some problems.

Cabo San Lucas

He hadn't slept in almost twenty-four hours and he was tired, but he had to sail ten miles to the southwest just to clear Todos Santos Bay and round Banda Point. He sailed another ten miles away from the coast before falling asleep, thinking about the 860 miles he had to sail to reach Cabo San Lucas. When he woke, the wind had shifted to the west and he was heading in toward the coast. Even before the sun rose above the horizon he could see land. He was much closer than he wanted to be and he was heading in the wrong direction. He changed course but kept close to the coast. As the sun rose, he saw that the coast was brown and bare. There were no landmarks, no way of telling where he was.

He knew that he couldn't continue like this. He had to have a better idea of where he was. Latitude. He needed to know his latitude. He knew, in theory at least, how to do it. After setting a course away from the coast, he went below and got out *The Elements of Celestial Navigation* and began reading the chapter on the noon sight. He read it through twice and then got out the sextant. In the locker, behind the sextant, he found three bottles of Jack Daniels whiskey. It seemed that they were supposed to go with the three cartons of Lucky Strikes. More gifts for the Port Captains, probably. He went back to his navigation. He seemed to have everything: the chart of Baja, the *Nautical Almanac,* and the sextant. He went through the procedure in his head again. It seemed simple enough. Now all he had to do was wait for noon.

He got out the fishing box that he had found a few days earlier and began to prepare a lure. To get the yellow feathers fastened tight took about an hour. He let the fishing line out past the log spinner, hoping that they wouldn't get tangled. He tied the end of the fishing line to a piece of shock cord, so he could tell at a glance if he had hooked a fish. He was so hungry for fish that he didn't want to eat anything else, but he knew that the way to catch a fish was to eat, so that he wouldn't be hungry. He checked his course and went below to make pancakes. He was getting better with his pancakes. He had advanced beyond the rubbery stage and he would be very happy now if he could just get them to rise a little. He could see that jam would probably be the first thing he ran out of.

A half hour before noon he took the sextant on deck and began to practice bringing the sun down to the horizon. He had to keep bringing it down until it stopped going up. That was noon. He waited. Patience was not a virtue at sea; it was part of the pace of life. The pace was set by the movement of the sun and the four to five knots of the boat. The sun reached its zenith and he went down to the chart table to plot his latitude. He seemed to be about where he thought he was. In the next few days his confidence in taking a noon sight increased. When he was to seaward of Cedros Island, he thought of going into Torugas Bay, but he didn't have a chart of the harbor. He remembered from coming up the coast on the *Astrolabe* that the entrance to the harbor was narrow. So he decided to pass it by and continue down to Cabo San Lucas, another 500 miles.

The following day he caught his first fish. While pulling it in, the line got tangled with the log spinner, but at least he didn't lose it. The fish looked like some kind of tuna; he just wished it wasn't so big. He had fried fish for the next three meals and he still had to throw most of the fish back in the sea. Taking noon sights and catching fish made him feel more comfortable about being alone on the boat, made him feel that he could actually cope with it, the boat and everything. But the feeling soon left him, for this was the day he found the pistol fastened to the ceiling of the navigation locker. It was a Browning semiautomatic .22 caliber pistol. It was loaded. This was the first find he made that puzzled him. He knew that Jack didn't like guns and never kept one, and a pistol didn't seem to have any purpose on a boat. But it meant something, or Jack wouldn't have put it there for him to find. He was tempted to throw it overboard, but if that was a mistake, he couldn't retrieve it. He unloaded the pistol and put it back in the navigation locker where he found it. He spent the rest of the day thinking about what he was supposed to shoot.

When he rounded Land's End, and entered the bay at Cabo San Lucas, his first surprise was the number of yachts anchored in the bay, particularly the 161-foot schooner *Goodwill*. His second surprise was the difficulty in anchoring next to them, for the bottom fell away abruptly from the shore. The first time he dropped his anchor too far out and it didn't catch, so that he drifted in too close and bounced his keel on the bottom. In the end he set both anchors, realizing that he would have to keep a close eye on the wind. The Port Captain came right out. He didn't want any money—just canned meat, cigarettes, and whiskey. Skip gave him a canned ham and a carton of cigarettes, which—he realized later—was too much, and pretended he didn't have any whiskey. The meat and the cigarettes seemed to be enough for the Port Captain.

As he was pulling his dinghy up on the beach, a gang of small kids rushed up to help him, shouting and laughing. He thanked them and then headed up the beach toward the village to look for some fresh fruit and vegetables, but all he could find this late in the afternoon was half a dozen oranges. When he got back to the beach, the gang of kids rushed up again to help him push his dinghy back in the water. He kept one orange for himself and gave the rest to the kids, who ran off up the beach, again shouting and laughing. Later he learned that the stocky kid with the reddish hair was their nominal leader. He was called Mario, and as they ran up the beach, with Mario at their head, he realized that they were shouting "Mario! Mario!"

Later he decided that he needed some kind of routine to give his days structure, the way being at sea structured his time. In the mornings he worked about the boat, doing small jobs. He sewed a split seam in the staysail, put a new splice on the end of the topping-lift that had parted a few days before reaching Cabo, and spent a number of frustrating hours fiddling with his navigation lights before he got them working again. It was much warmer now, even warm enough to swim. In the fo'c'sle he found diving equipment: mask, snorkel, fins, and a spear with a sling. He checked the bottom of the hull and found a bad gouge on the starboard side where he had scraped the breakwater in Half Moon Bay. He'd have to get that repainted at some point. Before noon he usually went ashore to shop for fresh food. In the afternoons he took long walks, either on Médano Beach in the bay itself or, crossing the point, on Solmar Beach where waves that had crossed the Pacific crashed on the shore. He also copied out his logbook and sent it to Anna, telling her where he was and thanking her for the charts. Once he rowed out towards Land's End to go spearfishing, but he couldn't handle the Hawaiian sling, and besides, the water wasn't that warm.

For the most part, the people on the other yachts were friendly, but he was a little shy of them after his experience in Ensenada. Finally, he approached a couple of them to trade books. He didn't want to read the books Jack had put on board. But he couldn't get anyone to trade books with him, mainly because Jack had put only hardbound books in the bookshelf and no one would trade them for paperbacks; in fact, they wouldn't take them at all. He made the mistake of saying he hadn't read them, and they insisted that he had to keep them. They wouldn't trade anything for paperbacks, except other paperbacks, so there didn't seem to be any way he could get something to read, without reading Jack's books. He made an exception for *The Elements of Celestial Navigation*; that is, he decided it really wasn't a book like *Typee,* but a tool. He kept it in the chart drawer, along with the *Nautical Almanac.*

He got to know Fred and his wife on the ketch *Omoo,* but they didn't have any paperbacks. They were people who didn't seem to read. Fred liked to spend his time making things or fixing the things he had made. He had made his own self-steering gear but it wasn't dependable and he spent a lot of time worrying over it. Fred was fascinated by the self-steering gear on *Jest,* and so one day Skip took Fred for a sail to demonstrate it. While they were outside the bay, as a kind of afterthought, Fred showed him how to take a sun sight, going through the entire procedure from using the sextant to working out a line of position. The results weren't very accurate because Skip hadn't been checking his chronometer. Fred showed him how to do that and encouraged him to study the rest of *The Elements of Celestial Navigation.* Fred was rather exacting and sometimes he got lost in the description of details, pointing out, for example, that an error of four seconds in time could cause an error of one mile at sea. But in the end, both he and Fred were satisfied that he could go on and practice taking sun fixes on his own.

A few days later, in the evening, Fred roasted a pig on the beach. He was so proud of paying only twelve dollars for it that he wouldn't take any money from anyone. So crews from the other yachts came, bringing beans, potatoes, salad and beer. Skip sat on a log, in the shadows just outside the light of the fire. Someone had given him a bottle of Carta Blanca, which he didn't drink, but poured into the sand at regular intervals. He felt good sitting there, somehow content with the world and his surroundings, as if he could be part of these people, or at least as if he could be part of their world of cruising boats. He knew that his age was a problem for most of them, that they felt he was too young to be doing what he was doing. But a few of them, like Fred, treated him almost as an equal, and he felt he could trust them, at least with some things.

After Easter the wind shifted to the south and the anchorage became exposed. A number of boats began dragging their anchors until, in some cases, their keels were banging on the bottom. Fred came by and told him that most of the yachts had decided to leave, and those going south were heading for Mazatlán that afternoon. His anchors were holding, so he decided to say goodbye to Mario and his gang before leaving, mainly because he wanted to give him a present, a hatchet he had found on board, which was of no possible use to him. After a few days in Cabo, he had begun to realize that Mario actually lived on the beach, in a shelter made of driftwood and corrugated sheeting. There were adults around, mostly older women, but the kids seemed to lead a rather unrestrained life. They had so little that he wondered what they lived on. But despite the poverty, Mario seemed to find a joy in just being alive. Skip liked to go ashore sometimes just to see Mario and his gang race toward him. When he held out the hatchet, Mario became serious for the first time since he had met him. Then, with a shout, he took the hatchet and, raising it with both hands over his head, raced up the beach, his gang following behind him, shouting "Mario! Mario!"

Just then someone he knew only by sight, from the *Valerie Queen,* asked him if he was John Johnston, and if so, there was a letter for him at the post office. He ran to the post office and picked up a letter from Anna. It was rather thick, so he decided to wait to read it. Most of the other yachts where already heading out the bay and he wanted to go with them. It wasn't until he had cleared the bay and set the course for Mazatlán that he opened the letter:

Dear Skip:
I was surprised and delighted to get your letter. I thought that you wouldn't remember. I enjoyed your Haiku Logbook very much, particularly your Scylla and Charybdis from March 20:

Barren land to port
to starboard the empty sea—
sailing between them.

I've sent you a $100 dollars, partly so that you will continue to write me. But I also want to help support what you are doing. As you can imagine, your departure has caused quite a sensation. It all came out in an interview in the San Francisco paper, which I've enclosed. I find it hard to believe that anyone has a father like that. Jack left on the *Astrolabe* not long after you did. The rumor running around is that he is headed for Hawaii. So it will take him months to get back. And now I don't see how he will ever find you. I really feel that I know what you are trying to do, that you feel that the *Jest* is part of your patrimony and you want to use it your way and not Jack's. (Everyone calls him Jack, even those like me who have never met him.) Whatever you do, keep writing. I wish you all the luck.

Love,
Anna

So Jack left for Hawaii. Did that mean the black Cadillac in Half Moon Bay wasn't his? He'd have to think about that later. What Anna said was probably true, but only partly. *Jest* wouldn't be his patrimony until he no longer had to run from Jack. Maybe that was what Anna felt. The money made him uneasy, though. Was it a gift or a loan? Jack said that when a man gives a woman money, he is buying something. What did it mean when a woman gave him money? He'd find out some day.

There was actually more to Anna's letter, but it was mainly about Pete and their boat *Ariel*. He had the feeling that Anna was one of those people who liked the idea of yachts but didn't like to actually sail them. He'd probably never see *Ariel* again. He unfolded the newspaper clipping:

Rite of Passage
Interview with Johnston "Jack" Johns
By Mary Befame
MB: You have told your son to sail a 35-foot boat by himself to Hawaii. Why?
JJ: The initiation process of our culture has been preempted by high school. Football, rock and roll, the Junior Prom, the parents' car: these have become the symbols that mark the transition to adulthood in our culture. Today's teenagers couple in the back seat of their parents' car and think they have become adults. As a result, our youth has lost the sense that sex has to be earned. We need to return to a world before *Coming of Age in Samoa*.
MB: So you have sent your son on an initiation rite? Isn't that dangerous?
JJ: That's why our teenagers fail to undergo an adequate initiation. There's nothing dangerous about high school, except drunken driving. Look at the high school role model, the football star. He goes from high school to middle age. He never grows up.
MB: Some go on to college. . . .
JJ: That's advanced high school, a mating ground for the rich, so that they can keep their money within their own class.
MB: Those are strong words coming from a college professor.
JJ: I'm not a college professor. I do research and I write. "Independent scholar" is the usual label.

MB: Let's get back to your son. Do you think he is prepared for this challenge?

JJ: What he doesn't know, he can learn. Necessity is the mother of education.

MB: Are you in radio contact with him? How is he doing? Is he afraid?

JJ: He has only a radio receiver on board, mainly for getting the time from Greenwich, so that he can rate his chronometer. As for fear, the word is not in the Johns' vocabulary.

MB: You have said that if he makes it, he will be the youngest person to sail from California to Hawaii. What if he does not make it? What if he falls overboard and drowns?

JJ: Isn't it better to fail now than to discover at forty that your whole life has been a failure and a waste, that you have become nothing but a forty-year-old teenager, always dreaming of that last high school football game?

MB: One final question. What will your son do once he has reached Hawaii?

JJ: He will get a tattoo.

The interview suddenly brought Jack very close, right into the cockpit. He felt that Jack was watching him again. He didn't know how. Maybe somebody was watching in Jack's place. He'd have to pay more attention to the other boats when he got to Mazatlán. Most of what Jack said in the interview was just Jack-talk, much like the talk about his book *King and Kinship*. Skip hadn't actually read the book, but there had been enough talk on the *Astrolabe* for him to know what it was about. More important, though, the very fact of the interview itself meant that Jack was serious. Jack had committed himself, publicly, to the idea of his initiation. Jack would be after him, would eventually find him. For the time being, though, Jack was far downwind from him, and he could only smile at that.

Mazatlán

When it was dark he could see the lights of the other boats ahead of him, but by midnight they seemed to have outpaced him and he was alone. In the morning the wind died down and it was nearly calm. None of the other boats were in sight. He was about to go below to sleep when he noticed a large patch of broken and confused water, and he wondered what was going on below the surface. As he sailed slowly through the patch, he saw that it was a feeding frenzy: thousands of small fish were being eaten by tuna, and in turn, the tuna were being eaten by sharks. Blood was everywhere. He thought that this was a good chance to catch something, so he threw his fishing line with the yellow-feathered lure into the water. Almost at once he caught a tuna that must have weighed about thirty pounds, for he had to struggle to get it on board. He cleaned the fish but since he had already eaten a breakfast of oatmeal and bananas, he waited for lunch to fry it up.

The following day he spotted a large sea turtle to leeward sunning itself on the surface of the water. The wind was light, so he slowly drifted up to it. As soon as the turtle sensed that *Jest* was approaching, it went into a panic, waving and splashing its flippers, trying to dive below the surface of the sea. He watched it swim into the dark water below. Later, he spotted more turtles sunning themselves, but he gave them a wide berth so as not to disturb them. Once, coming up the Mexican coast on the

Astrolabe, Jack gaffed a sea turtle and, along with two crewmen, hauled it on board. But instead of butchering it himself, Jack told Skip to do it. Jack said that learning to eat what nature offered was important for learning how to survive. Survival was one of Jack's favorite topics, and whenever Jack started talking about it, Skip knew that Jack was about to make him do something he didn't want to do. The turtle, lying defenseless on its back, was about 150 pounds. He had to drag it forward to the bow, kill it, cut it open, and carve out the meat. When he killed the turtle by cutting off its head, he knew he would never forget the look on its face, a look that reminded him of the word "sacrificial." Later he had to eat his share of the turtle, and later still he hoped that he never dreamed of that turtle or its ancient and hopeless face.

In the light winds, it took him four days to sail the 197 miles from Cabo to Mazatlán. During the passage he practiced taking sun shots, and for three days running he was able to advance his morning line of position to get a fix at noon. As he passed the Faro lighthouse on the north side of the Mazatlán harbor, the anxiety he had always felt while entering a harbor, especially a strange one, was nearly gone. He could see the boats from Cabo anchored in the harbor, and as he brought *Jest* into position off the starboard quarter of the *Omoo*, he felt as if he had arrived at a place where he wanted to be.

One morning, about a week later, the *Aeolus*, a 45-foot, center-cockpit ketch, came in and anchored outside of *Jest*. He saw a man with a woman and two small kids go ashore. He went ashore a few minutes later, mainly to walk around the market. As he took his usual route over the hill to town, he saw that the couple with the kids had gone along the coast. He liked to walk through the big covered marketplace. Somehow the sheer mass of produce, the oranges and limes, the tomatoes and onions, and the numerous varieties of beans and bananas, all piled high, plus the constant activity, made him feel as if he was in the middle of a festival. He walked up and down the aisles until he had seen everything at least twice. The stalls at the end of the market were less interesting, containing mainly clothes and utensils, but he stopped at one stall that sold parrots. He hadn't noticed this stall before and he watched the green parrots carefully as they perched in their bamboo cages. He tried to imagine such a parrot on *Jest*. He even had a name for it: Mario. But for some reason he wasn't able to visualize a parrot on the boat. The bamboo cage found no place, even though he tried to imagine it in various parts of the cabin. He didn't buy anything, nor had he planned to. And the parrot could wait until he found a place for it.

He went out the east side of the market and walked until he came to a more residential part of town. The streets were narrower and there was more shade. He looked through an open doorway and before it was closed he saw another world, a garden with palm trees and a fountain, surrounded by a verandah. Across the street he saw a woman comforting a child, then noticed that they had just come out of a dentist's office. He stopped outside a high wall, with bars on the windows, as so many building and houses had. He could hear children singing. It was a school. It was very pleasant here, and cool, but also foreign. A group of girls between ten and twelve, all in blue school uniforms, came down the street toward him. They were completely absorbed in their own chatter, and they parted and flowed past him on both sides, as if he were an inanimate object. The thought came to him that he could never belong to this place. No matter how hard he tried, no matter how good his Spanish became, he would always remain invisible.

He came out onto the plaza in front of the cathedral. It was suddenly hot. The cathedral seemed hermetic, to be guarding some secret, and it would be pointless for him to go inside and investigate. He began to walk back toward the harbor. This time he took the road along the shore, and when he was almost abreast the two small Hermanos islands, he recognized the couple with the two kids, walking ahead of him. At the pace he was going he was rapidly overtaking them. At first he thought they were the picture of a happy family, each carrying his share of the provisions acquired on their shopping expedition. As he drew along side, though, he realized that they were all overburdened. He introduced himself, saying he was from *Jest* and asked if he could help them carry some of their bags. They quickly loaded him up, with more than he thought was appropriate, saying they were Russell and Sandra Buchanan from Los Angeles. But it wasn't far to go now and the Buchanans seemed to be nearly exhausted. After they reached the harbor and loaded everything into their dinghy, they invited him out to their ketch for lunch. He found both the lunch and the ketch somewhat disappointing. Sandra prepared tuna sandwiches, something he ate frequently but usually only at sea. He decided the center cockpit was a waste of space. Instead of one large cabin, there were two smaller ones with the cockpit between them, taking up the widest part of the boat. But, he assumed, since they had two small boys, it made some sense to have separate cabins.

After lunch the Buchanans mentioned that it was their anniversary and then Sandra asked him if he could "look after Billy and Sammy for a few hours. The boys are really no trouble. They go to bed by themselves as soon as it is dark. All you have to do is be here, in case something happens." He found that he resented being asked to babysit. He wanted to refuse. He felt that if people went cruising with their kids, then the kids were their problem, and he didn't want them to be his problem. But the Buchanans had a way of both pleading and insisting. And since he had already helped them with carrying their provisions, he felt caught. So he finally gave in, especially after they promised him ten dollars and, more importantly, a paperback book, *Gone with the Wind.*

When he got back to his boat, Fred rowed over. Fred had promised to give him an old pair of his wife's nylons. Fred had warned him that there could be all kinds of trash in the diesel he bought in Mexico, and he could save himself a lot of trouble by using a nylon to filter it out when he filled his fuel tank. He wanted to give Fred a bottle of whiskey but Fred wouldn't take it. He took part of a ball of marlin instead. Fred said that the marlin didn't cost as much as the whiskey, but it was more valuable. As he sat in his dinghy, Fred nodded toward the *Aeolus*, and said, "I saw that you visited the Buchanans. We don't visit them." After Fred rowed away, Skip realized that Fred had given him some advice.

At about half past six he rowed over to the *Aeolus*. The boys hadn't been fed and neither Russell nor Sandra seemed to be ready to go ashore. He had to help Billy and Sammy with their scrambled eggs and potatoes. His instructions were to get the boys to put their pajamas on before it got dark and then send them to their bunks. Billy and Sammy appeared to be docile kids, and he thought he could just sit in the cabin and read a book. But as soon as their parents were ashore, they began to scream, fight, and even throw things. Sandra had mentioned, while leaving, that she would appreciate it if he could clean up and do the dishes after the boys were in bed. He hadn't planned to do any such thing, but now the plates were on the cabin floor and Billy and Sammy were tracking scrambled eggs and potatoes all over the place.

He told them once that if they didn't stop he would hog-tie them. When this threat had no effect, he grabbed the younger one, Sammy, and tied him to the table stanchion, using one of the nylons he still had in his back pocket. It took him longer to get Billy cornered and tied in the forepeak. After cleaning up the mess on the cabin floor, he decided he would probably have to put their pajamas on them himself and then tie them in their bunks. At some point, he thought, they would exhaust themselves, stop their screaming, and fall asleep. He untied Billy, since he couldn't get his pajamas on him otherwise. He had to first threaten to spank him on the butt and then actually do it before he could get the pajamas on him. The spanking seemed to calm Billy down, so he left him in his bunk and started to untie Sammy. While handling Sammy he thought it was strange, first that they screamed only nonsense, that is, they didn't threaten to tell their parents, and then they went completely passive as soon as he spanked them. Either that was the normal procedure, or it simply shocked them into submissiveness. Just as he was putting Sammy in his bunk, Billy jumped up and ran out of the cabin. Skip went after him and found that Billy had locked himself in the aft cabin. When he went back to the forward cabin, he found that Sammy had gotten up and locked himself in the head. Since they were both quiet now, he felt this was an acceptable development, and he decided to simply wait for the Buchanans to return. The parents could deal with their kids and the locked doors.

He found *Gone with the Wind* on a shelf between *Civilization and Its Discontents* and *Peter Pan*. It had over a thousand pages, and as he thumbed through it, the name "Johnston" seemed to jump out at him, General "Old Joe" Johnston. He began to read at that point: "Atlanta had nothing to fear, for General Johnston was standing in the mountains like an iron rampart." He paused for a moment, glanced up at Freud and Barrie, then read on about how Johnston seemed to disappoint everyone, except the men who fought for him, as he slowly retreated south. He fell back from one position to another so many times that it seemed as if Sherman was never going to catch him. Maybe that was what Old Joe was up to: as long as he kept falling back, Sherman was less of a threat. No matter how close Sherman got, Old Joe only had to keep moving, keep falling back, because if Sherman couldn't catch him, then he couldn't defeat him. Skip could see that the whole point wasn't about winning but about not losing.

He was still following Johnston's retreat into southern Georgia when the Buchanans returned, much later than they had said they would. He told them where Billy and Sammy were. They didn't seem to be surprised or even concerned. Sandra apologized for being so late and remarked that Skip's parents were probably waiting up for him, although they hadn't seen any lights on *Jest*. When he told them that there was no one on *Jest*, that he sailed alone, they seemed surprised and their attitude suddenly changed. Russell went through the cockpit and into the aft cabin. He seemed to have some way of unlocking the door from the outside. At the same time, Sandra went to the head and opened it. Sammy was asleep sitting on the toilet. She picked him up and sat down on the toilet herself, with Sammy on her lap, then she closed the door. After a few minutes, Skip decided it was time to leave.

In the morning he realized that he had forgotten to take the book with him when he left the *Aeolus* the night before. He puttered around the boat for a while, getting ready his jerry cans, one for fuel and the other for water. And when he decided it wasn't too early, he rowed over to the *Aeolus*. Sandra appeared suddenly in the cockpit, with a very red face, and started shouting at him to get away from their boat.

"You fucking pervert. Don't you dare come near this boat. You fucking child molester. Get away from here. And take your fucking nylons with you, you fucking pervert bastard."

He had forgotten about the nylons and was glad to get them back. Other than that he couldn't understand what Sandra was shouting about. At first he thought she wasn't serious, that she was putting it on because he hadn't washed the dishes as she had suggested, or because she didn't want to pay him the ten dollars for babysitting. But finally he realized that she wasn't going to stop shouting until he rowed away and disappeared from her sight. Although he suspected that something was wrong and that it was more important than dishes or ten dollars, he found that he was, more than anything else, disappointed when he realized that he wasn't going to get the paperback book.

When he saw that their dinghy wasn't tied aft of the *Aeolus*, he rowed ashore and started to take the coast road into town. About half way he saw Russell coming toward him. Russell, as he came up to him, had a very serious face, a face that Jack sometimes made when he was about to give a lecture.

"You could have told us that you sail alone."

"What's going on?"

"It's well known that those who sail alone lack certain moral standards of behavior. You can see it in Slocum and all the other single-handed sailors. Just read their books."

"What. . . ?"

"Look, we found your fetish, and I must say that nylons are very common and show a certain lack of imagination on your part. And Billy and Sammy told us how you undressed them and fondled them. I would really like to know what else you did, if you took your own pants down as well, but you are probably going to deny the whole thing."

Skip was automatically reaching into his pocket for the nylons when it suddenly occurred to him what Russell was implying. The situation was impossible and he just wanted to get as far away as he could. He stepped around Russell and started walking toward town. Russell turned and nearly shouted after him.

"When the others hear about your pederasty, you'll probably have to leave even the Mexican street kids alone."

He walked for over an hour along the coast until he decided that he would have to leave Mazatlán as soon as possible. But when he got back to the harbor around noon, the *Aeolus* was just motoring past the breakwater. They were headed south and since he didn't want to meet the Buchanans again, he changed his mind and decided to stay a few weeks and then sail for some obscure harbor.

Later he realized that the Buchanans hadn't had time to say anything to anyone in the harbor. But he found himself avoiding yachts that came from the south. He was so tied up about the Buchanans that he couldn't talk about it, even to Fred, though he had the suspicion that Fred didn't care for them. So he stayed on *Jest*, filled his fuel and water tanks, and began to read Slocum's *Sailing Alone Around the World*.

It was about a week later when he woke suddenly in the early morning hours. Someone was knocking on the hatch. When he slid the hatch back, he could see that it was still dark. The clock then struck two bells. Five o'clock. There was a woman in the cockpit.

"I want to come with you. Please, let me come with you."

The woman was wet. She had, Skip decided, swum out to *Jest* and climbed over the side. He motioned her below and gave her a more-or-less clean towel, and then a pair of his shorts and a T-shirt. Turning his back, he started the stove and put water on for tea.

"I don't care where you are going. I just have to get out of Mazatlán."

Her name was Adele and she had a story to tell. It was mostly about her boyfriend, who was jealous and who had threatened to kill her numerous times. This time he seemed to be serious. She pulled up the T-shirt she had just put on to show him the cut on her side. He didn't see any cut and he noticed that she didn't seem to notice.

When it was his turn to talk, he said he was headed for San Diego, that it was cold up north and that she would need a lot of warm clothes. He didn't bother to say anything about a passport. She seemed discouraged for a moment. She wasn't from Mazatlán, she wasn't even Mexican but Panamanian, but it turned out that she knew someone who could give her some clothes. He tried to sound encouraging but then concerned as he told her that the Port Captain was coming on board this morning, some time between ten and twelve o'clock, "to inspect things." She seemed to get the suggestion that the Port Captain shouldn't find her on the boat, for she said she wouldn't be back from getting the clothes before twelve.

It seemed settled. He fried up some eggs and warmed up some tortillas. At about eight o'clock he rowed her ashore, still wearing his shorts and T-shirt. Adele had left a pair of sandals on the dock, which she put back on before walking towards town. As soon as she was out of sight, he started for town as well, but taking instead the road over the hill. At the market he bought fresh food, fruit and vegetables, as much as he could easily carry. On the way back to the harbor, he stopped at the Port Captain's office and got his clearance papers. By ten o'clock he had the anchor up and *Jest* pointed out to sea. As he cleared the breakwater and began to get the sails ready, he thought about the difference between the sea and the land. The sea he could prepare for, the land was a different matter altogether.

Tres Marias

He remembered Fred talking about the Tres Marias and that the southern island, Maria Cleofas, was uninhabited. Suddenly he had a strong urge to go to an uninhabited island. The chart showed that Maria Cleofas was about 110 miles to the south. With a good wind he could be there the next morning.

Maria Cleofas was low and green, and as soon as he had anchored, he rowed ashore in his dinghy. The stillness on the island was noticeable, and it was emphasized by the shushing sound of the small waves breaking on the shore. He walked along the edge of the beach toward the northern point of the bay. There seemed to be a flock of birds there, but they didn't fly away as he approached. They didn't even retreat. Suddenly he was among them, a lot of duck-like birds that gathered around him. He squatted down to touch one, then picked it up and put it back down. The bird seemed unconcerned. He picked up another and petted it. He began to laugh. He was obviously the first human the birds had encountered. They seemed to want to stay near him. He toyed with them for a while but soon grew bored and began wondering what the fish in the bay were like. Maybe he could try to spear one.

He walked along the shore until he came to where a creek emptied into the bay. The creek was dry and he walked in its bed toward the jungle. When he reached the jungle he noticed that the birds had stopped following him, and that they had, in fact, suddenly disappeared. The trees were high enough for him to walk underneath. The stillness was now even more noticeable. He often stopped to listen but he heard nothing. After he had gone a few hundred yards into the jungle, there was a loud thud behind him, as something dropped from a tree he had just passed under. He spun around. It was a large lizard, a greenish-gray iguana. The iguana was sideways to him, moving up and down, puffing noticeably as its neck bulged. He stepped away from it and decided to go back to the beach by passing it to the right. He had taken only a few steps, though, when he saw out of the corner of his eye another iguana to his left. Then a third dropped from another tree to his right. There were in fact more than three. The jungle was suddenly alive with them. He rushed past the first one, running now for the beach. When he reached the beach, he hoped that none of the birds got in his way, for he didn't want to step on any of them. He jumped in his dinghy and rowed hard for *Jest*, but when he got there he simply sat in the cockpit. By sundown he had decided that it was the birds that had fooled him. They had fooled him into thinking the island was something it wasn't. He wondered if the iguanas ate the birds. That would seem to explain what he felt in the jungle, in the presence of the iguanas.

He didn't eat and he slept badly. He dreamed his old nightmare, the one he hadn't had for years. It was the nightmare that came to him after he had seen *The Thing*. At the end of the movie, the Thing comes down a corridor toward an electric mesh, and that is how his nightmare always started. Then suddenly the corridor was in a hotel with elevators at both ends. He ran for the elevator at his end, got in, and pushed the up button. When the door opened again, on a higher floor, the door of the elevator at the other end of the corridor, also opened. But it wasn't the Thing that stepped out, nor was it Jack, though that was how the nightmare usually developed. This time it was a large male body with the head of an iguana. As always, he woke up at this point.

He drank some tea and waited for sunrise. Then he gathered a few things together: a length of quarter-inch rope, a wire coat hanger, matches, salt, and his knife. Then he took out the .22 semiautomatic, loaded it and put the box of shells in his pocket.

As he entered the jungle, the sun was still low and the light slanted through the trees. He saw the iguanas much sooner this time but they wouldn't let him get close. As he approached, they slowly moved off into the underbrush. Then he saw one in a tree, on a branch that was just about at eye level. It seemed about to drop to the floor of the jungle, so he quickly aimed and fired. The bullet hit the iguana in the back of the neck and it fell to the ground and began to crawl off. He emptied the clip, aiming for the head but hitting it mainly in the back and neck. He reloaded, trying at the same time to keep up with the iguana as it continued to crawl away. Now he walked up to it and emptied the semiautomatic again, this time hitting the head nearly every time. The iguana stopped moving forward but it still twitched. When it was done, he tied the rope around its neck, using a stick to lever it up so he wouldn't have to touch it. Then he began to drag it to the beach. But he hadn't gone far when the head fell off and the rope came free. The end of the rope was bloody, so he cut that part off. He tied it again to the iguana, this time just behind the front legs. He used a stick again.

When he got to the beach, he dropped the rope and gathered wood to start a fire. Then he went to work on the iguana. He cut off the tail. As he had expected, the tail by itself wasn't so threatening and he was able to slit and peel the skin off of it. He used a board he found among the driftwood and cut the tail into chunks. The tail had more meat on it than he had expected and he realized with some annoyance that he wouldn't be able to eat it all. He used the coat hanger to skewer the pieces of meat and then placed it over the fire, using some rocks to hold it. He wanted the meat to be well done and when he finally took it off the skewer, it was almost scorched. After letting the meat cool, he salted and slowly ate a few pieces. He had forgotten to bring water. He ate about half the tail, throwing the rest up the beach. He let the fire burn down, and then hesitated because at first he couldn't decide what to do with the coat hanger. He threw it in the water. There were no birds on the beach.

When he got back to the boat, he had a great desire to read. He read Hiscock about masts and spars and running rigging, and then slept without dreaming. When he woke in the morning he remembered what Jack had said about the heroes of Chinese legends: they could eat anything, even toads and bat-demons. Then he began to cook his breakfast: eggs, pancakes, and papaya. After he had eaten he raised the anchor and left the bay.

Acapulco

A few days later, he woke knowing that something was wrong with *Jest*. The mainsail was flapping as if it had ripped. The angle of the sun slanting through the skylight meant he had slept later than usual. He glanced at the telltale compass above his bunk. *Jest* was far off course. As soon as his head was above the aft hatch, he stopped. The coast loomed dark above him and off the lee bow the Pacific swell was breaking over a rock. The wind had shifted and the mainsail was sagging, though the two didn't seem to be related. He brought *Jest* into the wind, then he tried to start the engine. Although the starter motor turned over, the engine—for the first time—refused to start. He looked at the mainsail again. The halyard had parted. That's why the sail sagged and flapped. He had to take in the jib and the staysail. Then he pulled the mainsail down, using all his weight to gain a foot at a time. Once it was down, he released the toping-lift, letting the boom fall on the cabin. He didn't look aft, at the coast or the breakers, as he untied the toping-lift from the end of the boom and then tied it to the head of the mainsail. He hoisted the mainsail again, using the toping-lift, and began to beat off the coast.

His mouth was very dry. When he realized that it had not been the fault of the self-steering gear but a shift in the wind that had sent *Jest* toward the coast, he set the wind-vane again and went below for some water. At first he thought the hand pump was broken, then he realized that the water tank was empty and he could hear his supply of fresh water sloshing around in the bilge. He took a can of apricots on deck, opened it and drank the juice, swallowing the apricot halves whole. Or swallowing them half, he wondered? He had five gallons of emergency water, and after checking that it was safe, he went below to look at the chart.

When he had gone to sleep that morning, he could still see the light flashing off Manzanillo. The dark headland, now off his lee quarter, was Cabeza Negra. He decided to head farther away from land, where there were fewer things to run into, and approach Acapulco more from seaward. It was four days from Cabeza Negra to Acapulco, and late one afternoon, he sailed through Boca Grande and into Acapulco Harbor. He had been to Acapulco before on the *Astrolabe*, so he knew where he wanted to anchor, just to the north of the yacht club. But when he entered the harbor, he saw that the *Aeolus* had anchored there before him. He didn't want to be anywhere near the Buchanans, so that meant anchoring near the commercial wharf, which was convenient for going into town, or behind the Peninsula, which was safer when the wind blew from the south. Jack had anchored between the two, between convenience and safety, but the *Astrolabe* was bigger than *Jest* and needed more room to swing at her anchor. Maybe he could anchor for a few weeks by the commercial wharf, until he got tired of being near town, and then move over to the Peninsula. But he knew once he anchored by the commercial wharf he wouldn't move. So he brought *Jest* up to the Peninsula, giving her enough room to swing, and dropped the anchor in four fathoms of water.

He looked for the *Omoo* because Fred would tell him, or at least give him a hint, if the Buchanans were spreading rumors about him. There were a number of other yachts, very few of them familiar, but the *Omoo* was not among them. He saw the schooner *Valerie Queen*—she was unmistakable with her topmasts and Herrschoff bow. He didn't feel any urge to go into town and he didn't know any of the other boats well enough to visit them, so he sat in the cockpit, thinking about what he should do the next day.

He decided he would rig an awning over the cockpit. He had to reeve a new halyard for the mainsail, but it wasn't urgent. He had to remember to check the fuel filter more often, so that the engine wouldn't refuse to start, as it had off of Cabeza Negra. And he had to solder the copper pipe that had come loose, so he could fill his water tanks. That wouldn't take long. He had everything he needed on board and last summer he had soldered all the joints himself, except the one that had come loose: that was the one Jack had done when he had shown him how to do it.

In the long run, though, he had to make some money. He didn't need much, just enough to buy fresh food and fuel and pay harbor fees. But there weren't many ways he could make money. He couldn't see how he could work for the Mexicans, and so that left the other American yachtsmen. As he knew, most cruising yachtsmen did their own work, for it was part of being a cruising yachtsman. But he had to try them because he wanted to avoid the alternatives. Which were to sell off the supplies and equipment on *Jest*, or to write to Anna again.

After a few weeks he was down to his last few pesos, but he hadn't been able to find any work. As he had expected, none of the Americans on the other yachts seemed to need any work done that they weren't ready to do themselves. Once he got up early and rowed over to the yacht club, when none of the officials were around, and bought a block of ice. He tried to peddle it to the other yachts, but in the end he only recuperated the cost of the ice, plus a small chunk of it for himself. He also tried to offer his help with shopping, especially to those who knew little or no Spanish. But it seemed that they didn't want, or even need, any help. They didn't shop at the large open market where they had to bargain, but at the supermarket where everything had a price tag.

When a new boat, the *Dolphin*, came in and anchored next to *Jest*, he waited a couple of hours and then rowed over.

"Hi. I'm looking for work."

"Well, you've found Walker."

"Walker?"

"Yes. And all the work you see on this boat belongs to me. And if that black boat over there is yours, then it looks like you have enough work of your own. You ought to be over there right now, scraping that black paint off the topsides and painting them white. What's the name of your boat—I can't quite read it from here—*Nest? Rest? Pest?*"

"*Jest.*"

"What kind of name is that? You ought to be scraping that off too. Change it to something more nautical, something more oceanic or mythical, like *Quest.*

"*Quest?*"

"All you have to do is drop the "J" and add "Qu." Of course it will be a little lopsided and lean to port, but you could fix that by adding "II" on the starboard end."

"Two?"

"*Quest II*. That's the name a cruising boat anchored in Acapulco should have."

He had thought about the name before, wondering if Jack had named the boat *Jest* or if that was the name it had when Jack bought it. He kind of liked *Quest II*, and maybe if he changed the name it would also change his luck. But he couldn't just paint over the name because it was carved in a wooden plaque that was fastened to the stern. When he took the plaque off, he saw that he had to scrape the paint off the stern and give it a new coat. First he scraped for a while, then he burnt the paint off with the blowtorch. It was only after he had the stern sanded smooth that he noticed there wasn't any black paint on board, only white. So he painted the stern white, two coats of primer and two of finish.

He was trying to make a stencil to paint the new name on the stern, when Fred hailed him. He hadn't seen the *Omoo* come in, but he was glad to see Fred and invited him aboard. Fred asked about his trip down from Mazatlán and talked about his own trip. He told how the Buchanans had to leave Puerto Vallarta because Sandra got angry in a hotel lobby and started to "swear like a trooper" at everybody in sight, including the Mexicans who were guests at the hotel. Fred had seen it, at least the latter part. The porter had pleaded with him to come to the hotel and take away the shouting American woman. But it was Russell who finally took her out of the hotel and back to the *Aeolus*. Skip had noticed that, although the *Aeolus* was anchored close to the yacht club, the Buchanans never went there, and that no one seemed to visit them.

All this time Fred ignored the several stencils of "*Quest II*" that covered the cabin table. Instead, Fred picked up the plaque with "*Jest*" on it, looked at it for a while and then said, "The carving is done very well and the gold leaf adds a nice touch to the name." Without waiting for Skip to respond, Fred climbed into his dinghy and then, after setting his oars in their locks, said, "I was wondering when you were going to get around to doing your topsides. White is much better in the tropics. It reflects the sun."

Burning the black paint off the topsides of *Jest* was hard work. He had to do it from the dinghy, which refused to stay in place, and he had to avoid burning the wooden planks under the paint, but it was work he knew how to do. Jack had him burn, scrape, sand, and paint on both the *Astrolabe* and *Jest*. He had a little more than half the port side cleaned off when Fred asked him to do the topsides of the *Omoo*. Fred said he would give him $80 and some charts, if he would burn, scrape, and sand both sides. Fred said he would do the painting himself. So Skip finished cleaning off the port side of *Jest* and put two coats of primer on it before starting on the *Omoo*. Before he had finished one side, he had offers to do the topsides of two other boats. Eventually he had so many offers that he never got a chance to finish *Jest*.

The people at the yacht club said that the rains would start on July 1 and on the morning of July 1 it started to rain, and it rained all day. He was between jobs. He was supposed to start on the *Horizon,* but now with the rain, he might never get started. Besides, he was a little tired of working and he had all the money he needed for a while.

A few days later he was in town walking across the plaza in front of the cathedral, carrying a shopping net full of mangos, when he ran into Fred. Fred said that he had sorted through his charts and he could give him the ones he didn't need. So he went with Fred into the post office. Fred asked for his mail at the general delivery window and after the woman behind the counter gave him a few letters, she turned to Skip, so he asked if there was any mail for him. There was a letter from Anna. While Fred was busy with his letters, he opened it and read through it. There was some gossip about people and boats he didn't think he knew, and then "Friends in Hawaii tell me that the *Astrolabe* hasn't turned up yet." Hasn't turned up yet? It's been over two months. Suddenly he felt that Jack was close by. He couldn't really listen to what Fred was telling him as they walked back to their dinghies. When they reached the *Omoo*, Fred handed him a bundle and for some reason the inflection in Fred's voice caught his attention, "mostly of the South Seas." He looked down at the bundle of charts, searching for a label. "I just wanted to tell you that Walker has promised to tutor you in French."

"French?"

"You'll need some French in Polynesia. That's what they speak there."

"I wasn't planning to go to Polynesia. Besides, don't they speak Polynesian in Polynesia?"

"Of course. But only the Polynesians speak Polynesian. Everyone else speaks French. And Walker is going to Tahiti too, so he can continue your lessons there."

He rowed to *Jest*, and on the cabin table he untied the bundle of charts and glanced through the titles: South Pacific—Western Portion; Marquesas Islands to Tahiti; Tuamotu Archipelago; Approaches to Tahiti and Moorea; Samoa Islands to Cook Islands; Islands and Reefs between Samoa, Fiji, and Tonga; Fiji Islands; New Hebrides Islands and New Caledonia; Papua New Guinea—Port Moresby to Cape Deliverance.

He hadn't really thought about where he would go after Acapulco, or even when he would go. He left the charts on the table and rowed to the yacht club. Ever since he started working on other boats in the harbor, he had been able to use the yacht club facilities, especially the showers. He assumed that the yacht club officials thought he belonged to one of the boats that had paid the yacht club fee. He went out the main gate and walked across the peninsula to Caleta Beach. He sat on the sand and a beach vender brought him a green coconut with the top cut off. He sipped the coconut water and stared at Roqueta Island, trying not to think of the charts on his cabin table. Toward sundown he noticed a large yacht sailing in through Boca Chica. The yacht was almost in front of him, between the beach and Roqueta Island, when he saw that it was a ketch with a very tall mizzenmast, almost as tall as the main mast. He got up and started to run toward the yacht club. If he was lucky it would be dark when he got underway, darker still when he went out, passing Jack as the *Astrolabe* was coming in.

Twilight is short in the tropics. He said that to himself over and over, as he got the anchor up and started out of the harbor. He stayed close to the peninsula because he wanted to show Jack his port side. It was white, and with the awning up and the dinghy trailing behind, instead of on deck, he hoped that *Jest's* profile would be just different enough that Jack wouldn't recognize it. When he saw the *Astrolabe,* she already had her navigation lights on. She was under power and heading almost right towards him, as if Jack wanted to anchor the *Astrolabe* in the spot that *Jest* had just left. As the *Astrolabe* passed him, he heard

Jack's voice: "Stand by the anchor." Then behind him he heard the anchor chain rattling out and he knew Jack had not recognized him, had not expected him to be going out as he was coming in.

When he was abeam the light at La Yerbabuena, heading south, he secured the anchor, took down the awning, and hoisted the dinghy on board. The lights of Acapulco were astern as he went below to set a course for the Marquesas.

Nuku Hiva

He sat at the chart table making calculations. It was 2,860 miles to Nuku Hiva. If he averaged four knots, he could make 96 miles a day and reach Nuku Hiva in about 30 days. If he averaged five knots, he could make 120 miles a day and reach it in about 24 days. If he averaged six knots—but he could never average six knots, not for 2,860 miles. He went on deck and looked at the horizon. Visibility was closing down. To windward the horizon was already lost in a cloudbank. *Jest* was up to more than five knots. Soon she would be doing six knots and then he'd have to think about releasing the wind-vane and steering himself. He went below and put hot water on for tea and soup, then he got the storm trysail out of the forepeak.

By evening he was under trysail and staysail, and *Jest* was still making over five knots. The lee rail was often in the water and he had to do the steering now. The waves threw the bow off and when it fell off too far, water came aboard. He was already soaked and by midnight he would be too cold and too tired to steer. Before that happened, he decided to take in the staysail and heave-to with the trysail. He lashed the wheel and went forward, hooking his safety harness to the mast. He got the staysail down and then went below and slept.

For five days he wore his harness. Each day he steered, sailing under trysail and staysail. Each night he hove-to and slept, or tried to: everything below was wet. Each evening he worked out his position by dead reckoning. In five days he made 280 miles, one-tenth of the way to Nuku Hiva. At this rate it would take him 50 days. He had water for 60 days.

When the weather cleared enough to use the self-steering gear again, he hung his bedding out to dry, except his pillow. He threw it overboard; he had decided to learn to sleep without a pillow. The mangos were going bad, so he sat in the cockpit and ate all seven of them. The bananas, hanging in a bunch from the skylight, began to ripen all at once. He made banana bread and banana pancakes. He fried them and steamed them. He ate them mashed with condensed milk. In the end, he threw half of them overboard, including all the ones he had boiled in canned strawberry juice, a gift from the *Horizon*, the boat whose topsides he never got around to doing.

He was down to oranges and onions so soon that he began to brood about how much canned food he would have to eat before reaching Nuku Hiva. Even canned peaches no longer appealed to him the way they used to. It was with the thought of fresh fruit and Nuku Hiva on his mind that he stared at the books that Jack had stocked in the bookcase. He had read *The Sea Wolf,* so he began leafing through *The Cruise of the Snark,* until he spotted the word *Marquesas.* He began to read from there: "in the thick of a heavy squall, the wind shifted suddenly to the southeast. It was the trade at last. There were no more squalls, naught but fine weather, a fair wind, and a whirling log." That's where he wanted to be too, in the southeast trades. The next chapter was called "Typee" but it was about Nuku Hiva. He began to read, looking for references to fruit. But the first time London mentioned eating was a reference to cannibalism. Then London began talking about race, and he remembered Jack saying that anyone who talked about race was a racist. First London said the Marquesans were a dying race and then he said they were a mixture of different races. So that there "are more races than there are persons, but it is a wreckage of races at best." This seemed somehow odd, the idea of both dying and mixing, but then London had nothing good to say about the Marquesans. They were disease-ridden, mostly with tuberculosis, but also with such exotic diseases as leprosy and elephantiasis, and their island had become a "howling, tropical wilderness."

Then in this howling, tropical wilderness London decided he wanted to drink a coconut, but instead of getting the coconut himself, he persuaded a Marquesan to get it for him:

> The cluster of nuts at the top was fully one hundred and twenty-five feet from the ground, but that native strode up to the tree, seized it in both hands, jack-knived at the waist so that the soles of his feet rested flatly against the trunk, and then he walked right straight up without stopping. There were no notches in the tree. He had no ropes to help him. He merely walked up the tree, one hundred and twenty-five feet in the air, and cast down the nuts from the summit.

Skip wondered what the Marquesan, a member of that dying and mixed race, thought about the inevitable white man who could sail three thousand miles across an ocean but couldn't walk that last one hundred and twenty-five feet to get his own coconut.

He had been trailing a line with his best lure, hoping to catch a fish, when one morning, just before sunrise, he heard something hit the mainsail and plop on deck, and then he heard the same sound two more times. On deck he found three squid and put them in a bucket of sea-water. In San Francisco, only poor people ate squid, but as Jack said, poor people eat better than rich people. He cleaned the squid and cut them into rings. At first he thought he would just throw the feet away, then he remembered that they were called tentacles rather than feet, and so he cut out the eyes and what looked like a beak and added the tentacles to the pile of rings. He decided to sauté the squid in oil with a little minced garlic and parsley—he had a jar of dried parsley—and serve them on noodles.

He had been averaging about 90 miles a day when he entered the doldrums and the winds became light and variable. At first he motored when there was no wind at all, but later he decided to turn the engine off and catch what wind he could in the frequent squalls that darkened the horizon. Chasing squalls was often frustrating, for at first there wasn't enough wind and then there was too much. But eventually he hit a storm that marked the southern edge of the doldrums, and after a last series of squalls swept past him, he reached the southeast trades and the first pleasant weather since leaving Acapulco.

He cut his hair the day he crossed the equator. After-ward he took a saltwater bath, using dish soap and a bucket, washing himself, he thought, in the name of the ill-tempered Neptune. From then on his days had a rhythm of their own, and he realized that he no longer noticed the clock. It was a brass ship's clock, fastened to the bulkhead, next to a matching barometer. Sailing down the coast, he had hated it because it chimed the hours and half hours, and he had let it run down off of Mexico. In Acapulco he had taken it off the bulkhead and tried to give it to Fred on the *Omoo*. But Fred wouldn't take it, and in the end he put it back on the bulkhead, wound it up and reset it. Fred had told him that when he began to hear the chimes without noticing them, he would be at home on the boat. He reached this point when he hit the southeast trades. He got up before sunrise and made tea. Later he ate pancakes or oatmeal, usually with applesauce and condensed milk. Then he cleaned up, checking the bilge and sometimes the battery, when he remembered. He took sun sights in the morning and then waited for noon to work out his position. He usually made pan bread and cooked rice or beans for lunch and then slept until evening. He got the Greenwich time in the evening, when the reception was better. Then he ate whatever was left over from lunch and tried to eat something fresh, but even his onions and potatoes had given out. Usually he stayed up late, sometimes the entire night, sitting in the cockpit.

The squid, landing almost fortuitously on deck, reminded him of a story he had once read about a dog that wandered aimlessly around, waiting for food to fall out of the sky. Now that he was in the southeast trades, the squid became important, not just because he liked to eat them, but because they broke up the rhythm of his day, a rhythm that was marked by *Jest* rising up on the long Pacific swell and sliding down again in a rolling motion. His sense of time and place became lost in the motion of that Pacific swell, as that motion took on its own meaning, independent of where he had been or where he was going.

Then one day everything changed. He sighted Ua Huka beneath a heavy layer of clouds. Later that day, just before sunset, he sighted Nuku Hiva, its dark and ragged mountains clearly outlined by the setting sun. He hove-to that night, and the next morning he passed Tikapo Point on the southeast end of Nuku Hiva, and less than an hour later he rounded Mataupapuna Island, at the head of Taiohae Bay. When he lost the wind inside the bay, he took in his sails, motored up the bay and anchored. It had taken him 37 days from Acapulco, averaging 78 miles a day.

There were two other yachts anchored in the bay: a 65-foot staysail schooner called *Nimbus* and Walker's ketch the *Dolphin*. He wondered how Walker got to Nuku Hiva before him. He also wondered why he was in Nuku Hiva, and for the first time in weeks, since leaving Acapulco, he thought of Jack.

He got his dinghy over the side and rowed ashore to get clearance at the gendarmes. Afterwards, he went to the store and bought some bread, a baguette. He felt good walking on a broad path under the trees, for it slowly began to sink in that he had made it to Nuku Hiva. Then he came upon a man sitting under a tree, carving what looked like a war club. The man had elephantiasis. His left leg and foot were swollen to nearly twice their normal size. The man looked up and smiled and said, "Bonjour." Skip saluted him with his baguette and said, "Bonjour," before continuing on his way back to the beach.

When he got back to *Jest*, one of the men on the *Nimbus* rowed over to gossip. "I'm Les. Walker, over there on the *Dolphin*, said you might be coming in. So you sailed all the way from Acapulco by yourself. I couldn't do that, not if I lived to be a hundred." Les provided him with all the usual facts: there were two couples and eight children on board the *Nimbus*, and Les was the owner's brother-in-law. They were from Seattle and had sailed to Nuku Hiva from Los Angeles. The owner didn't want to go to Mexico for some reason. After Les had talked for ten minutes or so, he invited Skip over to the *Nimbus* for dinner.

That evening Skip noticed that the *Nimbus* had a lot of room. There was a long companionway below, with cabins port and starboard. The table in the main cabin sat twelve easily, though not everyone was there for dinner. The owner was there, a large, friendly man, but not his wife. Skip sat next to Betty, one of his daughters. She was sixteen, the same age as Skip, and as she started to talk to him, he was reminded of high school.

"How was your trip from Acapulco?"

"Well, you know, first it was wet every day and then it was sunny every day."

"Nothing much happened? Nothing broke? Things are always breaking on our boat."

"Well, the jibstay came off at the masthead, and I thought for a while I was gonna lose my mast, but I. . . ."

"Don't you miss high school?" She had to ask him twice before he could work out an answer.

"No, not really."

"I can't wait to get back to Seattle. I dreamed that we got back to Seattle and that I had missed three whole years of high school and none of my friends would even talk to me. My mother says I shouldn't have dreams if I don't like them. Do you dream about things you don't like?"

"Last night I dreamed about cockroaches."

"Cockroaches?"

"They ate and drank everything on the boat. Then they dried up and crumbled into dust, cockroach dust."

"I hate cockroaches. My father hates them, too. That's why we didn't go to Mexico. What happened in your dream then?"

"I woke up and was very hungry and thirsty."

The next morning Skip rigged the boatswain's chair and repaired his jibstay. The shackle had simply come loose. Afterwards, he rowed ashore to go to the store. Just before he landed, Walker shoved off from his boat, so Skip waited for him.

"Hey, Walker, how did you get here before me?"

"Let me tell you, Skip. I left just after you did and sailed a great circle course. You probably sailed a rhumb line, and then I bet there were times when you were hove-to. I was never hove-to. Eddie and I stood watch and watch, even when it was blowing hard."

"Who's Eddie? You were still looking for crew when I left Acapulco."

"Eddie is Eduardo Maria Casagrande. I picked him up the day I left. He was just bumming around on the beach."

Skip wondered if Walker had talked to Jack but he didn't know how to ask without having to explain why he wanted to know. They had started walking up the path to the store. When they passed the man with elephantiasis, Skip mentioned *The Cruise of the Snark* and what London said about Nuku Hiva.

"Well," Walker said, "Jack London is an example of what we could call the poetic justice of natural selection. His beliefs were a bagatelle of Nietzsche, Darwin, and the superiority of the great white race. As he saw it, Superman shouldn't waste any time or pity on the diseases and devastations of the Pacific Islanders. But his idea of natural selection was never broad enough to encompass himself, so like many of the Islanders he despised, he died young, at the age of 40, of kidney failure exacerbated by pellagra. This was all the result of a bad diet while sailing around the South Sea on the *Snark*. In other words, they couldn't get Superman to eat his vegetables. There is a lesson there somewhere."

Just then Les came up. "Hi, are you going to the Chinese store?"

"Yes, but why do you call it the Chinese store?" asked Walker.

"Because it's owned and run by a Chinaman."

"Yes, but what if it were owned by a Frenchman. Would you call it the French store?"

"What do you mean?"

"I mean it's the only damn store on the island."

"Yeah, and it's owned and run by a Chinaman."

When they got to the store, Skip asked Walker to ask the Chinese storekeeper in French what the Polynesians liked most in his store. The storekeeper silently pointed to the cans of corned beef that lined most of one shelf. In addition to bread, Skip bought a can of corned beef and on the way back to the beach, he gave it to the man who was sitting under the tree, carving a war club.

He was still wondering if Walker had talked to Jack, if Walker knew what charts he had, and if Walker was following him. So he asked him about Fred.

"I've been wondering about Fred. Did he ever leave Acapulco?"

"Fred is never going to leave Acapulco. All that talk about not being able to make up his mind about whether to go to Panama or the South Seas is just talk. When he gets tired of Acapulco, he'll go back to California."

"You think so? Anybody else come into Acapulco after I left?"

"I left the day after you did. Remember? I was pretty busy getting ready to leave, so I didn't have much time to notice any boats coming in."

Walker was lying, of course. There wasn't any way he—or anyone else—could have missed a new boat, especially the *Astrolabe,* no matter how busy he was. That meant Walker had probably talked to Jack. More than that, he probably talked to Fred, too. That's how Walker knew he was going to Nuku Hiva. Fred told him about the charts. As he got in his dinghy and rowed out to *Jest,* he wondered what it meant. He should probably get away, leave the Marquesas altogether. Jack was probably just over the horizon, waiting for him to get into some kind of mess and then suddenly appear, as if out of nowhere. He could get away as soon as he wanted, even that evening. All he really needed to do was finish filling his water tanks.

That evening, though, there was a feast and all three yachts were invited. As Les explained, the couple that was giving the feast were called Hina and Joe. Les found Hina very funny, mainly because what few sentences she could say in English always ended in "no bullshit," as in "You come to my party, no bullshit." Hina was from Hiva Oa and like many Polynesians, her dream was to go to Papeete. When an American yacht stopped at Hiva Oa and offered to take her to Papeete, she jumped at the chance, but first she had to get permission from the governor of the Marquesas, who was in Nuku Hiva. But when the yacht got to Nuku Hiva, the governor refused to give her permission, so Hina had to get off the yacht. As she had no means of support and no way to return home, the governor let her work in his house. Then Hina was caught stealing a butcher knife from the governor's house and put in the jail. In the same jail was Joe, who was there for stealing one of the governor's pigs. After a few weeks, Hina became pregnant, so Joe and she were let out of jail to start a family. Now they had three kids and they wanted to celebrate their marriage anniversary.

Skip decided to bring a bottle of whiskey, which he gave to the first Polynesian he met. The whiskey disappeared without any sign of acknowledgement, and he assumed that it was the wrong thing to bring. Skip was hoping Eddie would show up soon and that he could sit next to him. But eventually he had to take a place next to Betty. Instead of a table, huge banana leaves were laid on the sand. The dishes were coconut shells, and much to Skip's delight, he could use his fingers. There was pig, chicken, breadfruit, poi, and some strange vegetables. Skip ate everything that was put in front of him. After a while he asked about Eddie.

"He and Barb are together," Betty said. "He's taking her for a moonlight row in the dinghy."

"There's no moon now."

"That doesn't matter. They just want to be alone together. Don't you think he looks like Frankie Avalon? I think Frankie Avalon is so good looking. Don't you like him?"

"I like James Dean."

"But he doesn't sing."

"Buddy Holly, then."

"Oh, I don't like the kind of hair Buddy Holly has, and he wears those awful glasses. I don't think he's my type. Besides, he's dead."

"Along with The Big Bopper and Ritchie Valens. Do you think Eddie and Barb will show up?"

"No. Eddie wants to come with us on the *Nimbus*, but I don't think Dad will go for it. It's too bad. Eddie is a lot of fun, even though Barb monopolizes him all the time. You should have heard him at lunch tell about this guy he sailed with before he got on the *Dolphin*. Eddie makes him sound like some kind of Captain Bligh. He's got different genoas and spinnakers and he's always having them changed, even in the middle of the night. Then he has a cocktail hour but no one gets to drink anything except him. Eddie says he lies in his bunk, watching a repeater compass and if you steer just ten degrees off course, he cuts your cocktail privilege. Eddie said that by the end of the first two days, everyone had lost his cocktail privilege. But the worst part is that this guy then gets everyone in the cockpit at five o'clock and drinks a gin and tonic, while the rest of them have to sit and watch. It must be crazy on such a boat. I think Eddie called it *Astronaut* or some-thing."

"*Astrolabe.*"

"What?"

"The boat's called *Astrolabe.*"

"Do you know it?"

"Yeah. Excuse me while I take a little walk."

The next morning he found the port side of his deck covered with fresh fruit: bananas, papayas, mangos, coconuts, limes, and a large citrus fruit—larger than a grapefruit—that he didn't know the name of. The whiskey, as it turned out, was the right thing to bring to the feast after all. After eating a papaya with lime, he finished topping off his water. It was easy but dull work, and as the sun got higher, he put on the straw hat that he had bought at the store. By midmorning he was finished and he began getting ready to put to sea when he saw Les row Barb over to the *Dolphin,* pick up Eddie and then row them both ashore. Skip got in his dinghy and followed them. He saw

Les go off to the right, in the direction of the store, and Barb and Eddie go off to the left, in the direction of the path that led up the valley to the mountains. This was the only path that led out of the valley, so it wasn't unusual that he'd be on it too. He thought he would just hang back a little, out of sight, and then suddenly come upon them, pretending to be surprised. At first the path followed the stream that flowed down from the mountain. It was very pleasant in the shade, and he saw a few banana trees and then his first papaya tree. It was very thin and straight, with a bunch of leaves at the top, like a coconut tree. Under the leaves was a cluster of green papayas. For some reason the sight of the papaya tree made him very happy.

When the path began to turn into a series of switchbacks, he began to hurry, but when he reached the ridge, nearly out of breath, there was no sign of Barb and Eddie. The path branched and he went to the left, which he assumed led to Taipivai. At this height, at the top of the island, the landscape was more like a broken plateau with long grass and few trees. The southeast trades blew through the grass. After walking up and down ridges for about an hour, he came to a small fruit tree. After breaking open one of the egg-shaped fruits, he realized it was a guava tree. He ate as many as he could and then tucked in his shirt, so he could carry about a dozen more.

At the guava tree he decided to go back. He hadn't seen anyone, let alone Barb and Eddie. He suddenly felt strange, more alone than he had ever felt before, even at sea crossing the Pacific. Then he knew what it was. The boat. He was far from *Jest,* farther than he had ever been since leaving San Francisco. He hurried back to the first ridge where he could look out on the bay and see the three boats floating at anchor in the tropical blue water. He decided to get off the mountain and back to the bay as quickly as he could. He would leave Nuku Hiva that day, before sunset. He didn't need to talk to Eddie. But as he headed down the path that led back to the bay, he suddenly came upon Eddie with his arm around Barb, who had her face hidden in his shoulder.

"Eddie?"

"What'cha want, kid?"

"I just wanna ask you, did Jack talk to Walker in Acapulco?"

"Jack talks to everybody. Walker talks to everybody. Everybody talks to everybody. So what, ok? Now get lost."

Tahiti

As soon as he cleared Motumano Point, he set a course for Pago Pago, over 1,800 miles to the west. He had told both Walker and Les that he was heading for Tahiti, because that was where they were headed and that was where they expected him to go. He had even said that he might stop at one or more of the Tuamotu atolls. This would give him, he hoped, enough time to disappear somewhere beyond Samoa. That was his plan, to disappear somewhere beyond Samoa, though he didn't know yet where that somewhere was.

His course would take him north of the Tuamotu Archipelago, then just south of Flint in the Line Islands. It was good weather, with *Jest* rolling just enough to make him set up a lazy guy to keep the boom from swinging with the roll. He watched the flying fish, tickling the waves with their tails to get up speed, before sheering off to port.

He quickly fell into a routine that left him with a lot of time, so he decided to read another one of Jack's books, one called *Omoo*, because that was the name of Fred's boat. Fred had told him that Omoo meant rover. But according to the Preface of the book, Omoo referred to the wondering men called "taboo kannakers." This seemed more expressive than rover, for a taboo kannaker was someone who could travel from island to island without being attacked, and more important, without being eaten. This is what most yachtsmen expected, or at least desired, when they arrived at an island: not to be attacked and not to be eaten.

The weather continued fair and life on board was easy for five days, but on the sixth day out of Nuku Hiva he woke to find almost a foot of water in the cabin. He pumped it out and then lifted the cabin flooring. At first he couldn't find where the water was coming from, so he plugged up the limber holes to isolate the compartments of the bilge. The water was coming in somewhere in the main cabin, and since he couldn't see anything, he guessed that a seam had opened under one of his freshwater tanks. Even if he could stop the leak temporally, he had to get *Jest* to a port where he could get her hauled out. That meant Papeete, which was now almost due south of him.

He drank as much freshwater as he could, filled all his pots, and checked his emergency water supply, then emptied his lower water tank into the bilge. Only when the tank was empty did he realize that he could have taken a fresh water bath. He unfastened the tank and manhandled it forward. He couldn't see anything, but the bilge was still slowly filling up. He put the water tank back and then took the starboard settee apart, opened the valve of the upper tank and let it flow into the lower one. When he lifted the tank up, he found underneath it one of Jack's hidden treasures, a long, flat package that was tightly wrapped in plastic. He threw it up on the bunk and returned to the leak. It was as he had expected: the water was seeping in at a seam. He couldn't think of any way to stop it, so he put the tank back. If it didn't get any worse, he wouldn't have to pump for more than a few hours a day.

But each day it got worse. By the time he had cleared the Tuamotus, leaving Mataiva atoll to windward, he was pumping four hours a day, two in the morning and two in the evening. Papeete was 160 miles away, about two days at the most. But the next day he was hit by a storm and blown west of Tetiaroa without ever sighting it. He was hove-to for three days, and each day he had to pump more. When he finally cleared the pass at Papeete, he was pumping eight hours a day.

Once *Jest* was moored in Papeete, she stopped taking on water. Skip spent those first few days in Tahiti mostly on the boat, trying to forget all the pumping he had done and letting his hands heal. He looked out across the bay to the reef, with its line of white breakers. To the right was the main harbor, with its shipyard and slipway, closer were the docks for freighters, the occasional cruise ship, and the Moorea ferry. Next to him, in a line, were the other yachts, moored like *Jest,* with their bows out and their sterns tied to the seawall. Behind the seawall, separated by a strip of grass, ran Boulevard Pomare. To the left, the bay extended out to the channel that ran between the island and the reef in the direction of Faa'a. There was no exit there. Farther out he could see the breakers on the reef near the pass. The pass was the only entrance to the bay, which made the bay seem like a trap.

He couldn't get out of Papeete until he got *Jest* repaired, but that would cost more money than the $94 he had left from Acapulco. Besides, he needed that to live on. There was an English film company on the island making a movie called *Tiara Tahiti.* He recognized one of the actors who had played Captain Nemo in *20,000 Leagues Under the Sea,* and this made him hope that he could get a job as an extra. He went to where they were hiring for a nightclub scene and watched as everyone who looked and dressed European was hired to eat, drink, and dance. He said he could do that, but they said there were "no kids in the night club scene."

A few days later he thought he had a job working on the schooner *Pilgrim,* which was charted for a cruise to the Leeward Islands. He was ready to go as deckhand, when, overhearing how much the cook was going to be paid, he asked how much he was going to be paid. The owner of the *Pilgrim* looked at him somewhat surprised and explained that usually people paid him to sail on his boat, that he was making an exception for Skip by letting him come for free. But for free Skip could sail his own boat, though he didn't bother to say that.

As a rainsquall came in from the west, Skip was sitting in the cockpit protected by an awning. He was looking at the pass, thinking that Jack was coming, and when the *Astrolabe* appeared in the pass, she would plug it up, stopping any escape. He was still brooding about Jack when the squall cleared off to the west and a ketch suddenly stood in the pass. When he realized it wasn't the *Astrolabe,* he sat down again and watched it enter. As it came closer, he realized it was the *Dolphin,* and eventually Walker dropped his anchor and backed down next to *Jest.* Skip was looking for Eddie, but Eddie wasn't on board, at least he wasn't on deck. Instead, there was a Polynesian, sitting in the hatch doing nothing. He watched as Walker went ashore and walked off with Maurice, the gendarme who took care of the yachts.

A few hours later he saw Walker in Viama's, drinking coffee. Before he could say anything, Walker told him there was mail for him at the post office. Skip thought it might be from Anna. She must have guessed that he was in Papeete, since Papeete was one of the two places where he was most likely to turn up. The other was Panama. But it wasn't from Anna. It was a $500 money order from Margaret. There was no letter or note, just the money order, which meant, as he knew, that the money was from Jack, for Margaret was Jack's factotum. She might also be, or more probably have been, his consort. Once, when trying to decide what Margaret's relation was to Jack, he had looked up a lot of words, and although "factotum" and "consort" weren't exactly what he felt Margaret was, they were the most suitable words that he could find.

As he walked back, he saw that Walker was still in Viama's, now drinking Hinano beer. He wanted to find out what happened to Eddie, so he asked Walker about the Polynesian on the *Dolphin*. Walker said, "That's Tiriki. I picked him up in Mahini and brought him to Papeete so he could find a big, fat wife. I assumed he could speak French because every time I said something to him he said, 'Oui, Papa.' I also assumed that he could cook—he said, 'Oui, Papa' when I asked him—but I never found out whether he could or not because he was seasick all the way from Mahini. Aside from that, Tiriki is a wonderful fellow, the only fellow I know who smiles even when he's seasick."

Just then, Les joined them and began talking about the destruction of Tahiti. "Captain Cook said on his first visit—no, his second visit—that the white man had ruined Tahiti. And look here at the example." He gestured to Tiriki who was walking by. Actually he was strutting by, with an immense smile on his face. Les was referring to how he was dressed. Walker had given Tiriki some old clothes and Tiriki had cast off his pareu and T-shirt and put on a white dress shirt with a black tie. He also had on a pair of white boxer shorts—and nothing else.

"But this does not illustrate ruin. Tiriki is displaying, like his forefathers, his incorruptible simplicity and naturalness. And before you call him naïve, consider whether his simplicity is not also a natural satire of our own mode of dress. As soon as we reach the tropics and begin to 'go native,' the first symbol of civilization that we discard is the wearing of underwear. It is uncomfortable, unnecessary, and probably unsanitary. Tiriki is not only adapting our cast-off symbols of civilization, he is rubbing our noses in the display of our loss."

But he had stopped listening to Walker, for Tiriki suddenly reminded him of the description in *Omoo* of Papeete over a hundred years ago. Then it was common to see Polynesians proudly wearing various items of European clothes. Especially noticeable were the men parading up and down the road, wearing coats with pareus instead of trousers, and one young man who wore an old pea-jacket buttoned up to the chin, sweating in the tropical sun, but smiling, as Tiriki was now smiling. Tahiti hadn't changed that much.

"Look who's coming in, the *Aeolus*. It's getting so full here we'll all have to go to Bora Bora to avoid the crowd." Skip turned and saw the *Aeolus* looking for a place to moor at the end of the line of yachts, away from *Jest*. Before Walker could take up the topic of the Buchanans, Skip got him to agree to help him make the arrangements to have *Jest* hauled out as soon as possible. When Walker asked him what the hurry was, Skip showed him the palm of his hands and said he was getting tired of pumping three to four hours a day.

He got *Jest* hauled out sooner than he had hoped. Since he had to save as much money as possible, he wanted the yard to work on the leak. The rest of the work he decided to do himself. So as soon as *Jest* was in the cradle and out of the water, he scrubbed the bottom. Before the yard had gotten out the two planks that had been gouged along the seam on the breakwater at Half Moon Bay, he was putting anti-fouling paint on the bottom. By sundown he was finished, except for the gap on the starboard side where the two planks were still missing. They wouldn't be ready until the next day.

He washed off and walked into town. He was looking for Walker, who had offered a bunk on the *Dolphin* while *Jest* was out of the water. He found Walker outside of Quinn's eating from a cart. Skip joined him, had a plate of food and then followed Walker into Quinn's. They sat at a table and Walker ordered beer. "How did you like your *poisson cru?*"

"What's that?"

"That's what you just ate. It's raw fish. Actually it's not raw. It's been marinated in lime juice, coconut milk, and onions."

"It was good, but listen, I don't want a beer."

"How do you expect to be a real yachtsman. It's not enough to sail around, even single-handed. You have to learn to drink beer and kiss women." At that moment, two Polynesian women walked over and sat down. Walker seemed to know them, at least he talked to them as if he did. The woman next to Skip was at least five or six years older than he was. Her name was Titi and when he explained that he didn't like beer, she got him a coke. Then when the band started up, she got him to dance. She laughed at the way he danced, and at first he was a little offended, because he was trying hard to do a very vanilla version of the bop, with none of his Jerry Lee Lewis flourishes, but then he noticed that Titi wouldn't let other women dance with him. When a slow dance started, Titi adjusted easily to his two-step. Walker wasn't dancing, but during a break, he tried to get Skip to dance with Tia, the other woman at the table. But Titi wouldn't let him. She monopolized him until, exhausted from working on *Jest* all day, he fell asleep at the table.

When he woke up, Walker and Tia were gone and his right index finger was stuck in a Hinano beer bottle. People were leaving and Titi led him out of Quinn's and up a side street. They went inside a low barn-like building, with a hall down the middle and stalls on each side, separated by thin wooden partitions that did not reach to the ceiling. She took him into one of the stalls where he could see almost nothing. On the floor was a pallet. She pushed him onto it and took his clothes off. He remembered that his finger was still stuck in a beer bottle and that he probably shouldn't wave it around. When Titi was through with him, she made him go out and take a shower in the open shed outside.

When he woke up in the morning, his finger was no longer in the beer bottle, but he couldn't remember when he had gotten it out. He left Titi sleeping and went outside. It was cool and the town was still quiet. At Vaima's he drank a large cup of coffee and ate two rolls. Jack wouldn't let him put milk or sugar in his coffee, so he never drank it before. But now he poured milk into it until it was muddy brown, and then added sugar. He could learn to like coffee this way.

Just before sunset Skip moored *Jest* again next to the *Dolphin*. The yard had put in the new planks, caulked and payed them. He finished painting the planks just before *Jest* was slid back into the water. He had spent most of the day burning and scrapping the rest of the black paint off the starboard topside. It went much faster working from a stage than a dinghy. Now he had one side painted white and the other with no paint at all. But all the black paint was gone.

He thought of going to Quinn's to meet Titi, but after taking a shower on the quay, he realized he was too tired, and after eating some bread and papayas, he fell asleep. The next morning he was sitting in the hatchway when he saw Titi climb out of the *Dolphin's* cabin, followed by Walker. Titi smiled and waved: "Bonjour." Walker was trying to look sheepish, then he just laughed and said in his rolling voice, "She's going to do my laundry."

Although he wasn't actually looking for Walker, he found him later in Viama's, but before he could think of anything to say, Walker started in. "What can I say in my defense. I confess to unpremeditated fornication. That's second degree sex, intended but unplanned. All done in the hot blood of the moment. In fact, where were you last night? You had *Jest* moored again at the seawall before sundown. You were expected at Quinn's. Women depend on such things, you know. They want a good time and they expect you to be there, to dance and buy beer." He paused and then said as an aside, "Actually, you're too young to spend money on women.

"That's why the women like us yachtsmen, instead of the French. With the French it's all work and no play. The French want colonies, they want to be able to go where they can have servants and get suntans. For them this is serious business. They lost Indochina and they're losing North Africa. So this is serious business. It's about colonialism and imperialism, it's about being in charge, and as long as the natives are happy to play their role as natives, the French are satisfied. But the French themselves haven't any time for play.

"But it could be worse. At least they do their nuclear testing somewhere else. Though, when I think of it, that new airport out at Faa'a they're building is worrisome. Who do you think is going to be using it? You won't see a lot of Polynesians flying Air France. And now that MGM and *Bounty II* have gone home, that leaves the colonialists, the Foreign Legion and the tourists. Remember, Skip, whatever else they say about us, we're not tourists. We're travelers. The difference is based on time. The tourist generally hurries back home at the end of a few weeks or months, but the traveler, since he doesn't belong more to one place than to another, moves slowly, over a period of years, from one part of the world to another.

"And we'll have to be moving again soon. The three months they allow us here go by fast. And then it's hurricane season. Where do you plan to spend the hurricane season?"

Skip knew that a lot of boats were going to Port of Refuge in Tonga, so he said, "Probably Tonga. But I may go on to New Zealand. Do you think I could get work in New Zealand?"

"Unlike Mexico, New Zealand probably has child labor laws."

"Child what? Look, I'd do anything except babysitting."

"What's wrong with babysitting? Isn't it easier than scraping topsides?"

"I've tried it. With the Buchanans. They accused me of messing with their kids."

"Ah. Kid messing. It sounds like what one does with kids, though with the Buchanans anything you do turns out to be something Freud has a name for and "messing" probably isn't one of them."

Skip decided to sail over to Moorea and anchor in Cook's Bay. There he could finish his topsides and at the same time wait to see if Jack showed up. He wanted to see Jack without being seen by him, so he didn't tell anybody he was going over to Moorea. He didn't tell anybody anything, especially Walker. Early in the morning he dumped his bucket and took his shower on the seawall in his pareu, and then topped off his water tanks. After he turned the water off, he looked down the row of boats moored with their sterns to the seawall. He had kept a list of the boats that came to Papeete that season. There was the *Pilgrim,* an old pilot schooner that was used in the movie. They had pasted *Dark Lady* over her name on the stern and used her in a scene where a man in a striped shirt falls overboard. They shot the man falling overboard at least a dozen times. Later, the *Pilgrim* went out to the Leeward Islands and was wrecked on the reef at Maupiti, west of Bora Bora.

There was the *Black Witch,* a 120-foot steel-hull schooner. She had come into Papeete with a paying crew of sixteen, plus the owners who were captain and mate. Now there was no one left on board, except the owners. It seemed the paying crew couldn't put up with the continual bickering between the two owners, which sometimes developed into a spectacular exchange of blows, since both men were big and hairy. Now they were out of money, living off their ship's stores and the girls in Quinn's, who got drinks for them off the tourists whenever a cruise ship came in.

There was the *Hurricane,* the same ketch he had met in Ensenada. After they arrived, the crew fought for three days. On the first day Jones and Whitman fought. On the second day Jones and the woman fought. And on the third day Whitman and the woman fought. It was mostly shouting, but it was loud and public. The woman spent a night in jail for tearing up a hotel room. When she got out, she left the *Hurricane* and when home on the liner *Mariposa*. Jones and Whitman stopped fighting and sobered up after the *Hurricane* nearly sank in her moorings when the seacock on the toilet broke and seawater flooded the cabin.

There was the *Nimbus* in from Mahini. The captain found cockroaches on her and so he anchored her out in the bay, sealed her up and released cyanide bombs in all the cabins. The two families spent three days in a hotel. The captain's wife, whom Skip had never seen, went off in one direction and Les, with a Tahitian woman, went off in another. Three days later, after the *Nimbus* was aired out and everyone was on board again, everything was back to normal, or at least as normal as it had been before, except that Barb had gotten pregnant, from Eddie it seemed, who had disappeared.

There was the *Diana* in from Panama. Captain Johnson, who said he was too old to do anything other than sail around the world, was now on his seventh circumnavigation. His two crew members left as soon as the *Diana* was moored, complaining that they had done nothing but pump nonstop for 67 days. Captain Johnson always found new crewmembers, though he never held them for more than one passage, mainly because he was an old-school sailor, which meant he overworked and underfed his crew.

The Buchanans came in on the *Aeolus* and managed to offend everyone in the harbor, including Maurice, the gendarme, which was considered unnecessary and selfish. Buchanan returned one night smelling—as the whole harbor could hear—like "a Tahitian whore." And after breaking most of what could be broken in the main cabin, his wife locked herself in the aft cabin and didn't come out for two days. Later she took the kids and left for California on the *Mariposa*.

And there was the *Dolphin* with a new crewmember, Hans, who had sailed his own boat, the *Seestern*, to Papeete and then out to Maupihaa in the Leeward Islands to visit where Felix von Luckner had wrecked the *Seeadler* during the First World War. When Hans got to Maupihaa, a storm came up and he wrecked the *Seestern* on the same reef. Now he was a man without a boat, which among yachtsmen made him a second-class citizen.

These were the boats and the people that came to Papeete that season.

Samoa

After spending a week in Cook's Bay in Moorea, where between rain squalls he finished putting two coats of glossy white on his topsides, he took the ferry back to Papeete. He needed some 12-volt bulbs for his cabin lights and a gasket for the pump on his kerosene stove. And he thought he would check the post office one last time and pick up some fresh bread. It was about sixteen miles to Papeete, and the other passengers, all Polynesians, were seasick during the entire crossing. He didn't see the *Astrolabe* until the ferry passed in front of the yachts moored along Boulevard Pomare. He had half expected to see her there, but it still made him flinch when he realized that he didn't want to be seen by Jack, or by anyone who knew him, which meant all the yachtsmen in the harbor. He couldn't get back to Moorea until the evening ferry, so he had to stay away from Vaima's, the market, the post office, and probably the Chinese restaurant, where he had planned to have lunch.

He bought his light bulbs and gasket near the shipyard and then thought about staying there until the ferry left, when M. Furneaux, who ran the shipyard, came up to him and began talking to him in English. This was a surprise because M. Furneaux hadn't spoken one word of English while *Jest* was in the yard being repaired. M. Furneaux asked him about *Jest,* if she was taking any water and then he reminded Skip to keep his deck wet so that the seams didn't open up in the sun.

"So what about your other boat, this *Astrolabe* we are going to pull out tomorrow. Did you scratch her bottom too?"

"The *Astrolabe* is not my boat. It belongs to someone with my name, but it's not my boat."

"Who has your name, but not your boat?"

"It's Jack's boat. When you see him tomorrow, tell him that I'll be in Huahine next week and I'll meet him there, or if he misses me in Raiatea, I'll try to be in Bora Bora within a month, but that I'm not thinking of coming back to Tahiti." He couldn't think of the name of anymore leeward islands, so he finished what he hoped was an undeliverable message, one that no one would even try to pass on.

Staying away from the waterfront, he walked around to the post office. He waited in the shadow of a tree, about a block away, and watched through the afternoon as most of the yachtsmen in Papeete came to check for their mail. Later he saw Jack come around the corner with his slight limp and enter the post office. He was inside so long that Skip was beginning to think he had left by some other exit. Then he came out with Maurice the gendarme. After a few words, Maurice walked off, but Jack continued to stand in front of the post office, looking down the street, just to the left of where Skip was hiding in the shadows. He knew that Jack couldn't see him because the sun was low and shining into his eyes, but he was still unable to move. He could see that Jack had that canny look that meant he knew someone was watching him. Then Jack turned and walked away toward the harbor.

That evening he got back to Moorea without being seen, and the next morning he was underway, heading for Pago Pago. It felt good to be leaving. Moorea was astern, and behind it lay Tahiti, where Jack was. It felt good, mainly because his plan had worked. Jack hadn't trapped him in Papeete Bay. He had seen Jack and the *Astrolabe,* and he didn't think that Jack had seen him. No one saw him except M. Furneaux. And he was sure that Walker and all the other yachtsmen thought he was headed for Tonga.

Pago Pago was about 1,200 miles to the west, and with the southeast trades, that meant about ten days. It was easy, lazy-guy sailing. It was also cockroach weather. Except when they scrambled across his face at night, Skip didn't mind the cockroaches. He even took an interest in the various things they ate, which—aside from the things he ate himself—included soap, tar, paint, glue, cockroach poison, other cockroaches, and everything he dropped on deck. He began to believe that cockroaches could survive on bilgewater. They were secretive creatures with mysterious habits. He couldn't discover where they went during the day, whether they had nests where they laid their eggs and performed other housekeeping chores, or whether they were individualists, living alone like hermits in the outer reaches of the boat's crevices. They had the disturbing ability to get into places that seemed impossible to get into. He kept his sugar in airtight plastic bags, but whenever he opened one, there was always a cockroach inside. He once unscrewed the lid of a honey jar and found three cockroaches embedded in amber. Another time he found a cockroach in a tube of toothpaste that, as far as he knew, he had never opened before. He admired their ability to survive. Slapping them with an open palm, he discovered, didn't even stun them. In fact, hitting them with any part of the hand was usually nothing more than an empty gesture, for they simply kept going. The only sure method of killing them—and he had to be quick—was to step on them, shift his weight to that foot, and then grind back and forth. Once, after washing his foot, he noticed that this procedure tended to leave a stain on his unvarnished floorboards. So he called a truce. He decided to accept them, observe them, and maybe learn from their tenacity.

One day he took out the long, flat package that he had found under the starboard water tank. It was a bolt-action rifle. He assembled it and fired two rounds from the boxes of ammunition he found with it. He had tried to sell the pistol to the guys on the *Black Witch,* but they didn't have any money, so he traded it for a case of canned corn, two cases of peaches, a case of evaporated milk, and, what he really liked, a case of canned coffee. The pistol had been new, but the rifle, he noticed, was not. It looked like it had been worked on: the barrel had been shortened, new sights had been put on, and the wooden stock was hand-carved. It had the look of something special.

Twelve days out of Moorea, about an hour after picking up the light at Breakers Point, he hove-to until morning. On the chart, Pago Pago Harbor looks like an upside-down boot, with the toe pointed to the west. It was almost a mile from Breakers Point to Goat Island Point, where he turned into the inner harbor, which was the toe of the boot. He motored past the commercial wharf and then anchored in three fathoms, in front of Fagatogo, as the town was called. The rain fell in torrents.

He stayed on *Jest* most of the time, reading *Coming of Age in Samoa.* After a few days Buchanan came in on the *Aeolus.* Later he met Buchanan in town, and he seemed very apologetic and even forced Skip to take the $10 he was never paid for babysitting in Mazatlán. Later still Skip found himself becoming the victim of unsought confidences. With the exception of Jack and, in his own way, Walker, he found that most sailors were men of few words, men of secrets, who told stories so as not to reveal their secrets and thus remain, essentially, silent men.

But Buchanan wasn't the first to unburden himself to Skip. In Papeete one day Les told him all the gossip on board the *Nimbus*. Skip was eating in the Chinese restaurant around the corner from Viama's when Les came in and sat at his table. He ordered pork chow mein and, without any preliminaries, launched into a monologue that was slightly disconcerting. He talked about "passion" and "duty," which seemed to be related to "lush tropical islands" and "the demands of marriage," and through it all he seemed to be grasping for some reconciliation between a life at sea and a desire for brown bodies, neither of which, it seemed, interested his wife.

Now in Pago Pago the rain showed no sign of stopping. Buchanan rowed over to *Jest,* and after accepting a cup of coffee, launched into his own version of the same monologue. It began with the advice that Skip should never marry one of his own patients, something Skip didn't think he would ever do, and as advice, it sounded like just the opposite of what Jack would have said. Buchanan talked a lot about his wife, about her "difficult period" and "how much she owes me," about "obsession" and "fixation," although it was not always clear whose obsessions and fixations he was talking about, for they seemed to belong to the world at large. But what did become clear, even to Skip, was that Buchanan had made Freud, or at least some of his ideas, a major part of his marriage.

They heard someone hailing *Jest* and Skip went on deck to see who it was. The rain swept in, falling in sheets from the opening of the harbor, and the far shore was all blurred. The *Dolphin* had come in and Walker was in his dinghy along side *Jest*. Skip invited him aboard and poured him a cup of coffee.

"What's this. Have I come all the way from Tahiti to interrupt the psychoanalyst at work?"

"We were just talking about marriage."

"Ah, marriage. I sometimes wonder if I miss the bliss of domestic bliss."

"Well, what do you do instead then?"

"You mean, what do I do instead when. In Mexico I worship the proud and passionate prostitutes. In Tahiti I worship the hedonistic hearts of the Quinn's girls. In between I keep a strong grip on myself. Now in Samoa I've heard there are plenty of charitable churchgoers, panting for my conversion. But you, Russell," jabbing Buchanan in the shoulder, "why did you ever marry the woman that left you?"

"Well, at first she needed me. She was young and very good looking, you can't imagine how beautiful she actually was. There just didn't seem to be any way I could resist her. On top of that, she was rich. Her father has oil wells."

"That's the wrong answer, Russell. My question was meant to be rhetorical and you should have said, "I loved her and she loved me." Life would be simpler if we kept it that way." Into Skip's mind popped the line from Ritchie Valens, "Oh how happy now, we can be."

But Buchanan wasn't listening. He was talking about his wife. "But what gets me is that I taught her everything she knows. Everything she knows about Freud. And now she accuses me of all the obsessions and fixations that I taught her."

"He who makes his bed with Freud must lie down with him. But imagine Freud in paradise. I can see him in Tahiti surrounded by dancers, the band playing a fast and suggestive tamari. The bare bellies calling enticingly. And here's Siggy, making observations about neurosis. You know that he thought savages were neurotics and that neurotics were neurotic because they lacked civilized behavior, that is, because they were savages."

"Is that so?"

"Yes, of course, that's so. Look in *Totem and Taboo*. In fact, that's the whole point of the book: neurosis is the lack of civilized behavior, where civilized behavior is defined as whatever the middle class was doing in Vienna in 1900."

As the days passed and the rain continued to fall with a natural persistence, he began to notice that whenever Buchanan came over to *Jest*, Walker came over as well, a few minutes later. Then he began to notice that Walker tended to bring up Freud, either to manipulate the conversation, or to provoke Buchanan, or both. It was probably both. Walker was up to something, and he was surprised that Buchanan didn't seem to notice. Skip guessed that Buchanan had met Jack in Papeete or had heard something about Jack that Walker didn't want Skip to know. He couldn't imagine what, though Jack had his share of secrets. Even some of his lies were secret.

One day Walker was invited to the Goat Island Club and he took Skip along as his crew, he said, because his own crew, a young man who left the *Black Witch* in Papeete, had nowleft him. The rain was falling again as they walked towards the Club. Walker pointed ahead and said, "The only time you can see Rainmaker is when it isn't making any rain."

"You mean that flat-topped mountain across the bay? On the chart it's called North Pioa and South Pioa."

"You've got one of those charts where they've tried to preserve the Samoan names, but even so, the cartographer just couldn't resist introducing English words into the Samoan landscape. This is what they call creeping imperialism. In a few years they'll stick a Rainmaker Hotel here and in another ten years, even the Samoans will be calling the mountain after the hotel."

Their host at the Club was a radio operator called Williams, and when Walker discovered that he was a self-proclaimed Samoanologist, he got Williams onto the topic of Margaret Mead.

"The whole point of *Coming of Age in Samoa* is to claim that if you allow adolescents to have sexual freedom, they will become well-adjusted adults. But this is simply a sexual sideshow in Rousseau's idea of the noble savage. Look, Mead describes aspects of adolescent sexuality that run counter to her argument. For example, the male rapist, the *moetotolo,* and the female virgin, the *taupo.* Both are important forms of behavior that are outside of sexual freedom. In fact, they could be seen as framing the concept of sexual freedom in the Samoan society. When we look for the underlying principle that links these two forms of behavior, both depend on violence and both restrict female homosexual activity. In other words, we can see that they are the means that a society uses to suppress matriarchal tendencies, especially as expressed in lesbianism. What it all comes down to, and what Mead refused to recognize, is that sexuality is repressed in society because society is repressive."

Later, walking back to their dinghies, Skip said that Williams, when talking about Margaret Mead, sounded a lot like Jack. "He ought to," said Walker. "He was practically quoting from Jack's article 'Of Mead and Men.' But he obviously didn't get Jack's point. Jack argues that if Mead is right about Samoan sexuality, then he's right, too. But obviously he's not right—who could possibly believe that stuff about lesbianism. So if Jack's not right, then Mead's not right either. It's a logical fallacy, of course, but Jack was only trying to get people to question Mead's authority. But all he got was ridiculed or plagiarized because everyone thought he was serious. Which in the end probably pleased him more than anything else."

He noticed that Walker had had a lot to drink. "You know a lot about Jack."

"Well, to tell you the truth, when Jack was still teaching we shared—not an office—but a building."

"Is that why you've been following me?"

There was a pause. "Look, Jack asked me to look after you, and. . . ."

"How did you know where I was going?"

"Jack told me." He paused again, realizing this time that he was probably saying too much. "We all knew you were going to Pago Pago because you said you were going to Tonga."

What was this? Was Walker Jack's agent? But Walker was looking at him, so he said, "Jack didn't tell you to look after me. That's not something Jack would say."

"Actually, he said I should take notes. I think you're to be a chapter in his next book, which he'll probably call "Coming of Age in America." Or maybe you're to be the whole book, in which case he'll probably call it *Coming of Age at Sea.*"

"Are you?"

"Am I what?"

"Taking notes."

"I'm always taking notes."

Fiji

He sat in the hatchway with his back to Tutuila. Jack wasn't chasing him. Jack was pushing him farther and farther. It was like the story Margaret told him, just before Jack moved him out of the house in Berkeley and into his own one-room apartment, above the garage in Sausalito. Margaret was sitting at the dining room table and he had come in and stood at the opposite end, with his left hand resting on the back of the chair. It was Jack's chair, now empty. "I remember once, you were standing like that and Jack was sitting there. You were about four-years old and you wanted Jack's attention. But he was talking, so you started to bounce up and down, holding on to his chair. After a while he turned to you and said, 'You want to bounce. Keep bouncing until I tell you to stop.' So you kept bouncing and bouncing. Jack thought you would want to stop after a while, but it seemed like you would never get tired. Finally he told you to stop, but you kept on bouncing and bouncing, not paying attention to anything. Jack had to hit you before you would stop. I've rarely seen him so angry."

This was one of his favorite childhood stories. Now he knew why. Jack lacked patience and he had beaten Jack because he lacked patience. It was a game, and Jack liked to play games, only he also liked to make the rules. So he had beaten Jack at his own game. Now Jack was playing another game with him, only instead of bouncing, it was sailing. He had reached the point where Jack said, "You want to sail. Keep sailing until I tell you to stop." But Jack lacked patience. Jack would tell him to stop, but he wouldn't stop. He had only to keep going. He didn't even have to hide, just keep going. At some point Jack would get angry. And then it would be over.

A tension that had been building up in him was suddenly released, now that he knew what he was doing, why he was sailing farther west. He could concentrate on enjoying himself because he didn't have to worry about anything except the sailing. And that was a simple matter. The sea didn't play games. It wasn't out to get him. It wasn't like Jack. It wasn't what Jack called a reality teacher. It was simply reality. He knew he could learn from it, but he also knew that, unlike Jack, the sea wouldn't try to teach him.

There was a string of islands and atolls about 150 miles east of Viti Levu. He had to pass through them and then cross the Koro Sea before reaching Suva. At first he wanted to take the Bounty Passage but decided against it. It was out of the way and more dangerous than the Lakemba Passage, which he reached on the sixth day out of Pago Pago. After approaching the north side of Lakemba Island, within two miles of the reef, he headed due west toward the southern end of Ngau Island. The next evening he watched the sun set behind Viti Levu and later that night he hove-to off the lights of Suva.

In the morning he tied up at the wooden dock of the Royal Suva Yacht Club, just behind the 70-foot staysail schooner *Oceanid*. The owner of the *Oceanid*, Bob Sterling, caught his mooring lines and told him if he had a yacht club flag and—looking aloft at *Jest's* mast—a British courtesy flag, he could use the yacht club facilities, which included a shower. Skip had a yacht club flag because Jack was a member of a San Francisco yacht club, but he had no British courtesy flag. Bob had a spare one to loan him, and after handing it to Skip he said, "Now all you have to do is convince the club secretary that you are white." After hoisting the yacht club flag to the port spreader, the British courtesy flag to the starboard spreader, and the American ensign on a staff at the stern, he had free run of the yacht club, so he went and took a shower.

He was very tired but before going back to *Jest* and sleeping, he stopped at the bar and had coke with ice. There were three men drinking at the bar, two were crewing on the *Oceanid,* an American and an Australian, and the other was on a South African yacht anchored out in the bay. Skip was slowly crunching his ice, enjoying its coolness, when the voices of the other yachtsmen suddenly grew louder. He hadn't been listening to them, though they seemed to be arguing about something. Suddenly the Australian's arm shot out and knocked the South African down. The American started cheering, and then the Australian knocked him down. Skip, who hadn't said anything, was just putting his glass down when the Australian knocked him off of his bar stool. At this point the club secretary came running into the bar, making a hushing sound, as if he were trying to quiet children and the Australian knocked him down as well. The Indian behind the bar hadn't moved or said anything and perhaps the Australian didn't see him.

The next day Skip had a black eye, but then so did the club secretary when he came to tell him that he was "persona non grata" for fighting, or as he said, for "being in a disturbance."

"But I wasn't fighting. I was just sitting there. It's all a misunderstanding."

"There is no misunderstanding. You were in a fight. Thus you were fighting." Skip wondered if the secretary was persona non grata as well, since he was also in a fight. But he thought that if the secretary couldn't see that for himself, it wasn't worth telling him. All it really meant was no more showers and no more ice. He took down all his flags.

Bob came over to apologize for his Australian crew. "He's a good crew. It's just that he has a very unfortunate way of conducting arguments."

"What was it about? The argument I mean."

"Fried bananas."

"Why didn't they just have a cook-off or something."

"No. Not that. Whether bananas cause constipation or diarrhea."

"I make them all the time and don't get either one."

"Maybe that's why you got knocked down." Bob invited him over for lunch to meet his family. But Skip was too self-conscious about his eye, so he said he couldn't. He was expecting someone. Maybe some other time. But the *Oceanid* was leaving the next morning and there wouldn't be another time, until many days and many miles later. And only then, after all those days and miles, was he to realize that he had missed an opportunity in Suva that day, that except for a freshwater shower or fried bananas or something, things might have been different. But as Jack said, that's how we experience fate, that except for some things, other things might have been different.

He would have left Suva the next morning as well, but he was waiting for the *World Traveler Magazine* people. When they arrived, it turned out to be a man named

Gordon who was both a writer and photographer and Anna, who had kept in touch with Skip ever since Half Moon Bay. Anna and Gordon liked the bar and veranda of the yacht club, and when the secretary learned that they were from *World Traveler,* they were given full privileges of the club. And when the secretary learned why they were in Suva, he invited Skip back to the club. The secretary came to him, his yellowish eye facing Skip's yellowish eye, and said, "You weren't fighting. You were just an innocent bystander. It was all a misunderstanding." Skip refused. This, he thought, was an argument he could win. "There was no misunderstanding. I was in a fight. Thus I was fighting." Besides, Anna brought him a coke with ice when he wanted one, and if he got up early, he could take a shower at the club before the secretary arrived.

Anna, he could see, was trying very hard to be nice to him. He usually ate dinner with her at her hotel, though he preferred the Indian curry houses. She went shopping for him, buying him clothes that he never would have bought himself and that he didn't think he would ever need. During the day he and Anna would sit around and talk, though they never talked about Jack, Pete, or as he realized later, what she was actually doing in Suva or how she was involved with *World Traveler.* Gordon, who looked like a small version of Teddy Roosevelt, sat on the veranda making notes. Skip assumed that Gordon was getting information about him from Anna, for Gordon rarely asked him anything. One clear day they took *Jest* out to take photos. Gordon chartered a powerboat, so that he could photograph *Jest* under sail. After about a week, Gordon said he could wrap it up with just a few questions.

"Let's begin with this. Why did you decide to sail across the Pacific on a small boat? You probably had to beg your father to interrupt your education and promise to continue studying at sea."

"Yes."

"Luckily your father is very farsighted and realized that learning to be independent and self-reliant is as important as learning history and algebra. And what better way is there to do that than to experience nature first hand. Does your father continue to encourage you?"

"Yes."

"Let's try this. What are you afraid of most?" He had to think about that, because at first it had been Jack but now he couldn't think of anything in particular. "Storms," Gordon said. "You're probably afraid of being hit by a big storm. So far you've been lucky, but somewhere ahead of you there's a big storm, a hurricane or typhoon." It seemed to him that Gordon had already written his article. He had seen issues of *World Traveler* before and he could see in his mind how the article about him would look. There would be four or five pages of photos—they were the most important part—and in between, sort of like tar poured between the planks, would be sentences such as, "He begged his father to let him go to sea and to experience nature first hand" and "He had been lucky so far, but somewhere ahead of him was a big storm, maybe even a hurricane or typhoon."

"Do you often feel lonely? With long stretches of ocean behind and before you, you probably spend long hours, thinking of the girl you left behind you." He sat there, he realized, with a blank look on his face, until Gordon said, "Your high school sweetheart?" Then he remembered Carol. She was so much like him that he had never noticed her until they went to see *Psycho*. His whole homeroom class decided to go, and he ended up in the back seat of someone's car, next to Carol. And, he realized now, she ended up next to him. So they sat together in the movie house because everyone else was pairing off and moving to different corners to be alone. During the shower scene, Carol grabbed his forearm with both hands and held on to it. Then, when the mother was suddenly turned around in her chair, Carol screamed—along with a lot of other people—and clutched him around the neck. At first he was embarrassed, and then he felt sorry for her because he realized that afterwards she felt she had made a fool of herself. Though now, when he remembered her hysterical tears and warm breath on his neck, he felt for her a certain affection. The following Monday, in school, she came up to him and said she was sorry for screaming. He pointed out that most of the girls in the class had screamed. But that's not what she meant and he knew it. So she said that next time she wouldn't scream. She was asking him to ask her for a date. But it never happened. Jack took him out of school to work on *Jest,* and although he called her twice, he didn't have a car. Besides, he didn't want to explain to her why he wasn't in school.

"Carol. Her name is Carol."

"Oh, we don't really need a name. She'll just be the 'someone' who's waiting for you to get back."

"To get back?"

"If this issue is successful, we'll probably be able to do at least two more, one for the Indian Ocean and one for the Atlantic, plus, of course, the final one."

"You mean back to San Francisco?"

"Where would you like to go? The Seychelles?" Gordon had turned to Anna. "Could you do an assignment in the Seychelles? You know, sign the contract and everything."

"Of course." She looked a little pained, and Skip noticed that she changed the subject. "If we expect to catch the early flight out tomorrow, we had better get packing."

By the next morning, Skip wanted to ask a few questions, but he didn't get the chance. Gordon had given him a camera and film and told him to take a lot of photos. Anna had given him $400 and told him to ask for more if he needed it, especially if it was for *Jest*. He liked the money. It made it easier to be independent of Jack. He began to feel, though, that *World Traveler* was trying to organize him. He didn't care what they printed. That was their business. But he didn't like being told what he was supposed to do or where he was supposed to go. Actually they didn't even tell him. They just assumed it, that he would sail around for a while and come out at San Francisco. It made him think of the proverb, "Out of the frying pan and into the fire." Which made him think of other proverbs, "Look before you leap" and "He who hesitates is lost." Was he getting away from Jack only to be caught up by *World Traveler*? There were other possibilities. There were always other possibilities. It was in the nature of things. But just now he didn't know what those possibilities were.

Nouméa

At sea his thoughts were like the waves, rising and falling, and also like the waves, he was never sure where they would arrive. After leaving Suva, he thought about Anna. She seemed to be acting as his agent, plus some kind of legal guardian, since he was still too young to sign a contract. If so, why didn't she just tell him, instead of playing the coy friend? What was she getting out of it anyway? If it was money, he didn't mind, as long as she gave him some of it. If it was adventure, such as flying to places like Fiji, he didn't mind that either, as long as she didn't try to tell him where she wanted to have her adventures. If it was romance, it must be with Gordon, but he didn't care about that and it wasn't any of his business anyway. These all might be reasons why she had taken him up. But he felt that there was something else. He felt that she was adopting him, though not in any maternal sense. She wanted something out of him, not so much out of what he was doing, but more out of what he was. But he didn't know what that was because he didn't know what he was, not to an attractive woman who was older than he was, and probably more intelligent, certainly better educated. So it bothered him, not knowing what it was about him that she could have any use for. Somewhere down the line, on the other side of some ocean, he probably would find out, and he probably wouldn't like it.

Nouméa was about 760 miles southwest of Suva. At first the sailing was easy, with the wind just aft of the beam. He made such good time on this point of sail that he ended up going farther south than he needed. When he changed course and headed north by west, the wind was almost dead astern. Since the self-steering gear didn't work well on this point of sail, he was in the cockpit steering. The wind picked up in the evening and he decided to set his course more to the south again, so he could put *Jest* back on self-steering. He was also thinking that he should probably reef. Then he fell asleep. When the squall hit, *Jest* jibed, breaking the mast. He woke to see it and the sails falling, almost in slow motion, until the entire rig crashed on the port bow and slid into the sea. At first he just sat there in the cockpit, then as *Jest* lay broadside to the wind, the mast began to beat against the hull. He tried to get the mast on deck, but with the sails and the rigging and the size of the sea, he couldn't handle it. Everything was one big tangled mess, plus the weight of the water in the sails made it too heavy. He got the cutters out and began cutting the rigging free. At first he tried to save as much of the rigging and sails as possible, but in the end he had to cut everything free. Then he left *Jest* lying a-hull and went below and slept.

In the morning he prepared breakfast, beginning with tea, then bananas with condensed milk, pancakes with strawberry jam, and ending with coffee. Afterwards he cleaned up below and then went on deck. The mast had broken about five feet from the deck. The boom was where he had lashed it to the port rail with about a foot of mainsail still attached to it. He had lost the jib, but the staysail had been furled to its club-boom and it was still there. *Jest* was drifting toward New Caledonia at about one knot. If he could jury-rig a mast with the boom, then maybe he could get steerageway and make a few more knots. The boom was light enough for him to manhandle and he had enough rope to rig it with double backstays. He set the trysail with a jury-rigged reef. That gave him steerageway. Then he set the staysail with a jury-rigged reef. That was even better and he could keep her on a course heading for Nouméa, about 200 miles to the northwest. That was four to six days, maybe more, for he would have to heave-to and sleep now and then. Then he would be close enough to Nouméa to motor in.

Sixteen days out of Suva and seven days after losing his mast, he picked up the light on Amedee Islet, which marked the pass through the barrier reef that encompassed Grande Terre, the main island of New Caledonia. In the morning he took down his sails and motored through the pass and on into Nouméa, where he anchored in Fisherman's Bay. Later the next day an Englishman by the name of Brown came out in an old rowboat and told him he could move over to the yacht club, where there was room at one of the floating docks. He invited Brown aboard to show him the way to the yacht harbor. The yacht club had a new floating dock but no club house. After they tied up *Jest,* Brown said, referring for the first time to the fact that *Jest* had been demasted, "That is a remarkable rig." When Skip didn't respond, Brown continued, "But it seems to have served its purpose." Skip invited him below and offered him a cup of tea, which he declined, and then a glass of whiskey, which he accepted. "Don't bother about the ice," he said, and Skip realized after a moment that Brown was joking, that Brown had seen immediately that there was no refrigeration on *Jest.* When Skip finished telling the story of how he lost his mast, Brown finished his whiskey and said, "Well, I'm looking forward to seeing your new mast."

For a week he didn't do anything except walk around Nouméa. He went into town every day or so to buy fruit and bread. In the late afternoons he walked out to the beaches where the French lay in the sun or drank in bars at the edge of the sand. He often stopped at the Bar Ritz and had a coke. He knew he should write Anna and tell her it was all over. *World Traveler* wouldn't be interested in someone who couldn't keep a mast in his boat. Besides, how was he to get a new mast, plus rigging and sails. He felt so stupid about losing his mast that he couldn't get the letter started. But at the same time, he also realized that if he didn't do anything, Jack would eventually show up. He didn't want that, but without a mast there just wasn't anything he could do, except go off and live in the hills of New Caledonia. For a week that was about the only thing he could think of.

In the early afternoons it tended to rain. He left his jury-rigged mast up, so that he could rig his awning. When he decided to extend his awning to the foredeck, so he could leave his hatch open at night, he noticed for the first time that there were two wires hanging out of the broken stump of the hollow wooden mast. Two wires didn't make any sense. One wire was for the masthead light. But the mast hadn't carried anything else that needed electricity. Where did the other wire go? There was an aluminum plate on the aft side of the mast, below the boom yoke. At times he had wondered what it was for. Now he took the screws out and lifted it off. Inside the mast was a series of battery packs—he couldn't think of what else to call them—and what, he began to realize, must be a radio. Probably a transmitter that sent out a signal, a particular frequency at a particular time. So the second wire was not for electrical power. It was an antenna for the radio. He wondered if Walker or someone else came aboard and changed the batteries when he wasn't around.

The whole thing was sealed in plastic. He put it carefully back the way he had found it and then screwed the plate back on, making sure the gasket was in place. The last thing he did was reach as far into the top of the broken mast as he could and cut off both of the wires. He threw the parts he had cut into the water.

Now he was in such a hurry that he forgot to take Anna's phone number with him and had to go back for it. At the post office he got through to Anna on the first try.

"Hello?"

"Hello, Anna? Can you hear me?"

"Who is it?"

"It's Skip. I've lost my mast."

"Where are you?"

"At the post office."

"No. I mean, what country are you in? Is everything ok?"

"I'm in Nouméa. I lost my mast but I was able to get into Nouméa with a jury-rig. Now I need a new mast, plus rigging and sails and everything."

"I see. Wait a minute." There was a pause, and as he waited he heard an animal-like whine in the phone line. "Here's what you do. Call me tomorrow at this time. Ok?"

When he called the next day he learned that *World Traveler* was going to pay for a new mast. It seems they expected him to lose his mast—or something similar—and that if he hadn't lost it, then they would have felt there wasn't enough adventure in what he was doing and that they wouldn't be getting their money's worth. As he hurried back to *Jest* so he could send off his sail plan, he thought it was too bad that *World Traveler* hadn't been there when he sprang the leak out of Nuku Hiva. That was an adventure. He wondered what else they expected to happen to him. It seems they were paying him to come as close to sinking or being adrift as possible. They expected all kinds of things to happen to him but that in the end he would survive. Or did they? Of course, if he died that was the end of the story. On the other hand, if they could get pictures of him sinking or lying dehydrated in his cockpit, shriveled up like a mummy, that would make a good story.

He met Brown on the dock one morning and told him he would be getting a new mast some time soon. Brown congratulated him and invited him up to his house for lunch. Skip accepted and then there was a pause before he remembered he was wearing shorts, T-shirt, and no shoes.

"I should change." Skip was trying to imitate Brown by not asking any questions.

"Very good idea. You'll be meeting my wife and her daughter."

Skip put on the pair of khaki trousers and the navy polo shirt that Anna had bought for him in Suva. Then he had to choose between the canvas shoes she bought him and his Mexican sandals. He decided on the sandals. He finished off by running his hands through his hair a few times and then washing his hands. He felt very dressed, almost as dressed as Brown, who had on a white shirt, with shoes and socks. They drove up in Brown's car. It wasn't far, just up the hill above the yacht harbor, but the car had to follow the road that went around the hill and up the far side. The house was at top of the hill, an old colonial villa that overlooked the town and the commercial harbor, but not the yacht harbor. That view was blocked by a stand of bamboo. Inside he met the wife and daughter, Catherine, who was about his age, which meant she was still in school.

Skip had never been in such a house before. The main room, the salon he guessed it was called, took up the entire front of the house. There were windows on two sides, some of them French, and on a third, a stairway leading to a landing that ran along the back of the house. There was a raised area at the back of the salon, under the landing, for dining. After a few words and a glass of something that could have been lemonade, Mrs. Brown sat at one end of the table, nearest to the entrance to the kitchen, and Skip was seated opposite her at the other end of the table. From his experience with Jack this meant that Mrs. Brown ran the household, that it was in fact her house, and Skip occupied not so much the seat of honor as the seat of scrutiny.

"So you are the son of the famous anthropologist Johnston Johns."

"Yes, ma'am."

"That's tongue, by the way. I hope you like it."

"Yes, ma'am."

"Wasn't Johnston Johns the American anthropologist who called us, the civilized people of the world, a pack of savages?"

"Well, he said that in some ways the civilized are more savage than the savages and that the savages are more civilized than the civilized."

"You would hardly say that the savages are civilized if you had ever seen a kanaka try to use a fork and knife."

"As Jack would say, have you ever. . . ."

"Jack?"

"Johnston Johns. Everyone calls him Jack. And he would say, have you ever seen a Polynesian watching a white man eat poi?"

"What are you trying to say?"

"Polynesians think it's ridiculous that we don't know how to use our fingers to eat poi."

"Well, I don't plan to eat any poi, certainly not with my fingers. Besides, this is Melanesia, not Polynesia."

"But that's not the point. It's like a Melanesian saying he doesn't plan on eating any tongue, so why should he use a fork and knife."

"That's exactly why they are savages. They don't even want to use a fork and knife. They would rather sit around drinking kava."

"As for that, a lot of French people sit around drinking wine." This was the first time that he had ever used one of Jack's arguments, plus the first time that he had ever had the desire to do so. Still, he couldn't see why Mrs. Brown was so upset with him that she barely spoke to him the rest of the meal. It couldn't have been the comment about wine, for there wasn't any wine on the table. But as he was to learn later, it was the wine. Mrs. Brown had what was called a drinking problem, a serious drinking problem, so serious in fact that if one of her Melanesians had had it, he would have been called a drunk.

When the meal was over, he thought he would have to leave, but Catherine didn't seem to be affected by her mother's attitude. She led him into the conservatory that ran the whole length of the back of the house. It looked unused. There were a few plants, but it was mainly full of old furniture.

"I don't understand why your mother was so upset."

"You contradicted her at her own table."

"What's that supposed to mean? We were just having a discussion about what Jack calls the Fork and Knife Argument."

"Besides, Mother thinks your English is bad."

"What's wrong with my English?"

"Before lunch you said 'could have went' twice."

"'Could have went'? What's wrong with 'could have went'?"

"It's ungrammatical. And what's really wrong with it is that you don't know it's ungrammatical."

"Huh. Do you want to hear how Jack ends the Fork and Knife Argument? First he gets the other side to commit itself to using a fork and knife for everything and then he says that most people—I think he says most cultures—use their hands in a lot of similar ways. For example, Jack would say, we don't use a fork and knife to wipe our butts." When he saw that she wasn't shocked, he said, "Actually Jack says 'ass' instead of 'butt' but 'ass' is vulgar." And when he saw that she still wasn't shocked, he said, "I must have told it wrong. You're supposed to laugh." This seemed to wipe out all that 'could have went' business and from then on they were on easy terms, sitting on an old sofa, watching the afternoon rains come in from the southeast. At least he felt easier once he became used to her tendency to look unflinchingly at him with her deep blue eyes, their darkness emphasized by her pale skin. Too pale, he thought, for someone who lives in the tropics.

The first thing she told him was that Brown, whom she called the Major, wasn't her father, making it implicitly clear that she didn't like him because he wasn't her father. Her father was French and lived in Paris. Her mother was born in St. Louis, but considered herself French. Her father and mother weren't married and never had been.

He felt flattered by her rush of confidences about herself and the intimacy it implied. At the same time, she said he was being ridiculous when she said she wanted to be frank and he said he was fine with being jake. It seemed that her humor didn't run in that direction. As he was leaving, she asked him if he could help her with her geometry. He could. Geometry was the only subject he had ever done well in at school. So she told him to come back on Tuesday afternoon.

He walked up the hill, following the path that ended at the drive that led up to the villa. Catherine met him at the door with a smile and a steady look; then she took his hand and led him back to the conservatory. She had on a white blouse and a long, dark skirt. It was one of those indistinguishable colors, somewhere in between gray and blue, even brown. He couldn't tell. He sensed that she had been uncertain about him coming and was now pleased that he had. While waiting for her to get her geometry book, he stared out the window at the garden. The geometry book was in French, which he hadn't expected because he hadn't thought about it. When she explained what the problems were, he looked at the diagrams and then told her the solutions. Sometimes he drew the diagrams for her. As she went to get tea, he thought it was funny that he had to leave school and come thousands of miles to help someone with her homework. It started to rain, blanketing the mountains, making the world smaller.

As they drank their tea, Catherine asked him, "Would you like to play a game? I ask you a question and you have to answer honestly. Then you can ask me a question."

"What if I don't?"

"It's just a game. Where you tell the truth."

"No, what if I don't answer. I mean, what if I don't like the question."

"It's not so terrible as that. I'll begin with something simple. Do you love your father?"

"No. I don't even like him."

"Why not?" She seemed surprised.

"Is it my turn now? That's not my question. Do you like it here in Nouméa?"

"No. I want to go to Paris, and I am going to Paris. Soon. Why don't you like your father?"

"Let's play the game this way. We get to ask each other just one question each time we meet. That way we won't wear the game out. So, what don't you like about Nouméa?"

"You just said you didn't want to play anymore."

"We're not playing. It was just a normal question. You don't have to give an honest answer."

She began to talk more about herself again, a little about school and living in Nouméa, but mostly about her mother. She talked about personal matters in an easy way that fascinated him, and that allowed him eventually to talk about himself, something he had never done before.

A few days later he got a letter from Anna, asking him to send the photos he had taken of being dismasted. He hadn't taken any photos. He had completely forgotten about the camera; in fact, he didn't even know how to use it. So when he saw Brown at the villa, which he often did, he asked him to go out with him on *Jest* to take some photos of his jury-rig. A few days later they went out and wallowed about inside the reef with the jury-rigged trysail and staysail set. As Skip had guessed, Brown knew a lot about photography. He probably knew a lot about a lot of things but preferred to remain as perfectly inconspicuous as he looked.

He had been in Nouméa for more than four months when he entered the conservatory and noticed that it was beginning to look like it was being used again. Catherine came in with some tea and a copy of *World Traveler,* the new issue with the article about him. She opened it up and said, "Here's a photo of you. You look like a skinny kanaka."

"I can't help it. It's mostly caused by sun and diet." There was a pause. "What if I were to call you a sophisticated Parisian."

"Well, what's wrong with that?"

"It depends on your point of view. It's like me saying what's wrong with being a skinny kanaka."

"Sometimes I think you are just mad. Too many days at sea. Here in the magazine it says, 'Loneliness rode with him for a hundred days, and throughout the longest nights. At times it was like something he could touch.' You never told me how lonely you were."

"I'm not lonely. If I had anyone with me on *Jest* they would be trying to boss me around. Then I would feel sorry for myself, which is probably worse than being lonely. Besides, I didn't write that stuff."

"What about this poem. It says you wrote it:

Diving with a splash
the bird of Pukarua—
rises with a fish."

"That's one of my haiku." He realized Anna must have given it to the magazine people. He didn't think Anna should have done that. He didn't want his haiku mixed up with the stuff Gordon wrote.

"Haiku? What does it mean?"

"This one is from a popular Tahitian song: 'Te Manu Pukarua.' It's about the birds of Pukarua. When the fishermen see them dive into the water, they know where to throw their nets."

"Are there any more?"

He looked out the conservatory window. It was a view he had become familiar with:

Bougainvillea
climbs the south face of the wall—
looking for the sun.

"It's nature poetry, isn't it? Could you do one about the hibiscus?"

"Where is it?"

"The hibiscus? There's one by the front door."

"I can only write from experience. And since I don't come in the front door, I haven't seen the hibiscus."

"But you recited the one about the bougainvillea, just like that, while you were sitting there."

He pointed out the window and said, "I've been watching that bougainvillea climb your garden wall for the past few months." She looked out the window, and he wondered if she was seeing the bougainvillea for the first time. He had thought of the haiku a few weeks before, but he didn't tell her that.

They sat next to each other on the sofa, drinking tea and watching the rain move in from the southeast. She asked him if he had known any native women. He asked what she meant and she explained the concept of carnal knowledge.

"Oh, that."

"Be frank. Have you?"

"What if I were to ask you that?"

"Really, we have nothing to do with native men."

We? She must mean Frenchwomen. "What about the guy that drives you home from school?" He had arrived early one afternoon and saw them drive up to the villa on a Vespa. "Do you let him pet you?"

"What do you mean?"

He explained the concept of petting.

"My mother says Americans have a number of vulgar habits."

"They probably do." But as far as he knew, being frank wasn't one of them.

It rained hard all afternoon and into the evening. She said there was no point in him getting wet. He could sleep on the sofa in the conservatory. She wanted him to stay and sleep there, though he didn't know why, unless it was her desire for secrets. She brought him blankets and in the dark he took his clothes off but couldn't sleep. Later in the night she came and told him her mother had come home "tiddly" again. Catherine was in her nightgown and as she bent over the sofa, her hair fell off her shoulder and over his arm as he lay there, and he realized that her hair had never been cut.

She looked at his pile of clothes. "Are you naked under the blankets?" He was, of course. Anna hadn't thought to buy him any underwear and he hadn't thought to wear any. But that was all Catherine wanted to know and she left after that. Their relationship was essentially a matter of talk, an intimacy of words and secrets, mostly her secrets. In the morning he left before anyone else was up.

When his new mast finally arrived by ship, Brown helped him get it transported to the yacht club and set up. He couldn't have done it without Brown's help, especially the tuning of the rigging. It took a couple of more days to reeve all the running rigging. When the sails were bent on and everything else was ready, he and Brown went out for a test sail. They sailed out to the lighthouse and except for a few minor adjustments, everything was fine.

They were all day out in the sun, so when they got back to the yacht club they were both tired. Brown seemed to have enjoyed it. Skip offered him a whiskey, and after the second one, Brown began to tell a story: "There was a man where I grew up, a man called Cooper who wanted to go sailing. He began to build a boat. It took him many years and when the boat was almost finished, he met a young woman and married her. He thought now he could go sailing with a mate, but at about the time the boat was finished—it was a beautiful 35-foot cutter and stood in his garden—his wife had a child. He thought that in a few years he would have a mate and a crew, but as the son grew old enough to go to sea, his wife had a daughter. All those years he kept working on the boat, keeping it up, and when the daughter was old enough, he put his boat in the water. Then the war broke out and the War Office requisitioned his boat. When the war was finally over and he got his boat back, it needed a complete overhaul, but then so did England. Like so many others, he worked repairing the war damage. In the meantime his boat slowly deteriorated and finally sank during a southeast storm."

At first Skip thought that Brown was talking about himself. But he wasn't. Brown was talking about him.

When Skip realized this, he tried to reassure Brown that he would leave Nouméa and continue his cruise. "Now that my mast is ready, I'll be leaving Nouméa. Catherine says she wants to go to France. Maybe I'll see her there."

Brown smiled. "That will be a good sail. Halfway round the world."

When he had his stores and water on board, he walked up the hill to say good-bye to Catherine. She wrote out her address and made him promise to come see her in Paris. He thought it typified their relationship: he had to promise to go to Paris to visit her, but she had never walked down to the yacht harbor to visit him on *Jest*. As far as he knew, she had never seen *Jest*, except in *World Traveler*. But he didn't want it any other way. He would remember the conservatory at the back of the villa for many days to come. It was the kind of memory out of which his past was to be formed.

Port Moresby

He didn't want to leave Nouméa, but there was so much pressure on him to leave that it seemed inevitable. Everyone he knew expected him to leave. Not only Anna and her *World Traveler* people, but also Brown and Catherine. Partly it was that article in *World Traveler,* plus he couldn't stay in Nouméa, now that they had supplied him with a new mast and sails. But he knew it was more than that. Leaving was part of the rhythm of his life on *Jest.* It was almost a year since he had left San Francisco, and he had thousands of miles behind him and twelve or more ports, so that leaving had become one of the things he did.

But still he didn't want to leave Nouméa. It was because of Catherine, and he had to ask himself if he was in love. Jack said he would be a fool about love, but then Jack said he would be a fool about most everything. He didn't mind so much about being a fool, but he didn't like the idea of proving Jack right.

He headed south, towards New Zealand. He averaged five knots and after three days he was about 40 miles northwest of Norfork Island when the wind first backed and then died. Without wind, the sails began to flop from side to side, slapping the rigging in the slow rhythm of the swell. He took them down. On the morning of the fifth day out of Nouméa he was surprised by the silence of the sea. At first he didn't think it was possible that the Pacific could be so calm, and as he looked out toward the horizon, he was reminded of the line from *The Rime of the Ancient Mariner*: "a painted ship upon a painted ocean." He had always wondered how an ocean could be painted. Now he knew what the line meant: it was motionless, for here, as in a painting, nothing moved.

Later a swell began to roll in from the northeast. It was so hot that he thought about going for a swim, but in the end he was afraid to leave the boat. On the third day of the calm he noticed that the barometer was falling. He knew a storm was coming, and while he waited for it, he decided to do what he had sailed so far south to do. The new mast, like the old one, had an aluminum plate on its aft side, below the boom yoke. He unscrewed the plate and took out the transmitter with its batteries. He knew that he had only to disconnect the batteries to disable the transmitter, but he felt that sailing 375 miles needed more of a gesture. He pulled the transmitter free from its antenna and threw it into the sea. The water was clear, and as he watched the transmitter sink, he half expected a shark to glide by and snap it up. Now he was ready to head back north.

The wind came up in the evening. By midnight he was headed north at five knots. By sunrise he was hove-to. By noon the wind was still rising. He knew he had to do something because *Jest* was lying over with her lee rail in the water, but he sat waiting, hoping the storm would peak. He realized he had become immobile with tension and was almost cringing when he heard a loud snap. The staysail sheet had parted. As he shoved the hatch cover back and put his head out, he was surprised by the violence of the storm. The air was filled with water, both rain and spray, and the wind was driving it horizontally across the deck. It stung his face when he tried to look to windward.

As he went forward, he crouched low, one hand on the lifeline and the other on the cabin top. A wave caught him at the shrouds and knocked him down. His harness held him. He pulled himself up at the mast, and fumbling with the halyard, he tried to get the staysail down. The club boom was whipping back and forth and the sail was torn at the clew. Once he got the staysail secured, *Jest* eased up a little but not enough. He crawled aft and got one of the mooring lines out of the cockpit locker. He tied one end to the spare main boom that was lashed to the lee side of the deck. Then he went forward again and ran the other end of the mooring line through the bow roller. Coming aft, another wave caught him, knocking him down again. His legs forked one of the shrouds, keeping him from going overboard. He got the spare boom over the side without fouling it and watched as it was swept out ahead of *Jest*. When the mooring line straightened out, the boom popped out of the water and began tumbling end over end until it was lost in a breaking wave.

He went aft and released the trysail sheet, and as it whipped back and forth, he went forward again and released the halyard and clawed the canvas down. When the trysail was almost down, another wave caught him and he held on with both arms around the mast. Slowly he became conscious of not being able to hold his breath any longer, but having to hold it anyway because the water kept pouring over him. When his head finally broke free, he was in a lull between the waves. The water was up to his waist, and as he looked out before him, there was only the mast and the sea. Then *Jest* rose out of the water as the next wave approached.

He crawled back to the cockpit and got a second mooring line out, tied one end to the five-gallon jerry can, the other end to the bow, and threw the jerry can over the side. When the second mooring line straightened out, the jerry can tangled with the boom, keeping it from skipping out of the water. He couldn't think of what else to do, so he went below. There was about a foot of water in the cabin. He started the engine and while he was pumping it out, another wave tumbled over *Jest*. And now, without any sails set and dragging the boom and the jerry can, she was still lying over with her rail in the water. He climbed back into the cockpit, put the engine in gear, unlashing the helm, and tried to hold the bow closer to the wind.

In the late evening, when he began worrying about his fuel, he felt the storm peak. He lashed the helm, shut down the engine and went below. He drank two glasses of water. He wanted a hot tea but it was out of the question because he was so cold and stiff that he couldn't get the stove going. He got his wet clothes off, found a blanket that wasn't very wet and fell asleep.

He slept until the following afternoon. There wasn't much water in the bilge, so the water during the storm must have come in through the open hatch. He drank three cups of tea and ate some crackers and a can of peaches before going on deck. The sky was overcast and the sea confused but he could set the trysail and staysail and then haul in the boom and the jerry can. He unbent the torn staysail and got the old one from below and bent it on. Then he set sail. *Jest* forereached enough for him to pull in his jury-rigged sea anchor. When he got the boom and the jerry can up to the side, he couldn't get them on deck until he cut the boom free. He didn't need the boom but he wanted the mooring lines and the kerosene.

He told Catherine to write him in Port Vila, but he couldn't make the New Hebrides now, not with the wind from the northeast. Besides, he didn't really want to go to the New Hebrides. That was Anna's idea. He had already studied the charts that Anna had ordered for him, so he knew if he wanted to go west he had to pass through the Torres Strait. He put *Jest* on a course for Port Moresby, 1,565 miles to the northwest, watched that she would hold her course in the cross sea, and then went below and made pancakes. He opened a can of strawberry jam and, with the pancakes, ate the entire can.

After a few days, the sea settled down and the wind shifted more to the east. On the first afternoon of sun he caught a yellowfin tuna and cut part of it into cubes and made *poisson cru* with fresh lime juice, pressed coconut milk, a chopped onion, and a large pinch of salt. His tomatoes had gone bad, so he threw them overboard. He fried the rest of the fish in corn oil with salt and pepper, squeezed lime on it and ate it with rice. He took his cup of tea into the cockpit to watch the sun set. As it grew dark he thought of the storm, but the emotion it caused was behind him, leaving only a single line running through his thoughts: A sea so vicious.

The closer he got to New Guinea, the steadier the wind blew and the better time *Jest* made. Fourteen days after the storm he rounded Paga Point and anchored in Fairfax Harbor. After the port officials left the boat, he studied the harbor. The wind blew steady from the southeast. To the left, off the port bow, was the town, hidden in the trees and other vegetation. To the right, in the distance, were a few outriggers sailing across the harbor. Down wind, at the lower end of the harbor, was a native village, partly built out over the water. He watched a powerboat pulling skiers around the harbor. It buzzed by him a few times, until finally, when the skier seemed tired, the boat came over to *Jest*. After the people in the boat asked him the usual questions—where are you from, and when are you leaving—they invited him over to the yacht club.

From then on he rowed over to the yacht club every day to take a shower. The club was large and dark inside, and in the afternoon, usually empty. At first he didn't trust himself to order anything to drink at the bar. But about the third day, after changing some money, he sat on a barstool and looked at the barman.

"Can I get something to drink?"

"Yes."

"What's in that bottle?"

"Lemon squash."

"What's in the bottle next to it? Orange squash?"

"Yes."

"I'd like an orange squash, please."

"Ice?"

"Yes."

"Soda?"

"Yes, everything."

"Gin?"

"No gin. Everything but the gin."

There was usually a table with men drinking beer. Some of the men were big and red and others were small and dark, but they had a similar look because they all wore white shirts and shorts. Usually they were talking, but now Skip noticed that they were silent, which made him realize that they were watching him. He got off the barstool, took his drink and began to look at the pictures on the wall. It wasn't like in America, for there weren't any captions under the pictures explaining who they were pictures of. He came to one that he recognized as Queen Elizabeth II. Next to it was another picture the same size, of a man with a high forehead and a lot of medals. He was about to ask who the man was when he changed his mind, deciding it was one of those things that you were supposed to know and thus shouldn't ask questions about.

The wind blew every day, especially at night, and when he got up in the morning he had to raise his anchor and move up a few hundred yards and drop it again. One night he dragged his anchor nearly half a mile. So he decided to move *Jest* over to the wharf to take on fuel. While waiting for the fuel truck, he sat in the cockpit and watched an outrigger sail in and tie up, almost under his stern. There was a man with three women, bringing their produce to the market. The man had holes carved out of the lobes of his ears. The women were different ages but they were all tattooed, including their faces and breasts. They unloaded their baskets and carried them off. Later, after the fuel truck had arrived, he was busy filling his tank, making sure it didn't overflow. After he screwed the cap back on the intake, he noticed that the man and women were back on their outrigger. They were sitting on the platform, passively watching him.

He stepped onto the wharf, walked over to where the outrigger was tied up and, like the four of them, squatted on his heels. They were chewing beetle nut, waiting for something, so it seemed to Skip, though he had no idea what it was. He took his Case knife out of his pocket and offered it to the man. The man slowly stood, took the knife and squatted again. He held the knife away from him and didn't look at it. After a few more minutes, Skip stood up and said, "Adios," which made him feel foolish until he realized it was as appropriate as anything else he knew how to say.

He climbed aboard *Jest* and went below, wondering if he had sailed nearly halfway around the world just to give a Papuan his knife. Then he wondered what he would do with it: use it to sharpen his nails, or carve a god, or stab a rival. All he knew was that he was as strange to the Papuan as the Papuan was strange to him. He doubted if he could even handle their outrigger.

He was sitting at the bar in the yacht club, drinking an orange squash. The beer drinkers were at a table behind him, talking about wogs and kanakas and boongs. He had been to the post office and the sail-maker. An Egyptian had repaired his staysail, hand-sewing a new clew so that it was stronger than before. It had cost him twenty Australian pounds. The repaired staysail was in its bag, on the floor next to his barstool. He decided to read the letter from Catherine that had been forwarded from Port Vila. She complained mildly about school and the bad weather, caused, as everyone claimed, by the American bomb tests. At the end she said that she missed their afternoons together. He thought about that, because he missed them too. He wondered if there was a chance of renewing them in Paris. But France seemed a long way off. He had decided that it would be faster going up the Red Sea and through the Suez Canal, than going around the Cape of Good Hope. The Red Sea, from the Gulf of Aden to the Gulf of Suez, was about 1,000 miles. It looked narrow on a map of the world, but it was about 100 miles wide in most places, except at the southern and northern entrances. He would have to order some charts in Darwin. Still, it was going to be hard, or demanding, as Jack would say. Always demand more than is demanded. Always require more than is required. Always expect more than is expected. He thought that Jack couldn't do that with every word: You couldn't always know more than was known. The voices behind him suddenly seemed louder. They were talking about the war and somebody called Kurtz.

"This one bloke, 'Kurtz' they called him—that wasn't his real name— he came down the Kakoda Trail, dressed like a wog, except he had dog tags and a .45. He didn't look like one of them. He was too big. Twice as big as them. And he was carrying a baby, and when they asked him what he had there, he said it was a king."

"It was King of the Wogs."

"Wasn't that the bugger with three wives?"

Were they talking about Jack? He knew the story of Jack's three Papuan wives. It was a major part of the book, *King and Kinship*. He also knew that some things in the book were not true and that many other things had been omitted. After the war, when Jack returned to New Guinea to do research on the tribe, he was unable to locate it and had to use another, completely different, tribe for his book. He knew this story because Jack used it once to illustrate a piece of advice he gave him: "Write your own history," Jack said. "Never let fate stand in the way of your destiny." But he had never heard anything about a Papuan child, a child that could be his brother, no, his half-brother. He wondered what Jack did with it. But when he began to listen again to the men at the table, they were talking about Papuan women, so he carried his staysail down to his dinghy and rowed out to *Jest*. He stowed the sail, got the anchor up and then headed for Paga Point. There were still a few hours of daylight, enough to clear the pass.

Thursday Island

He set course for the Bramble Cay Light. He was a little worried about getting lost in all the islands and reefs of the Torres Strait. Of course if he really wanted to get lost, he could head up the Fly River as far as he could and then start walking into the hills and mountains of Papua. Maybe in getting lost in the mountains, as Jack had, he would find what Jack had found. A place so remote he made himself into whatever he wanted. And a people so awed they made him king and gave him three wives. Or it was the other way around: through the three wives he had become king. It was a kinship through marriage that made him king. Or at least justified his accepting or taking the throne, or chair, or stool, or patch of ground where he sat his royal ass upon the sacred mud.

He thought he knew most everything there was to know about Jack. At least he thought he knew all he needed or wanted to know. He had learned not to ask Jack questions. That had always made him end up looking like a Bubba. So he had learned to watch and listen. And he thought he had watched and listened enough to know what there was to know. But maybe Jack had planted a lie at the bottom of everything and so everything he believed was based on that lie. For example, two things had always bothered him about his mother: no one ever mentioned her and when Margaret took him that one time to visit her grave over in the City, she seemed unusually nervous. She said she didn't want Jack to know what they were doing, but he was sure—at least now he was sure—that they couldn't have undertaken such a visit without Jack knowing about it, or probably more, without Jack planning it.

What if the body in the grave with the marker Cynthia Johns was not Jack's wife, but say his sister or cousin? What if Cynthia Johns wasn't even related to Jack at all, but just a convenient name with convenient dates? What if the grave marker itself, with its convenient name and dates, was something Jack had made and placed there for him to visit? Jack didn't even have to exchange it with some other grave marker. He could have just placed it there on the edge of the cemetery, as if some Cynthia Johns, some wife and mother, had actually existed. Yet he knew that Jack would just as soon tell an inconvenient truth as tell a convenient lie.

The weather was so hazy, making the visibility poor, that he never sighted Bramble Cay Light. He continued on dead reckoning, turning into the Great Northern Passage of the Torres Strait. He sat in the cockpit with the sextant, waiting for the sun to break through the haze. Each sun sight put him farther east from his dead reckoning position. A strong current was running through the straits and night was approaching. He needed an island. As the sun fell below the horizon, he sighted a spit of sand and anchored in six fathoms. In the darkness he could make out Dalrymple Light, so he knew about where he was. He went for a swim and then, after putting a fishing line over the side, he went to sleep in the cockpit.

He woke before sunrise and at first thought that his eyes were gummed up, making the world a blur. Then he realized that *Jest* was covered with birds. They roosted without moving, shoulder to shoulder on the lifelines, both booms, the spreaders, and even the masthead. As he stood up in the cockpit, the sun broke over the horizon, and the birds cried and flew off to the east, keeping low over the water. All that day he wondered whether it was he or the sun that awoke the birds.

The wind was on the port beam, and he sailed all day, passing Coconut Island, and then the Three Sisters to starboard. In the late afternoon he had the current as he came through the channel between Horn and Prince of Wales Island and anchored off the pier at Thursday Island. He wasn't met by a custom official, or an immigration official, or the harbor police. He was met by a doctor, who examined him, remarked on his excessive production of vitamin D, and then asked for his vaccination card. The doctor escorted him to his clinic and gave him four shots and a package of quinine. For the next three days Skip was sick and didn't leave his bunk. On the fourth day, while sitting in the cockpit getting some sun, a motorboat came along side and a young woman with a backpack jumped aboard.

"Hi, I'm Di. I'm coming with you to Darwin and I'm not gonna take no for an answer." There was a pause while she waited for him to say something. "You look awful."

"I've been sick."

"Good. I'm gonna help you."

"I'm just a little weak. I don't really need any help."

"I'm not gonna take no for an answer. First we have to get you out of the sun. What do you call that thing you use as an awning?"

"An awning. It's below, in the forepeak, on the starboard side."

"That's this side, right?"

"Right."

After a few minutes she came back with the trysail, which had come unfolded and was dragging on the deck.

"That's not the awning."

"How was I supposed to know? You didn't come and help me."

"You said you were gonna help me."

"You have to help me to help you. You go downstairs and rest while I string the awning up."

He went below and got in his bunk. At one time he thought there were only two types of women, nice women like Anna and nasty women like Mrs. Brown, Catherine's mother. There were of course beautiful women, but they didn't count because they existed only in fashion magazines. Now he had a new type, a nice woman who wasn't nice. As he listened to her stumbling about the deck, he puzzled over how an attractive woman could be so unattractive, then he fell asleep. She woke him up by trying to light the stove. She wanted to make him some tea, so he got up and lit the stove for her.

"You don't wanna use that pump. It's for saltwater. This is the one for freshwater."

"Why do you need saltwater in the kitchen?"

"For cleaning up. But I don't use it in port."

She wanted to make sandwiches for lunch, but there wasn't any bread, so he gave her some money and asked her to go shopping and buy whatever fruits and vegetables she could find. She had a difficult time rowing the dinghy ashore, mainly because of the current that ran through the anchorage. When she got to the dock, he timed her, from when she disappeared from view to when she reappeared again. She took over an hour. Maybe she had met someone. There was a good chance of that.

When she got back to *Jest,* she made tuna salad sandwiches. There were onions, tomatoes, and lettuce, so he didn't say anything about opening cans while in port. After lunch she told him to get back in his bunk and she would read to him. The sound of her voice put him immediately to sleep.

She woke him up to have tea again. He lit the stove and made the tea because she made it too strong. As soon as he sat down, she asked if he had any milk. He got out a can of condensed milk.

"Do you have any biscuits? To go with the tea."

He got out a large tin of assorted cookies. When he pried the lid off, they smelt remarkably fresh. "There aren't any more chocolate chip. I ate them on the way to Port Moresby."

"That seems pretty selfish."

"I can't be selfish by myself."

"What if you have guests and you show them a tin of biscuits like this?"

"I've never had any guest who complained about me eating my own chocolate chip cookies."

"That seems a little silly. You probably think you can go sailing off to any place you please and don't have to think of other people at all."

"Who should I think about and what should I think about them?"

"People who need help. You should think about how you could help them."

"Everybody needs help. I can't help everybody."

"You should do what you can."

"I always do what I can."

After tea she seemed to get bored with watching him cleaning up and said she wanted to go ashore. There was somebody she wanted to see. She wasn't back by evening, so he hung up an anchor light. Later he went to bed. She woke him up when she came back. In the morning she slept late. He was having coffee in the cockpit when she put her head out of the hatch.

"How do you feel today?"

"Good. See, I'm drinking coffee. Which means I'm not sick."

"Then we can leave in a few days."

"First we have to top off the water and take on some more food. Two people eat and drink twice as much."

She rowed back and forth, filling the water tank. Then after lunch he made her wait until slack water before he gave her a list and $20 in American money. He told her that she had to take her passport to change the money and that she could add anything to the list she liked. When she disappeared from view, he dove into the water and swam to the dinghy. There was a man with a red face on the dock as he climbed into the dinghy.

"Don't you know there are sharks in the water?"

"That's where I expect them to be."

He had the dinghy untied and turned around, heading back toward *Jest* before the man replied, now with an even redder face, "Bloody galah." Then Skip was too far away to hear what else he said.

Back on *Jest,* he quickly gathered up Di's things and stuffed them in her backpack. He noticed that she had left things all over the boat, as if she simply let things fall from her hand as soon as she was through with them. When he rowed Di's backpack to shore and heaved it up on the dock, the man with the red face was still there.

"Someone's coming to pick that up."

"Bloody galah."

He was tired when he got back to *Jest,* so after starting the engine he rested. Now that he had his dinghy, he had plenty of time. When he got his breath back, he would raise the anchor and head out to the Arafura Sea. Later he would stow the anchor and hoist the dinghy on deck. In Darwin he would send her a note: I don't take no for an answer.

Darwin

As he thought would happen, he began to find more of Di's things. There was a pair of khaki shorts in the fo'c'sle, under the storm trysail, and a hairbrush in the galley, in the rack next to the plates. Later he found the book she had been reading to him: *The Ugly American*. It was under the bunk she had slept in and next to it was the ballpoint pen she had used to underline certain passages in the book. Jack said there were two kinds of fools, those who read books and wrote in them and those who didn't read books but believed everything in them.

He looked at the title page of *The Ugly American*. He remembered seeing a book call *The Quiet American*. It was written by somebody called Green. Mr. Green reminded him of Mr. Brown and Mr. Brown reminded him of Catherine. Usually when he was reminded of Catherine, he set himself some task and chanted: busy hands make a busy mind. He decided to do a wash. There wasn't much to do: some shorts and T-shirts, a pareu and two dishtowels. The trick with washing with seawater was to wring everything out thoroughly before hanging it up to dry. He could have used some freshwater—Darwin wasn't that far—but as a matter of principle he didn't. He hung up his wash and sat in the cockpit, watching the day move as slowly as the boat.

Jest was barely making fifty miles a day when he cleared Cape Van Diemen on Melville Island and the wind died altogether. He took in the sails because they were just slapping against the rigging. He was about a hundred miles from Darwin. The name reminded him of something. He went below and took a book out of the second shelf. Charles Darwin, *The Voyage of the Beagle.* He wondered if it was the same Darwin that Jack said raised man up to the level of the apes. He looked through the book, but as far as he could tell, Darwin had never been to Darwin, but maybe the *Beagle* had because there was a Beagle Gulf north of Darwin. The next day he decided to motor for a while and ended up motoring the rest of the way into Darwin.

As he anchored inside of the *Oceanid,* the first thing he noticed about Darwin was the heat. The second thing was the tide. He rigged his awning and then glanced over at the *Oceanid.* At first he thought the heat was making him see double. Standing aft of the *Oceanid's* cockpit were two brown-haired women wearing white shorts and blouses. They looked like twins. He went below and got the binoculars, and looking through the cabin porthole, he tried to focus on the women, but he had never been able to see anything clearly through the binoculars. They brought the women closer but the image was blurred. He thought of rowing over for a closer look, but by the time he got his dinghy in the water, the women had gone below.

He wrote a letter to Catherine to tell her he was in Darwin and then went ashore to mail it. The tide was out and he had to climb up a wet ladder to the pier. After securing his dinghy, he looked up and saw the two women again, standing next to a car at the end of the pier. Bob Sterling, the owner of the *Oceanid,* was with them, and as he helped the women into a car, Skip realized that one woman was older than the other and that they looked alike because they were probably mother and daughter. They dressed in a similar manner, and wore their hair in a similar way. The car drove off, leaving a cloud of dust in its wake. Mrs. and Miss Sterling, departing.

After changing some money, and lingering in the air-conditioned bank, he walked about the dusty streets of Darwin and did a little shopping. When he got back to his dinghy, there were two girls standing on the pier.

"Is that your boat?"

"No, the smaller one is mine."

"Could we see it?"

"Ok. Hold this." And he handed them the bottle of orange squash and the bag of ice that he had picked up at the store. He got them to take their shoes off and then he held the dinghy as one got in the bow and the other in the stern. The tide was up, which helped. They were called Kate and Robin and they were mainly interested in him because he was a Yank, but they were much more interested in the boat. They wanted to know if he anchored at night. No, not every night. Only when he was tired and had to catch up on his sleep. Was he going to Sydney? They would do anything to go to Sydney, even sail on a boat. No, he wasn't going to Sydney. He was headed west. What did he do when a storm came, go into port? No, he took the sails down, went below and slept. It was a good time to sleep. Didn't he get depressed all by himself? What did they mean, depressed? You know, depressed, like when you don't know what to do with yourself. No, he always had something to do, and if there was nothing else to do he could always read or listen to the radio or just watch the sky.

While he was making some orange squash, the girls turned his radio on.

"What's that?"

"Don't you know? That's The Marvellettes and 'Please, Mr. Postman.'"

"Who's your favorite singer?"

"Living or dead?"

"You have a favorite dead singer?"

"Buddy Holly."

"Who else? I bet you say Elvis."

"I bet I don't."

"Listen. Here comes Chubby Checker and the 'Twist'. Do you wanna dance?"

"Then hold my hand."

"What?"

"Bobby Freeman. Top Ten in 1958."

"Can you twist?"

"Like we did last summer."

There wasn't much room to dance, but the twist didn't take much room. Two of them could dance, one at each end of the cabin, just beyond the table. They wouldn't let him stop, so they each took turns as he twisted the afternoon away next to the chart table.

Later Alan and Joyce from the *Jolly Swagman* came aboard with a bottle of gin. As the day moved toward evening, he decided to make something to eat. He hadn't expected anyone and hadn't shopped anything, so he made spaghetti. Joyce rowed to the *Jolly Swagman* and came back with salad and bread. She announced that another yacht had just come in. It was the *Dolphin* and soon after Walker rowed over. He had brought Di with him. As Skip put on another pot for more noodles, he tried to remember what he had done with the things Di had left on *Jest*.

When one of the girls said her father would "get up her" for being late, Skip rowed them both ashore, thinking that, like everybody else, the girls probably have strange fathers; certainly for a father to get up his daughter sounded strange. The tide was out again and it took awhile to get them both safely up on the pier. When he got back to *Jest*, everyone was gone except Walker, who had produced another bottle of gin from somewhere. Skip started to clean up and they talked a little about what they had done since they last met in Pago Pago. Skip asked him about Kurtz, telling him how he had heard the name applied to Jack. Walker turned around and studied the bookcase, then pulled out a book: *Heart of Darkness*. Skip had never thought of reading the book. He thought it was one of Jack's books on psychology.

"Oh no. Conrad is not our Polish Freud. He's our English Sartre. He didn't invent the literary unconscious. He invented the existential man, the man who believes choice is the essence of existence."

"What did Kurtz choose?"

"To become god. . . . Read it and you'll see the similarity between Kurtz and Jack that your friends in Port Moresby saw, a similarity that could be reduced to the unspeakable rites of an inscrutable man in an impenetrable jungle." With that Walker got up, climbed topside and fell overboard. Skip managed to get Walker into his dinghy without letting Walker pull him into the water as well, but he was as wet as if he had fallen in. He left Walker lying on the deck of the *Dolphin*, thinking that from there Di could take care of him.

The next morning, as he sat drinking his coffee and wondering when he could expect a letter from Catherine, he heard someone moaning in the forward part of the boat. "Who's there?" The response was more moaning, so he looked in the forepeak and found Di lying on his old staysail. "Are you sick?" More moaning. He saw that she had vomited in the bucket. She wouldn't move by herself and he couldn't move her by himself, so he would have to play nursemaid. He opened the forward hatch to let some fresh air in, emptied the bucket, and got her to drink some water. Later he got her to eat some dry bread and then some tuna. In the afternoon he was able to get her in the dinghy and then row her over to the *Dolphin*. He called from the cockpit, "Walker?"

"Make some coffee or go to Hell." Later, Walker sat up to drink his coffee. "How did you get Di over here? She must be worse off than I am."

"I made her some tuna fish."

"Why do you call it tuna fish? Do you know of some other kind of tuna besides fish?"

"It's just what people say."

"'It's just what people say.' Christ, the great *ad populum,* the fallacy of the herd and conclusive proof that man is still an animal because he does what all the other animals do."

"You sound like you feel better."

"You can go to Hell on roller-skates. Follow the Yellow Brick Road."

While rowing back to *Jest,* he thought about tuna fish. There were a lot of things that people say that don't make much sense. He remembered Jack saying once that horseback riding didn't make a lot of sense because there wasn't any other part of the horse that you could ride, besides the back. Then again, he thought, saying "horse riding" sounded strange. Which led him to believe that sounding strange was a lot worse than not making sense, especially when everybody was not making sense in the same way. He started thinking about camelback and elephantback, but his thoughts were interrupted by Bob, who was hailing him from the *Oceanid*.

Bob wanted him to keep an eye on the *Oceanid* for a few days. The crew was off on a holiday and Bob suddenly had to go to Sydney. As it turned out, Bob was gone for over two weeks. Skip rowed over to the *Oceanid* every morning, looked in the bilge—a different part each day—and ran the generator for an hour or so. After he found the toaster, he brought some bread and butter over, made toast, and listened to Bob's tapes. Most of them were jazz. He liked some of them, but most of them seemed to demand that he listen carefully, and he often found that he didn't have the patience. One day, in the bilge of the starboard cabin, he found an earring. A black pearl. Finders, keepers.

In the second week, when a storm blew up, he laid out *Jest's* second anchor and took down the awning. Then he rowed over to the *Oceanid* and took down her awning. Her second anchor wasn't rigged, and it was too big for him to handle alone, so he let out some chain on the main anchor. The ignition button in the cockpit didn't do anything, so he went down into the engine room. Just as he got the engine going, a strong gust hit the *Oceanid,* and he felt that the anchor wasn't holding. On deck again he saw *Jest* scooting back and forth in the wind. She was much closer in to shore than the *Oceanid,* and he hoped she would be safe. Another gust hit and the *Oceanid* heeled over, stretching the anchor chain out straight. Between the gusts, he let out more chain. He didn't know whether to go aft and put the engine in gear or stay by the anchor winch. He kept letting out chain between the gusts, until he noticed that the chain had turned rusty and he began to wonder how much chain was left. Then a strong gust hit and everything happened fast. The brake on the winch released, the last ten fathoms of chain whipped out, and the bitter end rushed into the bay. The *Oceanid,* free of her anchor, swung broadside to the wind and began to drift towards the lee shore.

He ran aft and after putting the engine in gear, he headed the schooner out of the harbor. When he was clear of Charles Point, he got the sail cover off the main staysail and raised it. Luckily, the *Oceanid* was rigged with winches everywhere. Although the gusts threw her bow off, she hove-to well enough. Then she had plenty of sea room, all the way to Africa. He went below and ate six slices of toast and opened, for the first time, some of Bob's orange marmalade. Then he drank a large can of tomato juice.

The cockpit had a dodger, so he got a blanket and some cushions together and catnapped there. About midnight the wind began to let up, and at five he started the engine again, took in the sail, and began to power back into Darwin. Then he remembered his dinghy, which he had tied astern. He cut the engine to idle and let the *Oceanid* drift. His dinghy was nearly full of water and about to go under. He didn't want to lose it, but he decided that going over the side to bail it out was not a good idea. He tied the end of the main sheet to the dinghy's bowline and ran it to the port wench. By cranking the bow of the dinghy up to the stern of the *Oceanid,* he was able to get enough water out of it to keep it from swamping.

When he reached the harbor in the afternoon, Bob and Walker came out in Walker's dinghy. They dragged for the anchor and picked up the chain on the fourth try. He was surprised that Bob wasn't angry with him. All he said was, "You brought her back." Jack would have been all over him for being a fool for losing the anchor. But Bob gave him a case of Wild Turkey whiskey. Skip would have preferred a case of tomato juice but he didn't tell Bob that.

A few weeks later, after the *Oceanid,* the *Dolphin*—without Di—and the *Jolly Swagman* had all left Darwin, he got a letter from Catherine. It was short. She was on her way to Paris and would write him next in Singapore. She hoped he would stop at Bali, so he could tell her about it. All the best, Catherine. He didn't want to go to Singapore. It was out of the way. The *Oceanid* and the *Dolphin* were headed for South Africa, and he was thinking of following them. He could write her from Darwin, if he had her address in Paris. He could write to Nouméa, hoping his letter would be forwarded to her, or he could write to the postmaster in Singapore, hoping her letter would be forwarded to him. But he decided that his chances of missing her letter were too great. He decided to go to Singapore.

Bali

When Skip looked back at his stay in Darwin, he realized that Walker was different; at least, the way he saw him was different. He wasn't afraid of Walker anymore. Well, not exactly afraid. He had never been actually afraid of Walker. But he didn't feel he needed to run from him anymore. It wasn't that he didn't think Walker wasn't spying on him, although "spying" was probably too strong and it wasn't any more sinister than Walker said: he was just keeping an eye on Skip. No, it was something else. Partly his changed attitude toward Walker was the result of bringing to the surface what he already knew, or at least assumed, about Jack. Jack always had backup plans, different ways of doing things, especially different ways of finding out things. In addition, Jack always seemed to have a number of projects going at the same time, projects that were the development of ideas he had, and Jack always had a lot of ideas. As Jack said, if you have a hundred ideas, only one of them has to be good. The problem Jack had, a problem that Skip could only glimpse, was that Jack didn't seem to always know which idea—among the many he had—was the good one.

So Jack probably had other ways of finding out where Skip was, assuming of course that he wanted to find out. And that was the other thing that seemed to be behind his changed attitude toward Walker. He knew that Jack had a way of becoming bored with some of his projects, of dropping them for a while and sometimes never picking them up again. And he knew that at some lower level Skip was just a project for Jack, some kind of sink-or-swim project, part of his work on contemporary adolescence. Jack liked to begin with what he called the received opinion, or even better, a proverb, and then turn it inside out, like the proverb about the horse: You can lead a horse to water but you can't make him drink. Well, you may not be able to make him drink, Jack said, you can sure as hell make him swim. Skip knew that he was that horse. But at the same time, he knew that he had been doing enough swimming in the past year to bring Jack's project to a standstill, if not to an end. And now either Jack would be bored with it, bored with the whole idea of trying to keep track of him, as he sailed farther west, across the Indian Ocean. Or the whole project was changing into something else. He hoped it was the first, that Jack was bored, but he was afraid that it was the second, that Jack would transform the sink-or-swim project of sailing to Hawaii into some other project. And what worried him more was that he didn't know what Jack had in mind, what new idea he may have come up with, and the longer he didn't know, the more it worried him.

The winds were light and from the south, as he sat in the cockpit reading the book that Walker had shown him, the one about Kurtz. He wore the straw hat that he had bought in Nuku Hiva to cut down the glare and throw a shadow across the *Heart of Darkness*. At the end of each page or so he looked up and surveyed the horizon, a thin line that separated the dark blue of the sea from the light blue of the sky, a line that in the distance held most of the world. He usually ignored the compass, for he had learned to tell if he was off course by the sound of the wind and the motion of the boat. Jack had installed a repeating compass over the starboard bunk where he usually slept. But except when he was near land, Skip hardly ever used it now. If the wind changed, *Jest's* motion through the water would change as well. He noticed that he relied more and more on his sense of *Jest's* motion and the sound she made, especially at night.

After finishing *Heart of Darkness,* he couldn't see much of a similarity between Kurtz and Jack, except that they both had gone into the jungle and bossed some people around for a while. Jack came out alive, maybe because he only wanted to be king instead of god. But the story puzzled him, not the part about Kurtz. He knew all about Kurtz, but he couldn't understand Marlow, the one who told the story. Kurtz chose to be god, but Marlow chose a nightmare, knowing it was a nightmare and calling it the nightmare of his choice. He didn't have to do that. What he had to do was choose the girl. That was the biggest puzzle. Why didn't Marlow marry the girl, Kurtz's Intended?

It was so simple, really. A man goes up an African river, into the heart of darkness, to get another man. He has all the usual problems with the boat and the people, both African and European. Of course he gets the man. But through no fault of his own, this man, this Kurtz, dies on the journey down river. That, however, is not the end. The man becomes a kind of substitute for Kurtz. He goes back to the city in Europe, where Kurtz was from, and visits his girl, his Intended. He tells her about the dead man, how he died and all. And anybody would think that she would put her hand on his arm, look into his sad eyes with her sad and perhaps even wet eyes. But no, instead of living sadly ever after, he goes through all that sadness to tell her a lie.

Instead of replacing the dead man's love with his own, he replaces the dead man's love with a lie. He tells her that Kurtz's dying words were her name, trading her name for Kurtz's horror.

If he learned one thing from the book, it was that he didn't want to be going up any river. But then again, wasn't Paris on a river? He could sail up that French river, right into the heart of Paris. It wouldn't be like going up that African river in the book. He wouldn't be going into any heart of darkness or unmapped territory. It would be just the opposite. Plus, what he liked best was that he wouldn't be going away from the girl but toward her.

The wind dropped and he was becalmed for a day, and when it picked up again, he began to make good time. After two weeks he sighted Sumbawa, then Lambok, and finally Bali. It would be dark by the time he reached the entrance of the harbor to Benoa, so he prepared to heave-to for the night. When darkness fell with tropical sudden-ness, he was surprised that he could see only one light on the island, which loomed off his port bow. There must be about a million people on Bali, but all he could see was one light. He wondered if that meant anything. Later in the evening, after baking some pan bread and eating it with strawberry jam, he sighted breakers to port. They shouldn't be there because he was at least six miles from land. He started the engine and then checked the chart, but there weren't any dangers marked on it. Then he saw breakers to starboard. He put the engine in gear and headed south and suddenly there seemed to be breakers everywhere. After he had run for about a mile, the break-ers seemed to disappear. He stayed awake that night, thinking about the breakers and where they came from. He saw in his mind the chart of Indonesia, the string of islands from Timor in the east to Sumatra in the west, with the Java Sea to the north and the eastern Indian Ocean to the south. There it was, the islands like a broken dam, unable to hold back the rushing water. In the morning it was clear to him that he would have to be careful of the tidal streams until he got into the Java Sea.

As he approached Benoa, small outriggers with white sails became more and more numerous. He didn't have a chart of the harbor and he was unable to spot any buoys marking the passage through the reef. With the binoculars he could see a freighter in the harbor, so he knew that he should be able to get in. He waited, hoping a pilot boat would come out for him, but instead the freighter came out. As he watched it, he realized that what looked liked birdcages on black poles were in fact channel markers. After the freighter cleared the reef, he entered the channel and zigzagged his way into the harbor. When he was through the channel, a launch came out and showed him where to anchor. It seemed quite simple; still, it was the first unfamiliar harbor he had entered without a chart.

When the launch came along side, he was overwhelmed by officials: harbormaster, emigration, customs, doctor, navy and their assistants, all in uniform. There was some confusion at first, because he didn't have a visa to enter Indonesia, but after filling out several forms and paying eight dollars, they said he could go ashore. At the customs office he declared $25, then he began looking for some way of getting to Denpasar. There didn't seem to be any buses or anything, but before he began to walk, a flatbed truck stopped and gave him a ride. From the back of the truck he could see the road leading through two rows of houses that were surrounded by mud and brick walls. He could see numerous temples and he realized that, for the first time, he wasn't in a Christian country. It was a strange country. Strange for him, although he realized he was the stranger. He saw men, like horses, pulling carts, and other men carrying pigs in bamboo cages that were slung beneath poles. Then he saw the bare-breasted women, threshing something: rice, he guessed. Several women pounded the rice with a long pole held vertically. They slammed the pole down with one hand and, when it bounded up again, they caught it with the other, all with a steady rhythm. Another woman tossed the threshed rice in the air and caught the freed grains in a round flat basket, as the breeze blew the chaff away.

The truck let him off at the outskirts of town and he walked to the covered market, where he saw more produce than he had ever seen before, even in Mexico. There were baskets of different colored powders; the reds and blacks, he guessed, were pepper, the yellow probably turmeric, but for the most part, he didn't know what he saw. Lunch was also strange. He went into a restaurant and, since he couldn't read the menu or make himself understood to the waiter—he didn't see anyone except Indonesians all day—he just pointed to an item on the menu. He was served what looked like raw ground meat with a raw egg on top. He paid for it without eating it and, since it only cost 25 cents, he pointed to another item on the menu. He was served what looked like the same thing as before, only this time it was cooked, so he ate it. Later, at the market, he bought a dozen eggs and a loaf of bread, then started back to Benoa.

As he passed each village, the people came out to stare at him and whisper among themselves. Soon a truck stopped and picked him up. This time he sat in the cab with the driver, who spoke some English. When Skip asked him why the villagers stared at him so much, the driver explained that they knew who he was, but they couldn't understand why he was walking along the road. The Europeans they had seen before always rode in cars. Then, a little later, a dozen policemen on motorcycles, with red lights flashing and sirens going, waved the truck off the road. The driver pulled over and everyone got out and stood at attention at the side of the road. Skip wanted to remain in the cab, but the driver was adamant. He came over and stood at Skip's window and shouted "Sukarno! Sukarno!" over and over, until Skip got out and stood at attention with the rest of the people at the side of the road. Then a line of black European cars with Sukarno and the leader of some other country roared past. Skip wondered why Sukarno called himself a president when he acted like a king. Perhaps it had something to do with black European cars. He decided he should read the rest of *The Ugly American.*

That evening he ate two fried-egg sandwiches, and then he boiled the rest of the eggs for five seconds and stowed them away. Although he had been in Bali only one day, he decided that he had been stared at enough, plus he had done enough staring of his own. Besides, he wanted to get to Singapore. Getting clearance from the harbormaster and the navy went quickly the next morning, and by 0900 he had the anchor up and was underway. But within a few minutes, after passing one of the channel markers to port, *Jest* was fast aground, with the tide just beginning to ebb. The pilot came out in a launch with a few of the naval officers and showed him a drawing of the channel. Two of the channel markers were missing. But Skip knew that it was mainly his own fault. He was in too much of a hurry:

he hadn't conned the channel properly and he hadn't paid any attention to the tide. Besides, it was Friday and the last time he had left port on Friday was Nouméa.

After getting into the water and looking at the bottom, he decided to lay *Jest* on her starboard side. So he swung the boom out to starboard and set his second anchor from the stern. By 1300 he was able to scrub most of the port side below the water line. At about 1900 he put the engine in reverse and started hauling on the stern anchor. He waited, for about as long as he could hold his breath, until *Jest* began to work free. But the night was black. There were no navigation lights, nor any lights at all except those on a freighter tied up at the wharf. So after he backed into the channel, he swung *Jest* around and started heading for the lights on the freighter. But *Jest* went aground again, on the other side of the channel. He got out the Coleman lantern and then got in the water and checked the port side for coral heads. It seemed to be free, so he swung the boom to port and waited until he could scrub the starboard side below the water line.

In the morning he backed *Jest* into the channel again and began slowly making his way past the channel markers. The people in the village opposite Benoa were all on the beach waving and whistling as he slowly steered *Jest* through the pass and into clear water. They must have thought that he had come to their island to entertain them, so he reached into the cockpit locker, got out his battered fog horn and blew four blasts: one long, one short, one long, and one short, indicating that he agreed with them.

Singapore

It was over a thousand miles to Singapore, a long way to go for a letter. He headed north, towards Borneo and when he was in the Java Sea, he headed northwest. He lost the wind off Cape Putung and drifted along with all the small fishing boats that surrounded him. One night, while listening to the radio, he heard about the crisis in Cuba: the United States threatened to sink any Soviet ships carrying missiles. He began wondering where he should go if they started a war. Indonesia didn't seem like a good choice, but then Singapore was a little too obvious. Looking at the chart, he could see that Singapore must be at the center of a lot of shipping. There was the northern part of Borneo that belonged to Malaysia. It looked like a fairly obscure part of the world. A few days later he heard that the Soviet ships had turned back.

He was making most of his miles during the three to four squalls that hit him each day. Still, he wasn't averaging more than fifty miles a day. He noticed that at night the small fishing boats didn't show any lights, and one dark night, during a squall, he almost ran one of the boats down. He saw a man quickly start a fire and then begin waving his arms. Skip headed *Jest* up into the wind and then fell off, leaving the fishing boat astern. The man must have been asleep, because *Jest* was carrying lights and could be seen from three miles off, even from a small boat.

When the sea was very calm, he used the engine, partly because the days were so hot, and with the engine on and *Jest* running at four to five knots, there was a little breeze. Eventually he entered the South China Sea and then headed west into the Singapore Strait. One morning, after twenty-three days at sea, he anchored off the Royal Singapore Yacht Club, hoisted the quarantine flag and waited for the port officials. There were a lot of ships anchored in the roads and he could see a number of official boats going out to meet them, but they all ignored him. Finally, when one boat came almost within hailing distance, Skip jiggled his quarantine flag up and down. It worked. The officials came aboard and he was cleared in a matter of minutes.

He rowed over to the yacht club dock, and after tying up his dinghy, he walked up the ramp to the clubhouse. The first thing they asked him was where he was from. San Francisco, he said.

"Impossible!"

"Impossible!"

It reminded him of a scene in the book he had just finished, *The Ugly American*. When the Ugly American told the French in Vietnam that Ho Chi Minh had built a road through the jungle, they said the same thing, "Impossible! Impossible!" Jack said that most people believe only what they want to, even to their own disadvantage. But even after it was generally accepted that he had sailed from San Francisco—after someone passed around a copy of *World Traveler*—they still looked at him with suspicion. A few days later, Joyce on the *Jolly Swagman* told Skip that it was probably his zoris—which he called flip-flops—that made the members of the yacht club look at him like that.

"Haven't you noticed that the white people here don't wear zoris?"

He met Joyce and Alan after he moved *Jest* over to the Kallang Basin where the other cruising boats were anchored. In addition to the *Jolly Swagman*, there was the *Tess*, the *Hyda Sea*, and the *Fairweather* at anchor in the basin. Within a few days Skip met everyone on the other cruising boats, except for the *Tess*. Skip knew there was someone on the *Tess*, but whoever it was, he never seemed to go ashore and he never seemed to have visitors. At the landing one day, Rick, who had just rowed in from the *Fairweather*, told him that the *Tess* was sailed single-handed, so a few hours later, after a rain squall had swept through the basin and Skip saw someone in the cockpit, he rowed over to the *Tess* and asked if he could come aboard. The man nodded, and when Skip introduced himself, the man simply said "George." Skip was curious because the *Tess* didn't have a self-steering rig. He noticed that all the lines led aft, so that the boat could be handled without leaving the cockpit. He couldn't get George to say much. When Skip asked him where he was from, George said Hong Kong, and when Skip asked him why he had stopped in Singapore, he said that he had money in a bank here. Becoming a little desperate, because he was also becoming uncomfortable, mainly because George wouldn't look at him, Skip blurted out that he had sailed alone from San Francisco, though he had stopped, he explained, in between. Skip wasn't sure, but he thought he saw a faint and somewhat sly smile appear on George's face. Then George said, but without looking at him:

"Did you ever talk to a fish? You have to call him first. You have to slap the side of the boat just right. Two slaps are best. And the lee side is best. When he comes you can talk to him."

"What do you talk about?"

"That's between me and the fish." Then George turned abruptly away and began staring forward, as if he were looking at something. When Skip looked, he saw the normal trash that the river brought into the basin after a rain, including now a huge dead rat, bloated and completely white, floating on its side. Later he was to see other dead animals floating past. A pig, a dog, and a cow were the ones he could identify. But what remained with him longest, what actually returned again and again in his memory, especially on long passages, was the image of the old man with his vague eyes and a worn, almost emaciated, body, the result of a life at sea. Skip could sense in that image what his own future might be, what he might become when he had sailed as many sea miles as that old man had. He might becomes a single-handed sailor who talked to fish.

When the 65-foot motor cruiser *Golden Dragon* came out of the Quam Bee boatyard and the slipway was free, Skip had *Jest* hauled out to check her bottom. He thought that she might have cracked something below the waterline after running aground in Benoa. Instead, they found a lot of dry rot in the stern planking, above the waterline. Mark Carver, who owned the *Golden Dragon,* introduced him to Ming, who had just finished a lot of woodwork on the motor cruiser. Ming said he could replace all the stern planks on *Jest* for $500. This seemed more than reasonable to Skip, but he didn't have the money, which meant he would have to write Anna, and, first of all, explain what he was doing in Singapore.

So he waited instead, and while he was waiting, he let Carver talk him into helping him take the *Golden Dragon* up to Penang at the northern end of the Malacca Strait. He had the feeling that this might be a bad idea because he knew that Carver wasn't much of a sailor. The first thing that Skip had noticed, when the *Golden Dragon* came out of the boatyard, was that Carver had put a mast on her in the attempt to convert her into a motor sailer. Carver said that he wanted to steady the boat, to keep her from rolling too much. But when they got out in the Malacca Strait and the first squall came up, the *Golden Dragon* almost rolled completely over. They never put the sails up again.

But Skip wanted to get off *Jest* for a while, to see what it was like, and besides, he thought that a passage up to Penang in a motor cruiser wouldn't take more than a few days and then another day to get back by train. It was actually the train ride that he was looking forward to. He had never been on a train before. But it turned out that he was gone more than a few days, mainly because Carver was a magician.

As Skip was to learn, Carver traveled from port to port, putting on magic shows. Later, when Skip arrived in Kuala Lumpur in a truck loaded with Carver's numerous black cases of magic equipment, he saw the posters: Mark Carver, World Famous Magician. On the poster Carver was holding his right hand out in front of him with a dove on his open palm and his left arm was stretched out behind him with a puff of smoke on his open palm. Skip tried to imitate the pose but found that he couldn't get his left arm in the same position. But the poster was one of the lesser illusions that Carver created about himself.

Carver had two women with him on the *Golden Dragon:* a tall blonde Australian named Anita and a very small and very pretty Malayan named Maya. In the magic show, Anita was Carver's stage assistant, the one who was on display, and the one who went into the audience for the mind reading act. Maya was the one who disappeared. She was so small and supple that she could fit into the secret compartments of the various contraptions that were wheeled on and off the stage by—much to his surprise— Skip himself. At one time, Carver also had someone to take care of the boat, but it wasn't clear what happened to him. Carver was never very clear about a lot of things, especially the past. He had recently come from Australia where he had put on shows for more than a year, traveling from port to port in the *Sea Fox,* a 72-foot schooner. He had lost the *Sea Fox* but it was never clear how. At one time Carver hinted at a terrible typhoon, at another time he hinted at a collision at sea, but Skip could never reconcile either version with the fact that Carver had been able to save all his magic equipment.

Skip was amazed, once he was on the *Golden Dragon,* how one thing led to another. Once they were in the Malacca Strait, Carver gave Skip the helm and went below. There was no autopilot, so he couldn't leave the wheel but had to stand there in the pilothouse and steer. Every time Skip put the boat into neutral and let her drift, so he could get a drink of water or check the chart, Carver would come running up to the pilot house as if some disaster were imminent. Then Carver would take the wheel for about fifteen minutes before giving it back to Skip and going below again. By the second morning, Skip told Carver he needed some sleep. This time he simply left the pilot house and went to his bunk in the forepeak. But he hadn't been asleep more than a few hours when he woke up because the engines had changed pitch. Carver was bringing the boat up to a pier at Port Swettenham, and he shouted at Skip to get the mooring lines.

After the *Golden Dragon* was moored, but before Skip could think about going back to his bunk, he was loading the numerous black cases of magic equipment onto a truck. Then he was in the cab of the truck, sleeping the twenty miles to Kuala Lumpur, where, after unloading the numerous black cases of magic equipment, he saw the poster of the world famous magician and met Su and Seah, two more members of the show. Su and Seah took him to a hotel and let him sleep for a few hours before waking him up and dressing him in black trousers and a white shirt, both far too tight, and a pair of Carver's old shoes, without socks. Then they took him back to the theater where Carver showed him where to hide the pigeons. He hadn't finished with the pigeons before the curtain went up and Carver, while making things appear out of no-where, pigeons, coins, cards, and silk—yards of silk—guided Skip in a stage whisper through the show. Skip's main job was to hand things to Carver and then catch them or pick them up after Carver pulled something out of them. At one point, Skip, holding a cylinder in front of him, walked up to Carver and whispered that he hadn't put a pigeon inside yet. Carver reached into the cylinder, pulled his hand out and waved it around, whispering that it didn't matter because nobody would notice. Then he pulled a few more yards of silk out of his sleeve.

That night, when the show was over, Skip returned to the hotel with Su and Seah, and after a plate of bami goreng they went to bed. There was only one bed in the hotel room, one big one, and Skip slept in the middle. Carver stayed with Anita and Maya in a different hotel, probably one with air-conditioning. Su and Seah slept in underwear that could have passed for two-piece bathing suits. Skip slept in his pareu, which he wore back from the shower. It had been a long day, so although he was a little confused about the way Su and Seah were treating him, he was too tired to give it much thought. But by morning he realized that they thought of him as something between a younger brother and a household pet. This was especially after they gave him the nickname No Hanky Panky.

For the next ten days Su and Seah were very good to him. It was a busy time with usually a matinee and evening show each day. They saw that he got enough to eat, that his clothes were clean, and that he took at least three showers a day. They teased him a lot but since he didn't understand most of it, the teasing didn't bother him. Besides, Su and Seah were very good natured, always laughing or at least smiling. But at the end of the show's two-week run, the two of them returned to Singapore. Carver didn't pay them. He wanted Su and Seah to follow him up to Penang, but they had promised to come only as far as Kuala Lumpur and they missed Singapore already. So Skip gave them money for train fare. He didn't have time to see them off; he was too busy loading the black boxes of magic equipment onto the truck to take them back to the *Golden Dragon.*

Carver's most famous act was mind reading and didn't involve any elaborate equipment. Anita would go into the audience and have people offer things for her to hold up, like pens and handkerchiefs and such. Carver was, of course, blindfolded but he could always tell what Anita was holding up. It was the one trick that Skip couldn't figure out, although he should have. Finally Anita told him: Carver simply looked under the blindfold. He had phenomenal eyesight, which Skip had already observed on the *Golden Dragon*. It was a good trick because it was so simple. Anita only had to make sure that she picked things that Carver could recognize and that she held them in a way that he could see them. Still, the show was not a success, and in Penang they had to close early. Carver wanted Skip to go on to Calcutta with him. He needed someone to help with the *Golden Dragon*. But for Skip that was out of the question because he simply couldn't think of leaving *Jest* for so long. Besides, he didn't trust Carver, who hadn't paid him anything yet. Although he didn't really need the money, not being paid made him mad, and being mad made it easier for him to say no to Carver. And then Carver made it even easier to say no by promising to teach him to be a magician, for Skip couldn't imagine anything he'd rather not be than a magician. Eventually Carver gave up trying to persuade Skip to go with him to Calcutta. He told Skip, the day before leaving Penang, that in the morning he'd pay Skip, after Skip helped him move the *Golden Dragon* over to the fuel dock. That, according to Carver, would make it easier for Skip to get off. That only made Skip suspicious. The *Golden Dragon* didn't need fuel and Carver never did anything for someone else's convenience. In fact, it wasn't even convenient. He also noticed that whenever Carver said something that wasn't true, he always made sure no one else was around, especially Anita. Still, Skip was somewhat surprised that Carver would try to take him to Calcutta against his will. He must really be desperate—but then, when Skip thought of it, he couldn't understand why Anita stayed on the *Golden Dragon*.

He woke just before dawn, got his bag and climbed noiselessly up on deck. As he thought, there were local boats about in the harbor and he waved one over to the

Golden Dragon. He always admired the way the local boatmen handled their boats with one long oar. And now he appreciated the way they could drive them without making any splashing sound. When the boat reached land, he paid the boatman and walked over to the ferry terminal. While waiting for the first ferry, he wished that he had left a note: Houdini was here. Or maybe: Houdini escapes. But Carver didn't have much of a sense of humor. He was like Jack in that he took himself very seriously. In fact Carver had a lot of things in common with Jack. They both liked to get people to do things that they normally would never think of doing. Then he began to think about their differences. Carver was better with his hands: he could take a man's wristwatch off while shaking his hand, without the man noticing it, and it didn't matter what kind of wristwatch it was either, whether it had a leather or metal band. Jack was better with words. He could talk a man into giving him his wristwatch, although Skip had never seen Jack try it. Jack probably didn't care about wristwatches. He was always generous, at least with money and equipment and things like that.

The train down to Singapore took about twenty-four hours. It was some kind of Hindu holiday, for the train was crowded with Indians. He was the only white person in the third-class carriage, and after a few hours he began to feel invisible. He thought a lot about Mark Carver, World Famous Magician, and overall he was rather pleased with himself. Although he was returning to Singapore without being paid, like Su and Seah, at least he wasn't going to Calcutta. He had held his own against a magician, a master of deceit.

When the train pulled into Singapore early in the morning, Skip walked to the post office and waited for it to open. There was a letter from Catherine, which she had sent from Paris. It was just a few lines: She was getting married in two months to somebody whose name Skip couldn't read. That was it. He left the post office and walked toward Kallang Basin. He walked the whole way, without thinking of anything, until he got back to *Jest*. He looked below, checked the bilge and the battery, started the engine and then sat in the cockpit, letting the engine hum in his mind.

They had only talked about love once; that is, she brought it up only once. It was when she was being frank. "Do you think that when two people are in love, each knows what the other is thinking?"

"You mean telepathy, like in *The Demolished Man?*" She hadn't heard of that novel. "Or do you mean does each know what the other feels?"

"Of course, feeling. You can't lie with your feelings, can you?"

"I couldn't." But as he looked at her, into her deep blue eyes, he saw that she could. And that, he realized, was a problem.

He knew as well that he had occupied a special position in her world. He was outside the normal life of French colonial habits and expectations, which made it possible for her to tell him things that she couldn't tell anyone else. She would often say, "Don't tell anyone this" or "Promise to keep this a secret." But who was he to tell? He never met any of her friends or anyone else she knew. Their relationship was even confined to that particular room, the conservatory, and after their first meeting he always came and went through the French doors that led into the garden at the back of the house.

She was secretive, probably manipulative, and certainly humorless—that was the worst, being humorless. That, more than anything else, was what she had in common with Jack. He hadn't thought of that before. So the question was why he had been so fascinated by her. Had been? Then he remembered the conservatory. And their talk. Their talk had created a web of words so thick with intimacy that he could touch it—palpable, that's how he thought of it, palpable. And even that word she had given him.

Now he wasn't going to sail up the Seine and conquer Paris. Should he write her? What kind of letter? He didn't want bitter memories. Sadness was better, sad memories. The memories you keep become your past. Had Jack said that? Or had he made it up himself? Was he beginning to sound like Jack? He let the sound of the engine seep into him some more. Then the haiku came to him, as he was thinking only about the humming in his own mind, and it came to him as if he had already written it:

The red hyacinth
standing before the closed door—
bowed down by the rain.

He tore the last page out of his logbook and wrote it down in pencil. She had made fun of him because he wrote letters in pencil. But he did his chart work in pencil, and he calculated his position in pencil, and he wrote his logbook in pencil, and so he wrote his letters in pencil. He wrote with a pencil. That's what he was, a guy who wrote with a pencil. And that probably made all the difference. He walked back to the post office and mailed the letter, realizing that he had not only come to Singapore to receive a letter, but also to send one.

Immediately he felt completely empty, as if he had nothing to do, nothing to get ready, nowhere to go. He walked about until he came to a movie house that was playing *Tiara Tahiti*. Somehow the movie seemed familiar, and after studying the poster for a while—starring James Mason and John Mills—he realized that it was the movie they were making when he was in Tahiti. He went in, hoping to see the nightclub scene that he had tried to get into.

Later, walking back along Orchard Road, he heard Su and Seah calling to him. They had seen him from afar and were trying with some difficulty to catch up with him. They asked about Anita and Maya and how he had finally gotten away from Carver. They seemed to have understood Carver better than he had, at least at first. And then they took him back to where they were staying. He was suddenly surprised at how late it was, nearly sundown. In the kitchen they ate bami goreng that an older woman prepared.

"You look sad." As always, he wasn't sure if they were being polite or teasing him.

"Yeah."

"You miss home. That's why you left the show."

Home? Where was his home?

"You sleep here with us, like in Kuala Lumpur."

"Yes, like in Kuala Lumpur. No Hanky Panky."

In the morning he discovered that they had a plan for him, a plan that would give him something to do. "You bring sailors and we give you money." There was a word for that. And in that word he saw his future. Just work in the evenings. Go around the bars. "You guys looking for some action?" An easy life. Does he collect the money or do the girls do that? They said they would give him money. After business he would sleep in the bed with the sisters, like in Kuala Lumpur. Big laundry bill. An easy life. It would be wonderful. Nobody would tell him what to do and everybody would despise him. He didn't know how he knew that, but he knew it as well as he knew anything he had ever known.

When he left Su and Seah, he said he would be back, but he wouldn't be back. He had something else to do. He had to leave Singapore, so he wrote to Anna to send him money to repair *Jest*. He didn't give any reason why he was in Singapore, but he knew she would send the money. So even before she replied, he got Ming to start work on *Jest's* stern. He hardly left the boat. He sanded and painted his cabin sides and top, to give himself something to do. Every day Ming brought lunch for his workmen, and Skip ate with them. He watched them as they tore the old planks off and began to replace them with new ones, working the whole time only with hand tools. Then the rainy season started, which slowed the work down. Then one day in May they were finished. He had already paid Ming two hundred dollars, and now he paid him the other three hundred. It was the best workmanship Skip had ever seen anyone do, and Ming was the most honest businessman he had ever met. The whole job was done on a hand-shake. Then he remembered the name on the stern. He had thrown away the name plaque because even it was partly rotten. So one of Ming's workmen, the one who could paint cardboard to look like teak, came out and painted *Jest* on the stern, using gold leaf.

Nicobar

The passage up the Malacca Strait was slow, but he wasn't in a hurry because he didn't feel he was going anywhere, he was just leaving Singapore. Besides, he had already sailed the Malacca Strait in the *Golden Dragon,* so perhaps for that reason the passage seemed uneventful, even uninteresting. He often didn't make more than 50 miles a day, most of it under power or during the infrequent squalls. Sometimes he anchored at night, close to the Malaysian shore. He spent most of the time thinking about where to go. He couldn't go to India because he didn't have any charts of India, plus he didn't want to be in the same country as Mark Carver. In the middle of the Indian Ocean there was a group of atolls, the Chagos Archipelago. The main atoll was called Diego Garcia, but it was British rather than Spanish. It looked about as far away from everywhere else as a place could possibly be.

It took eight days to get up to Penang at the northern end of the Malacca Strait. He decided not to stop in Penang. He remembered how bad the anchorage was, with a strong current running through the harbor and no protection from the squalls. He hadn't cared much what happened to the *Golden Dragon* when he was there before, but now he realized that he couldn't leave *Jest* alone in that anchorage. And since he had stocked up on provisions in Singapore, he decided to go on to the Nicobar Islands, which were 380 miles to the west, about the same distance he had just sailed from Singapore. But as soon as he turned west and moved into the Andaman Sea, the wind died and he spent the next day in sight of Penang. He had bought a wok in Singapore and every day, after the noon sight, he made bami goreng. Soon he would run out of onions and eventually he would run out of garlic and ginger, but he had plenty of noodles, dried shrimp, and dried mushrooms. He was looking forward to trying fresh fish with his noodles.

He powered until Penang was out of sight and then in the evening, when a light wind came out of the southwest, he put *Jest* on the port tack. He was adjusting the wind-vane when suddenly *Jest* was knocked down. The boom was dragging in the water and the deck seemed almost vertical to the sea. At first all he could do was hold on, and then he heard the jib sheet part. Keeping one hand fast to the starboard mooring cleat, he used his other hand to release the main sheet. *Jest* slowly rose out of the water and stood shivering before the wind. The first thing he did was grab his harness and put it on, then he went forward to take in the jib and mainsail. He noticed that both sails had ripped seams, but what surprised him was the sky. There wasn't a cloud anywhere. There had been no warning, just a sudden hard wind. He had heard about such winds before. Captain Johnson on *Diana* had mentioned them, calling them white squalls. Sometimes, he thought, black was better than white.

He let *Jest* lie a-hull as he pumped out the bilge. A lot of water had come in through the cabin portholes. Then he got the trysail out and hove-to for the night. He was a little dazed, or perhaps just a little exhausted. He had been in port too long, and it looked like he had to learn all over again what it meant to be at sea. As he lay in his bunk listening to the wind, he thought of one of the questions that Jack had often asked him. "What did you learn?" Now he thought of the question himself, and this time he had an answer: always wear your harness at sea, always.

In the morning the wind was still blowing hard from the southwest. He put up the staysail and tried to come about, but the sea had built up and *Jest* stopped dead in the water each time he brought her into the wind. So he jibed to get on the starboard tack and head a little north of west. He wasn't making much headway but at least he thought he wasn't losing any ground. *Jest* started to take on water because the bow, as she pounded into the sea, opened up her seams, especially those above the waterline. He realized that *Jest* had sat in the Singapore sun too long, but he couldn't do anything about it, except stop sewing every couple of hours and pump the bilge. After a few days the seams closed up and he had to pump only once a day. The wind continued strong, and when he was about 50 miles from Great Nicobar Island, he had to jibe again because he was too far north. But after heading south for a couple of hours, *Jest* was knocked down again, this time while carrying only the trysail and staysail. He let the sheets go and got the sails in. The harness saved him twice from going over the side. Then he ran off before the wind with nothing but the bare mast. He lost a lot of ground before heaving-to for the night.

A few days later the sun came out just enough for him to get a sight. At noon it came out again, so he was able to fix his position. He had logged over 600 miles since leaving Penang astern, but he was still 140 miles from Great Nicobar, which was about where he had been seven days ago. He was hove-to with the trysail up, but when he put the staysail up and tried to make some headway, the clew blew out and he hove-to again. Later, while trying to tune into Greenwich for the time, he caught a weather report that said there was a typhoon in the Bay of Bengal. He figured that he must be at the edge of it.

When the wind eased, he set the staysail again and made about 100 miles before it died altogether. He was about 40 miles from Great Nicobar Island, so he decided to power into the anchorage at Tinkat Champlong Bay. The moment he started the engine, he knew something was wrong with it. It sounded as if one of the cylinders wasn't firing, but since it didn't seem to be getting any worse, he headed *Jest* slowly towards Great Nicobar Island. He entered the bay in the late afternoon and noticed that it was wide but protected from winds from the west. There were no buildings or other signs of human habitation, only a deep green jungle, separated from the sea by a strip of white beach. He anchored in five fathoms but the water was so clear that he felt he could reach down and touch the bottom.

He brought all his bedding and clothes up on deck to dry, opened all the hatches, and rigged the awnings in case it rained. It had taken him thirteen days to make the 380 miles from Penang and he wasn't going anywhere for a while, not until everything on board was dry and he had finished repairing his sails and rigging. In the morning he took his facemask and fins and swam over to the reef at the southern end of the bay. There were lobsters every-where, and like the ones in California, they didn't have any claws. He swam back to *Jest* and sawed the handle of his broom in half. He never used the broom anyway, just a bucket of water to clean the deck and a wet cloth to clean below. He took about eighteen inches of stainless steel wire from his fishing box and made an eye at one end, threaded the other end of the wire through the eye and attached it to the broom handle. Then he went back to where he saw the lobsters. He slipped the wire loop at the end of the broom handle over the tail, from the back of the lobster, and when the lobster backed into its hole, the loop tightened and he pulled the lobster out. At first he thought he should have brought his dinghy to put the lobster in, but then he realized that he probably couldn't eat more than one at a time anyway.

After that he ate lobster every day. At first he ate lobster at every meal, but he found that no matter how he cooked them—and boiling was probably the best—and no matter what he put on them, the lobsters always tasted the same, and in the end he became thoroughly sick of them, so sick in fact that he never wanted to eat lobster again.

On the chart he noticed there was a river about five miles away at Laful, so he decided to see if he could get some fresh water. The engine sounded bad and he thought it might stop at any moment, but he couldn't do anything about it. All he knew about the engine was how to change the oil and clean the fuel filter; for anything else he needed a mechanic. After anchoring in Laful, he decided to take a look at the river, to see if he could get water before emptying his emergency water into the main tanks. He put his dinghy over the side and rowed to the beach where the river entered the sea. He left his dinghy there and began walking up the river. The water in the river was brownish in color and even had a rotten smell to it. He hadn't gone very far when he saw that he couldn't get his dinghy up the river because it was blocked with fallen trees. He could always float his canisters down the river, so he waded farther up the river, but the water was still brackish. He realized that on the one hand he was struggling with his fear of being alone in the jungle, for he had no idea what might spring out at him, plus the place was called Crocodile River. But on the other hand he was disappointed in not being able to get fresh water, not that he needed water so desperately, but that getting fresh water from a river was one of those things that he felt he should be able to do.

When he got back to the beach, his dinghy was gone. He walked the entire beach but in the end he had to swim out to *Jest*. In the evening he remembered that Slocum had put tacks all over his deck, so that he wouldn't be surprised by natives coming aboard the *Spray*. But there weren't any tacks on *Jest,* and he decided that screws wouldn't do. He went below and got out the rifle, cleaned it, assembled it, and then loaded it. He took the rifle with him to the cockpit where he decided to sleep. Nothing happened in the night, but in the morning he saw two natives in his dinghy coming toward *Jest*. They didn't look dangerous, so he put the rifle below. The natives didn't use the oars to row, but to paddle, as if his dinghy was a canoe, one in the bow, a boy about ten-years old, and the other in the stern, a man somewhere between twenty and forty, as far as Skip could tell. When they got to *Jest* they held on to her port side, not saying anything, just sitting there waiting. Skip decided that they were waiting for him to give them something. First he gave them some chocolate bars with almonds in them. The man and the boy, without looking at each other, both did the same thing. They unwrapped the chocolate bars, picked out the nuts and then threw the chocolate away. Then he gave them four cans of pineapple juice, which they simply let fall in the bottom of the dinghy without looking at them. Then the man stood up in the stern of the dinghy and pointed to the rag that he had around his waist, which seemed to be the only thing he had, except Skip's dinghy. Skip had six pareus from Tahiti that he had been saving. He gave a red one to the man and an orange one to the boy. They put the pareus on their laps and then the man took out a small tin—Skip didn't see where it came from—and using his finger, put some of its contents in his mouth, then he offered Skip some. Skip could see, by the state of the man's black and reddish teeth, that the tin probably held beetle nut. He wanted to refuse, but then they might leave, so he stuck his finger in the tin and then put his finger in his mouth. He turned away before taking his finger out of his mouth and most of the beetle nut was still on his finger, which he hid. After a few minutes he went below again, washed his mouth and finger, and got out a bottle of whiskey, from the case that Bob Sterling had given him in Darwin. He brought the whiskey on deck, loosened the cap and offered it to the man. The man drank about a quarter of the whiskey before passing out. The boy then let go of *Jest,* got the bottle of whiskey and, as the dinghy drifted off, drank about another quarter of the bottle before passing out as well. Skip dove in the water and towed his dinghy ashore. He hauled the boy out of the dinghy first and then the man. There wasn't any shade on the beach, so he covered them with the pareus he had given them, holding the cloth in place with the cans of pineapple juice and the half-empty bottle of whiskey. The whiskey was called Wild Turkey, and he saw for the first time how deceptive the label was, for no one ever thought of the turkey, wild or not, as being treacherous.

Seychelles

He prepared to leave Laful as soon as he had his dinghy on deck and secured in its cradle over the main skylight. When the anchor was clear of the bottom, the engine began making a dull clunking noise and then stopped. The mainsail was already up, so instead of trying to get the engine going again, he hoisted the staysail, and then let *Jest* run off on the starboard tack while he secured the anchor. Once out of the bay, he tried to head south, but the southerly wind was so strong that he decided to sail around the northern end of Great Nicobar.

The passage between Great Nicobar and Little Nicobar was about fifteen miles long and narrowed to less than two miles toward the western end. He had to beat through the passage, with his long tack to port. After a few hours, when he was more than half way through and about to tack away from Great Nicobar, a dugout with four men came out of the shadow of the island and began to follow him. He had been taking it easy, thinking about what he would cook for dinner. Now he set the jib, took the belly out of the mainsail by tightening the halyard, and released the wind-vane so he could do the steering. He steered for speed rather than pointing higher into the wind because the men in the dugout stayed in his wake, even when he tacked. They were gaining on him, but not enough to worry him. With one more tack to port he thought he could clear the western end of Great Nicobar; then he would be out of the passage. But when he made his last tack to port, the men in the dugout didn't follow him. Instead, they paddled into the wind to cut him off when he tacked to starboard again. And he had to tack to starboard because he couldn't clear Little Nicobar.

He set the wind-vane and went below to get the rifle. When he tacked back to starboard, he hoped he could clear Great Nicobar and outdistance the dugout. He was surprised that the men could paddle so hard for so long. It suggested a definite desire or need, even desperation on their part. Whatever it was, he knew that they didn't have anything he wanted.

When he saw that the men in the dugout were going to cut him off, he waited until they were about 200 yards off his port side and then he tacked away from them. But *Jest* caught a heavy sea while coming into the wind and she stalled, which gave the men in the dugout a chance to close up to him. He picked up the rifle and fired a shot over the dugout. At the same time, or perhaps a moment before, the man in the bow of the dugout suddenly stood up and raised his paddle over his head, but the moment Skip fired the rifle, the man fell back, collapsing in the dugout. The other men in the dugout stopped paddling. *Jest* fell back on the starboard tack and when she picked up speed, she passed the dugout within a 100 yards. A few minutes later she was in the Indian Ocean.

For the next week he headed southwest, trying to make as much southerly as possible, for he had to cross the doldrums and pick up the southeast trades before heading for Diego Garcia. It was easy sailing and there was little he needed to do, except cook, plot his position, and keep an eye on the weather. At first, when he thought about the incident with the men in the dugout, he assumed that the man in the bow fell backward from surprise. After all, he had stood up at the same moment that Skip had fired. Skip saw the paddle fly out of his hands as the man fell back, and it was possible, Skip thought, that he had hit the paddle, although he had aimed high over the dugout. It was only meant to be a warning, to let them know that he was armed. But as he thought about it more and more, he knew that when he aimed he hadn't calculated on any of the men standing up. In fact, when he saw that *Jest* had stalled, he had taken up the rifle and fired so quickly that he hadn't aimed carefully at all. He certainly hadn't calculated on the movement of the boat, he couldn't even remember if *Jest* had been rising or falling when he fired.

But what bothered him even more was the image of the man in the bow with the paddle raised over his head. He was much bigger than the native men he had seen in that part of the world, from New Guinea to Sumatra. He was big in the arms and shoulders, but mainly in the chest, like Jack. And as soon as Skip thought of Jack, he had to struggle to keep the image of the man in the bow from changing into Jack, a Jack with dark skin and cropped hair that looked like it had never been washed. But he had to admit that it was something Jack would do, dress up like an aborigine and chase him in a dugout, though he couldn't think of a reason why Jack would do it.

He hit the doldrums just before reaching the equator. He was a little concerned about his water supply, so he tried to collect as much water as he could during the squalls that hit him. But at the same time, the squalls brought the only wind, which meant that during the squalls he had to steer if he ever wanted to get out of the doldrums and into the southeast trades. He rigged his awning to collect rainwater, but when a squall hit, he was too busy handling the boat to deal with the water collection, so usually something happened. The wind ripped his awning or knocked his water canister over. Once he almost lost the water canister over the side, but in the end he managed to collect almost twenty gallons before he reached the trade winds.

It was over three weeks and over 1,200 miles when the wind came out of the south-southeast and he began to head due west. The next day he hooked a tuna, but it was so big he couldn't get it on board. He didn't have a gaff and the fishing line was so thin that it cut into his hands. If he hove-to he might have been able to get a line around the fish and use the winch to haul it on board. But he was making over five knots and he didn't want to stop, not even for fresh fish. Besides, it reminded him of the Goldilocks story. First there was no fish, then there was too much fish. So the next time the fish will be just right.

A week after reaching the trade winds he sighted land, just before sunset. But the next morning it was blowing a gale, right out the pass of Diego Garcia. The wind charts showed that no gales were predicted for July in the general area of the Chagos Archipelago, but he was hove-to under storm trysail, with his lee rail often in the water. The gusts must have been up to fifty knots, but more than that, the waves were enormous, the biggest he had ever seen. And *Jest* was slowly drifting toward the Great Chagos Bank. He waited that day and then through the night, but in the morning he could no longer see Diego Garcia. He thought he had enough sea room to wait one more day for the weather to clear, but when he tried to check his position, he found it impossible to use the sextant. The waves were so big that the horizon was usually hidden behind them, plus the deck heaved so much that he couldn't keep the sun on the horizon, even when he could find it. So when he sighted Egbert Island to leeward, he set the staysail, let out the sheets, and fell off until the wind was on his quarter. The Seychelles were a 1,000 miles to the west.

After he gave up on getting into Diego Garcia and headed *Jest* once again to the west, the days on board quickly fell back into their peaceful rhythm, a rhythm that was sustained by the steady wind that blew over his port quarter and the regular rise and fall of the sea that made *Jest* roll to starboard going down the face of the waves and then pause for a moment in the trough before lifting up again on the next wave. He was sometimes asked what he did at sea, out there in the middle of nowhere, as if they, those who asked him such questions, thought the sea consisted of some vast emptiness. But his world wasn't empty. There was the boat itself, with its multitude of parts, from its keel to its masthead, and every part had a name, plus a name for what it was made of and sometimes another name for what it did. Many parts of the boat had themselves parts that had names. The deck was made of teak and had a king plank and a devil seam that had to be payed. There was the mast with its rigging, the shrouds and stays, and the sails with their three sides, plus their three corners, all with their own names. There were no whatchamacallits on a boat. Then there were the variations in the wind and the sea and the different clouds and at night the multitude of stars and constellations. He had seen the moon disappear in the shadow of the earth and then the shadow itself disappear behind a squall. He had seen a waterspout swallow the Southern Cross and then spit it out again. He had seen a flying fish skim the top of the rising sun and plunge back into the sea. No, the sea wasn't empty.

The fishing was good that week, and by the time he sighted Frégate Island on the western fringe of the Seychelles, he had to throw them back into the sea and stop putting out his fishing line. He hove-to for the night and in the morning he sailed through the pass at Victoria on Mahé Island. The pilot boat met him inside the reef and towed him to the inner harbor, where he dropped his anchor and let the wind blow him back. He tied up, with his stern to the pier, next to the ketch *Diana,* which Skip had last seen in Tahiti. On the other side of the *Diana* was an 85-foot trading schooner. The passage from Nicobar to the Seychelles had taken him 39 days.

He walked down the Long Pier and into town, the land rolling under him as if he were still at sea. When he came to a bakery, he bought a loaf of bread, which he carried under his arm and ate pieces from as he walked around, looking at things. There was an old courthouse and post office, and at the center of town, there was a clock tower that looked like a replica of some larger clock tower in England. But the Creoles seemed unaffected by European time, as they moved in the unhurried rhythm of the tropics.

He walked back to *Jest* in time to see the trading schooner get underway. There were eleven men on the foredeck, hauling the anchor chain in. In the stern, a smaller man with short gray hair, not a Creole, stood and shouted. The mainsail and foresail were already set, and it occurred to Skip that the schooner didn't have an engine. When the anchor was up and down, the headsails were broken out and backed and the schooner, on a close reach, headed out toward the pass. The schooner would be back in a week, with copra and turtles.

He needed to get the engine fixed. During the storm in the Andaman Sea, water had backed up the exhaust pipe and gotten into the cylinders; at least that was what he assumed was the cause of the engine failure. At first he didn't think he could find anyone in Victoria who could fix it, but as it turned out, there were about a hundred Americans on the island, setting up a radar tracking station on the top of a mountain. Most of them worked for Philco of Palo Alto, just down the peninsula from San Francisco. He learned all this a few days later when he went to the Veranda Bar at the end of the Long Pier. The bar was upstairs, one large room with a veranda on three sides. Americans working on the tracking station spent the late afternoon and early evening at the bar, talking and drinking beer. Later in the evening they would all go to Sharkies, where there were women and music. Skip sat at the bar, with a glass of orange squash, listening to three Americans at a table near him. They were talking mainly about themselves. They were "the best," the best electrician, the best engineer, and the best mechanic. Skip went up and asked them if they could fix a Perkins diesel. They were silent for a moment, staring at him as if he were from another world, until one of them said, "Perkins, eh. It's a British engine. Where is it?" Skip explained that he had just arrived on a boat and what he thought the problem was. One of them stretched, another yawned. "What can you pay?" He had money, but from listening to them talk he knew that what he had to offer would not interest them, plus they didn't seem to be impressed with his sailing across the Indian Ocean. So he offered them the case of Wild Turkey that Bob had given him in Darwin. They didn't seem to believe him that he had a case of Wild Turkey. Probably didn't even believe him that he had sailed across the Indian Ocean. But the promise of a case of Wild Turkey was enough to get them to follow him down the Long Pier to *Jest*.

Skip broke out the case of Wild Turkey and set it on the table in front of them. He thought it was an impressive gesture, but then he realized he had probably made a mistake. All his cards, that is all his whiskey, was on the table, plus he had forgotten the man and the boy in Nicobar. "You said a case. There's a bottle missing. You've been drinkin' our Wild Turkey, eh?" Skip explained that he had traded the bottle for his dinghy. They said they didn't want his dinghy, that it probably wasn't worth a bottle of Wild Turkey, but they had to try a bottle first, to see if it was what the label said it was. Skip got out glasses and waited.

As they drank, they began talking about someone called Col. Lockjaw. He was the military officer in charge of the tracking station. Lockjaw wasn't his real name, but it seemed that he had a massive jaw, which he emphasized by smoking a large pipe. One American claimed that Col. Lockjaw could balance a full can of beer on top of his pipe, while it was in his mouth, of course. Another American claimed that he had seen Col. Lockjaw balance a coconut on top of his pipe, an unhusked coconut too. The third American claimed that he had seen Col. Lockjaw balance a sixteen-year-old Creole girl on top of his pipe, fully dressed.

"Who was fully dressed, Lockjaw or the girl?"

"And she was holding the coconut in her lap."

"While drinking a can of beer."

It seemed that Col. Lockjaw often went to the Veranda Bar, but Skip never saw him there, and he was disappointed to have missed seeing someone with such a tall-tale jaw.

When the Americans had finished the first bottle of Wild Turkey, they left for Sharkies. They never looked at the engine, they never even mentioned it. But a few days later, Skip returned from shopping and saw that the Americans had taken his engine out of the boat. So he began to work on the space where the engine had been. He cleaned the sump, checked for rot in the wood, and then scraped and painted all the places he could reach. While he was cleaning up on the pier, washing himself with the cold water from a hose, he began to notice a Creole girl sitting near the end of his gangplank. Every time he passed her, she said "pow," which he thought was a little funny, since it reminded him of someone getting hit in a comic book. Then he realized that she was saying "Paul." It took awhile for him to understand her, that she had met Paul at Sharkies and Paul had been nice to her or something, and she thought Paul was on *Jest* and she was waiting for him to come out. Skip tried to explain to her that Paul wasn't on *Jest,* that he was on the *Diana,* and that the *Diana* was half way to South Africa. But she couldn't speak English anymore than he could speak Creole, so she continued to sit there, waiting for Paul.

One evening, as Skip was walking down the Long Pier towards town, but not going anywhere in particular, he heard Fats Domino singing "I'm In Love Again." The music was coming from the warehouse, and as he looked inside, he saw that it was crowded with people. They were having a dance. It was a very different crowd from Sharkies, for there were no Americans and no bar girls. This was mainly, as he later learned, because there was no alcohol. They had an old record player, and Skip just stood and watched the people dance for a while, but when they played Fats Domino again, he went up to a Creole girl in a red dress, who had been not too obviously smiling at him, and asked her if she wanted to dance. As they danced, he smiled and she smiled, but he didn't say anything because he assumed that she spoke only Creole, and even when he asked her to dance, he assumed that she understood his intention but not his words. At the end of the dance, he discovered that he was wrong. He thought that he might as well dance with the other girls who had been standing next to the one in the red dress, but when he asked the one in the blue dress to dance, she only giggled.

"She doesn't understand English. Shall I tell her you want to dance with her?"

"No, you don't need to tell her that. I'd rather dance with you again." She was the prettiest of the girls that had been standing together, and since she spoke English, he thought they would understand that he wanted to dance with her.

"What shall I tell her you said?"

"Tell her I'm in love again."

Her name was Marie and she was, or was about to become, an English teacher. She had a very nice smile, and she looked very good in red, but Skip thought he would wait to tell her that. They remained together, dancing and talking, the rest of the evening. She didn't seem to have a boyfriend, as no one tried to dance with her the whole evening. He felt, in fact, that everyone else at the dance was purposely leaving them alone.

When the dance was over, he walked her home. They took the main road out of town to the south and then up the hill. It wasn't far, but when they came to the house there was no light. She said her mother and sister were down island, visiting. She was doing her teacher's training in the morning, but she was free in the later afternoon. Skip said he would like to come then and take her for a walk, and he knew by the way she smiled that he had said what she had hoped he would say.

The next afternoon, as he approached her house, Marie came out and met him. She said she had been waiting for him, giving him what he thought of as her sunshine smile. As they walked down the hill he noticed that she wore a red dress again, but a different one, with a lighter shade of red. It was a simple dress, with a firm fit at the bust and waist, leaving her arms bare, and with a wide, full skirt, reaching below her knees. He told her she looked very nice in red. That pleased her, and he was even more pleased because he had never complimented a girl before. He realized then (what he should have realized before) that she made her own dresses. On *Jest* he had a red and white Tahitian pareu with a hibiscus pattern. She would look good in that, and he hadn't seen anything like it on Mahé. He wondered where their cloth came from. England, or probably India. It was all so monochrome. He would give her the pareu, if the mildew hadn't gotten it, but then two meters probably wasn't enough material to make a dress with.

Becoming an English teacher seemed to be very much on her mind, and she asked him questions about English words and expressions that she had obviously overheard from the Americans working on the tracking station.

" 'Pissed off'? That means to be angry."

"And 'jerk off'?"

"That means to goof off."

" 'Goof off'? What does that mean?"

"It means to fool around." She smiled at that and he realized that he had to explain "fool around." "Actually, 'to fool around' is a little more general. It means to be doing something other than what you should be doing."

"That sounds like Antoine."

"Antoine is your friend?"

"Antoine is everyone's friend. He is a very big fool around."

The sun was still above the line of mountains that ran down the center of the island, and he could smell vanilla from one of the plantations, rising in the warm air off to his right. Perhaps because he had been around the Americans at the Veranda Bar and Sharkies, he found Marie one of the most unaffected persons he had ever met. She had no desire to leave the Seychelles, or even Mahé. At first he thought it was some kind of passivity on her part, a passivity that extended even to her attitude toward him, for she was so uninterested in where he had been or what he had done. Slowly he began to realize that it wasn't a passivity so much, but rather a view of life in which only the here and now were real. That was why, for her, he had no past.

She told him that her father, too, had sailed one day to Mahé, had married her mother and stayed. Her father was the captain of the *Dena,* a local trading schooner. His name was Kabir, Captain Kabir, and he was from Persia. This story made Skip see an emerging pattern: A stranger arrives in Mahé, and even though he is a sailor, he stays and marries a local girl and then becomes the captain of a local trading schooner. No, it wasn't a pattern but rather a ritual and he was in the middle of it.

When the sun fell behind the line of mountains and they had stopped at the banyan tree, he knew she would let him hold her hand now, but she would not let him kiss her, not yet, not until he had met her parents. Her parents would approve of him, for he saw that he fit the pattern, not so much because he was a sailor who could speak English, the official language of the Seychelles, but because he was neither a Creole nor a grand blanc, a member of one of the old French families. He had only to stay and everything would be arranged for him. A new family, including a new father. A Persian, no less, who would give him three fairytale tasks before letting him marry his daughter. They would be simple tasks, such as setting a course for the islands to the south, climbing the mainmast and setting the topsail, and standing at the helm and shouting at the crew as it hauled in the anchor. He would have to learn Creole, of course, but only enough to shout orders. And perhaps he would have to learn to walk more self-consciously, as he had seen Captain Kabir walk, after he had returned to Mahé from his last trip with a broken topmast. Yes, he would have to learn to walk like a man who carried his topsail in a gale.

He took Marie for a walk each afternoon, until one day, as he approached her house, she came out with her sister, Leah. Leah was younger than Marie and the most beautiful woman he had ever seen. It was a conscious effort not to stare at her. As they walked down the hill to the main road, Skip was in the middle, and Marie took his left hand, as was her habit now, and Leah took his right. The two girls talked about the dinner they would help their mother prepare when Papa returned from the lower islands. Leah often switched to Creole when talking about different foods, but Skip heard Marie mention papaya-flower chutney. He focused on that, trying to imagine what chutney made from papaya flowers could be like, while looking straight ahead. But he couldn't keep it up. He kept turning his head to the right. Unlike Marie's smile, Leah's smile was enigmatic. It could have meant anything, a certain self-awareness, or self-satisfaction. He knew then that he would often dream of it.

When he got back to *Jest* he noticed that the Americans had brought back his engine and reinstalled it. He put his hand on the cylinder head. It was warm, so he started the engine up and it sounded right. In some ways, so it seemed, the Americans were the best. He took a cold shower on the pier and then filled his water tanks. In the morning he picked up his clearance papers from the harbormaster, and passing the bakery, bought three loaves of bread. After he cleared the pass, he saw a sail to the south. The *Dena* returning to Mahé. He headed north.

Mombasa

He knew that he had been tested and that he had failed. But he simply couldn't take Marie for a walk every day; he couldn't go down the path that he assumed led eventually to marriage, while at the same time trying not to stare at her sister. Marie was very nice in her way, but one look at Leah and she possessed him, and she knew that she possessed him. The more he thought about it, the more he realized that he had to escape, not just from an awkward situation, but from Leah herself. He had to escape from the hold she would have over him. But then, maybe by escaping he had not failed a test but passed it. That would mean Marie had helped him, and that he had not only treated her badly, offering no explanation for his sudden departure, for no explanation was possible, but that he was also in her debt. He came to see that he was actually grateful to her, yet there was no way to repay her, and any attempt to do so, to write her for example, would make the situation worse and would make his debt to her greater.

He couldn't make up his mind whether to sail north or south, whether to sail up the Red Sea and through the Suez Canal or down to South Africa and around the Cape of Good Hope. So he sailed to Mombasa, 940 miles to the west. The trade winds held and he sighted the east coast of Africa after eight days at sea. The passage seemed short, but it was long enough for him to sort out in his own mind what the Seychelles meant to him, what he had learned, what mistake he had made, for he realized, once he accepted what he came to see as his disgrace, that in the long run he was one thing and not another, that he was a sailor and not an islander.

He didn't have a chart of the harbor at Mombasa, so he motored slowly through the pass and headed for the south side of the city. When he came to the Mombasa Yacht Club, he tied up to a mooring buoy. Ahead of him, tied to another buoy, was the *Oceanid*. He wondered what Bob was doing in Mombasa, for he should be in the Mediterranean or even the Caribbean by now. As he was to learn, the *Oceanid* had gone aground on the southwest coast of Zanzibar, and Bob had to repair not only the hull, he had also to build the slipway to haul the schooner out of the water so he could work on her.

The officials at the yacht club welcomed him, though as he sat at the bar, drinking an orange squash with ice, the club members seemed to be in a somber mood. The cause of this mood, as one club member explained to him, was the coming independence. So many white Kenyans had already left the country, so many more would leave in the next few months. When he left the bar and went out to the veranda, he saw a girl sitting in the shade, reading a book. It was the girl he had seen leaving the *Oceanid* in Darwin.

He walked up to her and said, "Jambo."

"Jambo. I'm Jo and you must be Skip, the Hero of Darwin. We saw you arrive yesterday and so I know all about you."

She hadn't asked him to sit down, but he hadn't talked to an American girl for almost two years, so he tried to see if he could get her to put her book away.

"I saw you sitting here reading a book, so I thought I'd come over and say hello." He looked down at the cover of the book. "*The Ambassadors.* Is it a book about travel?"

"Kind of," she laughed. "It's about an American who goes to Paris."

"And then he meets a French woman who makes a fool out of him."

"So you have read it?"

"No. But I know the story." He wondered if an American girl would make a fool of him.

"Could you row me out to *Oceanid?*"

"Sure, if we could make some toast. Hot buttered toast."

He didn't get any toast. It seemed the *Oceanid* had a routine, and breakfast was over and lunch wasn't ready yet. But when Bob and Jo's mother returned to the schooner, Skip was asked to stay for lunch. Bob asked Skip about what he had done since Darwin, but for most of the lunch Bob explained how the *Oceanid* had gone aground in Zanzibar, and all the problems he had had getting her repaired and back in the water again. After lunch, Skip and Jo went up on deck and sat under the awning.

"Robert was in fine form at lunch today."

"You call your father 'Robert'?"

"He's not my father," she said. "He's my mother's husband."

"Anyway, it was nice of him to invite me on the safari."

"He wasn't trying to be nice to you. He wants you to occupy me, so he can devote himself to Mother." Then she added, "Now that he has saved his boat, he wants to save his marriage."

"Oh, if you can see through him that easily, I must be completely transparent. Do you think you could like someone who isn't as smart as you?"

"I'm not smarter than you. I just know different things."

"Like books and people. What else?"

"That's already a lot, don't you think?"

"How long do I have to wait before you let me kiss you?"

"If you 'wait,' then forever. But it was unpredictable of you to say that. So let me see." She pretended to think a bit. "I'll give you a month."

"A month? You'll stay in Mombasa a month?"

"No, so you will have to hurry, won't you."

He thought it encouraging that she at least could talk about being kissed, so he tried to continue in that direction.

"I feel romance in the air. But I don't think your mother likes me."

"You shouldn't brag about not having a toilet or a shower on your boat. You know, you are already at a disadvantage because you sail alone."

"What kind of disadvantage?"

"It's strange and unsocial to live alone. You are like a hermit. You may be closer to nature, but you are further away from everything else."

"Help me out a little. How can I get your mother to like me?"

"She might tolerate you if you got a haircut, a pair of shoes, and accepted at Princeton."

"Maybe she'll settle for two out of three."

Bob rented a Peugeot, and the next morning they headed for the Tsavo National Park—to see the animals, Bob said. Although they were staying only one night in the park, they had managed to fill most of the last seat with a lot of luggage and two baskets of food. Skip had a haircut and new clothes. He felt a little self-conscious wearing khaki, especially in Africa, and especially on a safari, but Jo had insisted. He even bought the brown shoes she wanted him to wear, after he realized that it was important to her. She had called him obstinate, and when he said it was a virtue called persistence, she said that life at sea didn't necessarily carry over to life on land, and when he asked why not, she said that, well, you don't make friends with the sea. So he bought a pair of shoes and said that now she owed him a pair of kisses.

They stopped at the gate to the park, and Skip got out to take pictures of the tame hippopotamus and the baby elephant that the park rangers kept there. He hadn't taken many pictures since leaving Singapore, except for the fish he had caught. He had taken a picture of every one of them, trying to capture them in black and white before their colors faded. The ranger told Bob to be careful of the rhinos; they sometimes chased cars, and it was difficult to drive faster than 30 miles per hour on the dirt roads in the park.

Skip had never seen such a country. There were trees here and there, and bush, but it was mostly open, with a stream or pool now and then. He had expected to see a few giraffes or zebras, but he was astonished at the number of animals. There were whole herds of giraffes and zebras and elephants and gazelles and impalas and kudus and buffalos. He also saw dik diks, wart hogs, baboons, and jackals. Through his binoculars he spotted a cat lying in a tree. Bob said it was a lynx and Jo's mother said it was a caracal. Jo looked in her Swahili dictionary and said it was called a simbamongu. But everything was too far away to take a picture of. Without a telephoto lens, the animals would be just little dots in the vast savanna. Then they came around a bend and saw a small herd of elephants near the road. When Skip climbed out to take a picture, all the elephants moved into the bush, except a big bull that held his place, facing the car. Skip moved up to the bull as close as he dared and took a few pictures, then he imitated an elephant roar, just to see what would happen. The bull answered Skip's yell, raising his head and flapping his large ears back and forth. Then he charged. Skip took one picture and ran for the car. Bob was already driving away and Jo was holding the back door open. Skip jumped into the car and fell on Jo, while trying to hold his camera up. Jo's mother said something about almost being killed, but Bob was smiling and Jo was holding his hand in both of hers, and maybe he even got a good picture.

They stopped for lunch at a pond where there were supposed to be hippopotamuses. There was a picnic table under a large baobab tree, so Skip got out one of the food baskets and put it on the table, then they all went down to the pond to look for the hippopotamuses. Skip thought he saw two eyes sticking out of the water, but as he began to walk around the pond to get a closer look, Jo's mother yelled, "The food!" When he turned around, he saw that a troop of monkeys had climbed out of the tree and were plundering the food basket on the picnic table. Jo and her mother jumped about, waving their arms, but the monkeys didn't move off very far. Those who hadn't managed to grab anything were waiting for another chance, and a few even tried to reach the food basket that was still in the car. Bob rolled up the windows of the car, saving the one food basket, but the other was lost, most of it scattered around the table and under the tree. Jo's mother called the monkeys pests and was so disgusted with their behavior that she later refused to eat anything. But Skip managed to get a picture of a monkey holding a chicken salad sandwich.

In the late afternoon they arrived at the Kilaguni Lodge where they were to spend the night. Skip wondered about who was to sleep where. Since Bob had booked two cabins, there were, as far as Skip could see, several possibilities. Later Bob took him aside and asked him if he wouldn't mind sleeping in the car. Skip guessed that Bob wanted to share a cabin with Jo's mother, but Jo's mother didn't want Skip to share a cabin with Jo, even though the cabins had twin beds.

After dinner they sat on the veranda watching the animals at the water hole. To the west they could see Kilimanjaro, its white peak still lit by the setting sun. Skip thought everything so strange, the country, the animals, Jo and her mother, Bob and the car, plus being away from *Jest*. It was a different world to him. He was thinking how a rainsquall, so familiar to him, now seemed so far away, when Jo's mother said "Have you ever read 'The Snows of Kilimanjaro?' "

Somewhat startled, Skip replied, "I've read rain, but I've never had a chance to read snow." When he realized his mistake, he also realized that Jo's mother thought he was trying to be sarcastic. But she left the veranda before he could think of a way to explain himself. He told Jo that he had been thinking of rainsqualls, and "you can 'read' weather, can't you?" Plus he had never heard of a story about Kilimanjaro. Jo seemed skeptical at first, then she asked him if he had ever read Somerset Maugham. When he said no, she said in that case he had never read "Rain" either. After that he sat silently on the veranda until it was time for him to go to the car.

If he left the door open, he could stretch his legs out, so he had no trouble falling to sleep. Then later in the night he woke up. There was a lot of noise, crashing and yelling, and since he wasn't on *Jest,* he was disoriented. He saw some crazy lights jumping about, then realized they were flashlights being waved around; then he saw the large form of several elephants that had wandered up to the trees in front of the cabins. Some of the lodge keepers were trying to get them to move off, but the elephants didn't seem to be in any hurry, as they stomped about, crashing into trees. Bob came out to see what the noise was. He said something about elephants walking through his second honeymoon and then went back into his cabin. After it was quiet again, and as he was about to get back into the car, Skip heard Jo calling to him softly from her cabin.

"I thought maybe you would like to come in for a while. I can't sleep now after all that noise." She had on a cotton nightgown that covered everything except her hands and feet. When he came in and closed the door, she got back into bed.

"I'm wide awake now, too." He went over and sat on the unused bed.

"You are very different from the Skip described in *World Traveler.*"

"And you'd like to know how different? You want to know about my past, the girl in each port and all that?"

"Ok, let's start there. Have you ever been with native women?"

"Native of what country?"

"You know. The South Seas. Tahiti. Did you sleep with a beautiful Tahitian woman?"

"All Tahitian women are beautiful."

"Did you?"

"Yes."

"Just 'yes'? Not even 'yes, of course,' or 'yes, it was part of being in Tahiti,' or. . . I don't know. What was it like?"

"Why should I tell one woman what I did with another woman?"

"It's a question of trust. How am I going to trust you if I don't know what you are like? How am I going to know if holding hands means the same thing for you that it does for me?"

"What does it mean for you?"

"For one thing, it means affection."

"Yes. But isn't there some short cut for this? Couldn't we just kiss? Trust is bound to follow."

"Not for me."

"You just want to talk about it."

"Right now. I want to talk about what you did. With the women in Tahiti."

"I already told you that. Besides, I didn't do anything. She did it all."

"So what did she do?"

"She took me home. . . ."

"To meet her parents?"

"She took me home to take my clothes off and push me onto the bed."

"Did she actually push you?"

"I was young. I didn't know what to do."

"So what did you think?"

"What do you think I thought? I was young. I was self-conscious. Are we still working on trust? Because I'm ready to move on."

They talked far into the night, and Skip eventually lay down on the bed. They had reached a level of intimacy where they simply talked about themselves, Skip about Jack and Jo about her mother. At some point Jo turned off the light and not long afterwards Skip fell asleep on the bed where Jo's mother found him in the morning. The drive back to Mombasa was unpleasant. Jo's mother was mad at him for sleeping in Jo's cabin. Bob was mad at him because Jo's mother was mad at him. And Jo was mad at him because she was mad at all of them. The animals no longer interested them. Even when a rhinoceros chased them, swinging its horn at the side of the car and missing by a few feet, it didn't excite them enough to break the mood in the car. Skip didn't take any pictures.

Skip sat in his cockpit, watching the *Oceanid* and trying to guess when the schooner would leave Mombasa. He waited until one evening, just after the sun sat, when he saw Bob and Jo's mother go ashore without Jo. He climbed into his dinghy and rowed over to the *Oceanid*. When he hailed, the steward poked her head out and then, a few moments later, Jo appeared on deck. He asked her if she would like to go for a walk, and after going below to get her shoes, she appeared on deck again and climbed into the stern of the dinghy.

They took the road that led around the eastern end of the island that Mombasa was built on. There were a few buildings, but mostly it was open to their right, with some palm trees, then the shore, and then the Indian Ocean.

"We are leaving tomorrow."

"I guessed as much. Where are you heading?"

"First to Aden. Then up the Red Sea to the Mediterranean. Bob wants to leave *Oceanid* there for the winter.

Mother and I will spend the winter in Paris. What are your plans?"

"First I'll sail to Aden. Then up the Red Sea to the Mediterranean."

"Do you think it a good idea to try and follow me? You wouldn't have a chance to see me for a long time."

"When you return to the *Oceanid,* I'll be there."

"Are you trying to impress me with your decisiveness?"

"Decisiveness, determination, and devotion. But you have to help me. Say you'll wait, say you wouldn't go off with someone else until I see you again."

"How can you ask me that? We hardly know each other."

"Come over to this palm tree with me, so we can know each other better." He put his hands on her arms, just below her shoulders, and drew her face up to his. He wasn't sure if she wanted him to kiss her. He thought that she probably wasn't even sure herself. But he decided to take the chance.

"Ok, now we can do Fats Domino."

She made a face, something he had never seen her do before. "Why Fats Domino?"

"I Want to Walk You Home."

She laughed. "I thought you were going to say, 'Hello Josephine, how do you do?'"

"Well all right. I'll save that for later."

"Oh my soul. Don't you dare."

"Little Richard."

"Oh boy."

"Buddy Holly."

"I believe you."

"I believe *in* you. Jerry Lee Lewis."

"You can't keep it up."

"That'll be the day."

"Buddy Holly, again."

"Never felt like this til I kissed ya."

"Everly Brothers." Then she asked in a lower tone of voice, "How is this going to go on?"

"We'll follow the Book of Love."

"The Monotones?"

"Yes. Chapter one says to love her. You love her with all your heart."

"And chapter two?"

"We'll do chapter two when we meet again." He looked at her intently, brown eyes, brown, wild hair. At first he had thought that her eyes were a little too close together, then he saw the charm in them. More important, he liked the poise with which she looked at the world, and at this moment, with which she looked at him. It was this look, this poise that he would remember most. "By the way, I have this." He took a black pearl out of his pocket and handed it to her. "I found this in the bilge in your cabin when I was on the *Oceanid* back in Darwin."

"Oh, it's Mother's pearl. She let me wear it once and I lost it. She'll be pleased to get it back." And he thought that her mother was getting more than her pearl back. How could she be so different from her mother? But then, how could he be so different from Jack.

The next morning he watched the *Oceanid* slip her mooring and headed out for the pass. He wouldn't be able to catch her until she reached the Mediterranean and laid over for the winter. Beside, he was waiting for Anna to show up and prepare the next installment for the *World Traveler*. He hadn't written her while he was in the Seychelles, but when he reached Mombasa, he wired her because he knew then he would continue the cruise and that he would need the money more than ever. Anna said that *World Traveler* was sending her out to Kenya alone, and Skip thought that they should be able to do everything in a few days, including going out and taking a few pictures on *Jest*. But as it turned out, it took longer than he had thought. First, after *World Traveler* put her in charge of the assignment, Anna seemed to have acquired a sense of perfectionism. They had to go out on *Jest* three times before she was satisfied with the pictures she had taken. Then he had to recount in detail everything he had seen and done since Fiji. She made him get out his logbook and use it to give a day-by-day account. But what took the longest was the logbook itself. She wanted to take it with her, but he wouldn't even let her look at it. In the end he gave her three haiku to choose from and she gave him enough money to reach the Mediterranean.

Port Sudan

It took him fourteen days to reach Aden. He had a few squalls near the equator, but for the most part the passage was an easy one. The winds were light and the sea smooth. At first, after leaving Mombasa, he was a little impatient, but then he noticed that the current was carrying him between forty and fifty miles a day. The current carried him across the equator where the winds were variable and the sun stood directly overhead at noon. When he lost the current after passing Ras Guardafui on the Horn of Africa, the wind picked up and carried him across the Gulf of Aden and into the Inner Harbor.

He learned at the Aden Yacht Club that the *Oceanid* had stayed in Aden less than twenty-four hours. Aden was hot and dry and windless. He decided not to stay much longer than the *Oceanid* had. It was hotter than Darwin, which until Aden, he thought the hottest place in the world. The water on the dock, which ran in a pipe exposed to the sun, was so hot that he couldn't use it to take a shower until after three in the morning. The Arab women all dressed in black, in a head-to-toe chador, with a sheer material that they could see through covering their faces. The women seemed to favor light green and lavender for this. The only reason Aden was anything more than a camel camp, it seemed, was the large natural harbor that serviced the traffic passing through the Suez Canal. Cameras, watches, and radios were cheap, but fresh food was hard to find and expensive. Skip took on some stores, mainly canned goods, filled his water tank, and left Aden, heading for the Red Sea.

The second day out of Aden, Skip noticed a bubble forming inside the dome of the compass. This caused the compass card to swing erratically and even to get stuck, so he carefully unscrewed the fill hole and poured in some alcohol until the bubble was gone. He was on deck most of the time, keeping close to the Arabian coast. Then that evening, with the Hanish Islands to port, the compass fogged up, so that he couldn't see what course to steer. He found an anchorage between the islands, and then decided to sleep before rigging an emergency compass from the one that was fastened over the starboard bunk, even though he knew it wasn't very accurate. But later, when he woke just before sunrise, the fluid in the compass bowl was clear again. This continued for the next seven days, until he reached Port Sudan. Each evening his compass fogged up until after midnight, when it cleared up again. So in the afternoon he looked for a place to anchor, slept through the evening and the first half of the night, and then continued north up the Red Sea.

He hadn't planned to go into Port Sudan, but he needed to get his compass fixed. After tying up to the wharf, he went looking for the harbormaster, who turned out to be a friendly Englishman. The harbormaster said he would inform Mr. Sedgwick, who could help him with his compass and who would probably come by *Jest* the next day. Somewhat relieved, Skip walked into town. He found the market and wanted to buy a few kilos of potatoes, so he changed some money. He also bought some fresh beans and tomatoes. Near the market were a lot of camels that, he learned, could spit remarkably well.

In the evening a man and a woman appeared on the wharf above him, and when he looked up, he saw that they were about his age and both dressed in white.

"We heard you were here and thought we would come and say hello and take you off to the Club. That is, if you haven't any prior engagement."

"Prior engagement? Oh no, I've met all the local camels already."

"Well come along to the Club and meet the rest of the population."

They weren't brother and sister as he had thought, and the man wasn't really interested in Skip. He was just being polite for the woman's sake, escorting her down to the harbor to meet him. Inside the Red Sea Club, as it was called, it was cool. There was a fountain and a slight breeze from somewhere. The man went off to talk to someone, leaving Skip with the young woman. The transition was done so quickly, so deftly, from the heat of the harbor to the coolness of the Club, that he felt it had been planned, to bring him here and place him before this young woman whose name was Yvonne. He was thinking how very attractive she was when she began with one of those predictable questions that strangers tended to ask him and that made him feel like some wild animal that needed domestication.

"What do you do all day at sea?"

"What do you do all day in town?"

"Well, I still go to school. . . ."

"Before that, before you go to school, don't you first get up, then brush your teeth, then get dressed, and then eat breakfast? Maybe not in that order, but that's probably pretty much what you do, isn't it? Well, that's what I do too. And then you go to school and do some reading and writing and arithmetic. . . ."

"Maths, we do maths," but she was smiling.

"Ah, maths, of course. I do a little maths too, work out my position and write in my log. So I more or less do the same things you do."

"Do you visit your friends?"

"I'm always on the way to visit them."

"I see. You have been asked this before. And you want to say that your life is not exotic."

"My life is more or less like any other life, give or take a few nautical miles. Besides, what is a fresh, blue-eyed and fair-haired English girl living in Africa, in Sudan—of all places—doing calling my life exotic? I should be asking you about Bedouins, riding camels in the desert, and the searching for the source of the Nile."

He knew that once he got the sea out of the way, they could move on to something more personal. But Yvonne made it difficult for him by taking up a variation of the what-is-your-favorite-this-and-that line of questioning.

"What is the most important idea you have learned from your parents? Not something they have tried to teach you but something you have learned by watching them."

"Something you can't avoid learning?" From sailing to parents, he thought. Out of the sea and into the frying pan.

"Yes, some truth about life."

"From Jack I've learned about how things work. Or about the way we think about how they work. Or why things happen, or why we think they happen." He saw that taking the question seriously wasn't going to get him anywhere.

"What do you mean by 'things'"?

"Well, take cleanliness—this is just an example—how often do you brush your teeth? Once a day, twice a day. . . ."

"Twice a day. Is this a trick question?"

"No, no trick. So you've decided that twice a day is enough to be clean. Then along comes someone who brushes three times a day. Is he cleaner than you are?"

"You are trying to make me think I don't brush my teeth sufficiently."

"Wait. That's the point. You can never brush your teeth sufficiently because someone else can come along and brush his one time more than you. You see, what you think about things depends on the decisions you make—that you have to make, often without even being aware of it."

"You mean assumption. You are talking about assumptions."

"That's it. I'm talking about assumptions. If you assume that twice a day is sufficient to be clean, then it is clean. But it is still just an assumption."

"So this is what you do all day. You sit on your boat and think up ideas like this."

"To tell the truth, I usually sleep most of the day because I stay awake at night. It's gotten to the point where I can fall asleep at any time."

"Could you fall asleep now?"

"Now? No. You'll tickle my nose or something. Besides, I only do it at sea."

"Please. I want to see you fall asleep."

"It's too noisy in here."

"Plug your ears with this." She handed him a paper napkin. He tore it in half and stuck one half in one ear and the other half in the other ear, so that he thought that he probably looked like Dumbo the Elephant. Then he stretched out his legs, slouched down in the chair and shut his eyes. He thought that he could fake falling asleep. What could be simpler? But in fact he fell asleep almost immediately.

He dreamed that he had almost solved the barber's paradox. It was one of Jack's many challenges: The Barber of Seville shaves all the men who don't shave themselves. Who shaves the barber? The answer was just within reach, but he couldn't quite grasp it. Then something disturbed him and, as on *Jest,* he woke suddenly, fully awake. About a dozen people were standing around him, laughing. Some were laughing so hard that they were red in the face.

He stood up, touched a coke bottle on the table, pushed it away from him a few inches and said "Thanks for the drink." He then walked out of the Club. He was trying to remember the answer to the barber's paradox. It lay in an assumption. But what assumption? The laughter had disturbed his dream. The answer to the paradox was there, on the tip of something. And now he was wandering aimlessly around Port Sudan.

Sedgwick came the next morning, looked at his compass, clicked his tongue a few times and then took the compass away with a promise to return it "without delay." Which meant, so it seemed, the next morning. Sedgwick brought the compass back, resealed and refilled, and they took *Jest* out to swing the compass and check its deviation, something Skip had never done before.

Sedgwick was one of those men that Skip found very sympathetic. Usually English and middle-aged. Very polite and reserved, but very observant and, of course, competent. When Skip asked about the bill, Sedgwick told him he would send it, but Skip wanted to pay right away. Reluctantly, it seemed, Sedgwick sent his assistant to his office for some papers. Skip offered some tea and Sedgwick offered to show him a few places on the chart where he could find shelter farther north.

"I heard you were at the Club the other night."

"Yes. I had a coke."

"Will you be coming again tonight? That is, let me invite you if another member hasn't already done so."

"That's very kind of you. But I'm anxious to get off and there are a number of things I need to do first."

"Right, then. You'll be off tomorrow?"

"As soon as I can catch the harbormaster in the morning."

"I'll send him along then, if I see him."

Sedgwick hadn't been gone long when Yvonne appeared on the wharf above him, as she had the first evening, only this time she was alone.

"I wanted to say good-bye." She began to make some apology, but he didn't hear it, for as he looked up at her, standing above him in a white dress and with her blonde hair and blue eyes—he couldn't see her blue eyes in the fading light but he knew they were there—he saw not her, not Yvonne of Port Sudan, but a Woman and he knew in that moment the answer to the paradox: the Barber of Seville was a woman.

Then he noticed that she had stopped talking and had a curious look on her face, which he understood to mean that he had a curious look on his. He invited her aboard.

"You seem pleased to see me."

"I'm very pleased. You are just the woman I wanted to see. Would you like to look below? Just a moment." He hopped below and closed both his logbook and the door to the fo'c'sle.

"Here is where you read and write. Here is where you eat and sleep. And this is where you cook. This looks like a camp stove."

"It is a camp stove. But it works quite well."

"What do you cook? What did you have on the way from Aden?"

"I was lucky and caught a fish, a yellowfin tuna. So I had fried tuna steak with soy sauce and ginger, steamed rice, and green California asparagus. The asparagus was from a can, of course—I got a whole case of it in Aden—but the advantage of canned asparagus is that you don't have to cook it."

"No dessert?"

"Cornbread with peaches and cream. The cream was condensed milk. Would you like to try some?"

"You would make cornbread now? I would like very much to try some. I've never had any." He had her watch him from the cockpit, and when he had the dough in the pan, he asked her if she wanted peaches, apricots, or pineapple.

"What's best?"

"Peaches, peaches are always best."

Port Said

Tacking across to the Arabian coast, the jib sheet parted, and he sailed on under staysail and main. The seas were high, forcing *Jest* to lose way as she pounded into them. Tacking back across to the African coast, the staysail sheet parted, and he single-reefed the mainsail. He was sailing almost two miles for every mile he made good, and his gear was taking a beating, so he hove-to near the Arabian coast and waited for the wind to ease.

The wind began to ease the next day, and then it died altogether. As long as there was no wind and the sea was calm, he decided to use the engine and make as much northerly progress as he could. As he got farther north, he noticed that the ships coming from the north were closer together. And then it occurred to him that they were coming through the Suez Canal in convoys. Then the wind came up again from north northwest, and he had to tack again back and forth between Arabia and Africa. The seas were high again and in one twenty-four hour period, he lost five miles. It began to get cold, and now he wore a sweater, smelling of mildew.

At night the ships were becoming a problem. When tacking across the shipping lanes, he had to dodge them, coming into the wind to let them pass, which made him lose ground, and then trying to get across before the next ship came down. When he got close to the shipping lane, he turned on his spreader lights, and many of the ships flashed Morse code, in irritation it seemed, probably because they couldn't reach him by radio. He didn't know what they were saying or what they wanted, but his guess was that they thought he shouldn't be doing what he was doing, tacking across the shipping lane, but he also thought that they should be able to see that he had little choice.

It took him sixteen days to sail the 600 miles from Port Sudan to the Strait of Jubal at the southern end of the Gulf of Suez. The log read 1009 miles. The wind was blowing hard down the channel and the seas were so high that he couldn't make any headway, so he hove-to and waited for the wind to ease. But by evening it was still blowing hard and he didn't want to be at the end of the channel at night with all the shipping coming through, so he anchored in the lee of Shadwan Island and waited. He had become so tired that he was numb, but some primitive desire forced him northward, against the sea and the wind. His days and mind became disordered, and he even neglected his logbook. He wasn't able to think about anything, except the wind and *Jest* pitching into a head sea. Sometimes he felt there wasn't any reason to be doing what he was doing.

When he was rested, he decided to motor up the Shadwan Channel, which would give him protection from the wind until he reached the Gulf. But the wind was still blowing hard in the Gulf and he spent the next night and morning trying to pass the light on Ashrafi Island. He headed into the anchorage at Ummel Kiman and, just before sundown, he anchored behind a sand spit. The log read 36 miles. He waited for two days before the wind eased and he could head north again. When the wind died altogether, he powered for part of the day, but then in the evening the wind began to blow hard out of the north again, and he was forced to tack between Sinai and Egypt, averaging 25 miles a day under staysail and reefed main.

When he hove-to off the Egyptian coast, and the wind blew him over to Sinai, he anchored at Abu Zenima, just north of a wrecked cargo ship lying on the beach. He slept that day and all through the night. In the morning he went ashore, hoping to find some fresh food. A young man met him and led him into one of the low buildings that formed the village. Inside was a group of men who greeted him politely, and he sat at the open end of the semi-circle that they formed. He was served coffee in what he thought was a very small cup, and when he tilted it too far, he choked on the grounds at the bottom. The men smiled and laughed pleasantly, and someone brought him a glass of water. None of them seemed to speak English, so he asked for food, using his hand to signal what he meant, and then realized almost immediately his mistake, that they might think he wanted a meal. So with his other hand he waved in the direction where *Jest* was anchored in the bay. They brought him potatoes, eggs, butter, and much to his delight, a tin of English cookies. They wouldn't take his US dollars, so he went back to the beach and rowed out to *Jest*.

He fried the eggs and potatoes in the butter and felt that he hadn't eaten so well for days. Later, he got out the rifle, cleaned and oiled it, wrapped it in a new rag, and then put it back in its canvas cover. Then he slept again until the following morning. He ate eggs and potatoes fried in butter again and then rowed ashore with the rifle. The same men were sitting in the building when he entered. Again they greeted him politely and served him coffee. After he thought the appropriate amount of time had passed, he took the rifle out of its canvas cover, unwrapped it, and, holding it up, presented it to the headman. Skip could tell by the light in his eyes that the Arab was pleased. Then Skip handed him the rifle bolt, which he had taken out, and the two boxes of ammunition. The ammunition disappeared immediately, and he thought that it might be more valuable to them than the rifle. The Arab took the bolt and expertly rammed it home, then held the rifle over his head and, turning to the other men, said something, to which they all murmured in agreement. They were pleased and Skip was pleased. He had gotten rid of the rifle.

It was calm at anchor in Abu Zenima, but as soon as he headed into the gulf, the wind was blowing hard from the north. He crossed over to the Egyptian side, where he anchored at Marsa Thelemet and waited for the wind to ease. He was about sixty miles from Port Suez, and in his mind he saw himself crawling up the Red Sea and the Gulf of Suez on the chart, but when he sat in the cockpit and looked out at the wind blowing down that break in the desert, he measured the distance not in miles but in days. When the wind eased he used the last of his fuel to power north. Just before sunrise he raised the light at Port Suez and later that day entered the harbor in light winds and a calm sea.

He anchored in the small-craft basin, hoisted his dinghy over the side, and rowed ashore. He knew he was over-tired, he even felt a little dazed, but he wanted to get his harbor clearance before he slept. As he stood on the quay a moment, trying to get his bearings, a young Egyptian, well-dressed in slacks and white shirt, walked up to him, and said, "They shot him." He took both of Skip's hands in his. Tears were streaming down his face. "They shot the President." Then he walked away.

Skip was surprised by the man's emotions, then it occurred to him that there could be trouble. He rowed back to *Jest*, turned on his radio and fiddled with the dial until he got the BBC. He thought the man was weeping for Nasser, but it wasn't for Nasser but for the American President. Kennedy had been shot in Dallas. He listened to the BBC, trying to make some sense out of it, hoping to be told who did it and why. Then he fell asleep. He woke the next day, his radio still on, making a faint buzzing sound as the batteries had run down. Someone was on deck.

There was an official who asked for his ship's papers, and then asked him when he wanted to start his canal transit. Skip said as soon as possible, after he filled his fuel and water tanks. The official showed him where to take on fuel and water, and then got his papers to transit the canal the next day. Skip finally realized that he wasn't an official at all but a ship's agent. But he was very efficient. He told Skip that his Egyptian courtesy flag was too small and wouldn't do. So Skip bought a larger Egyptian flag, larger in fact than his American ensign. The agent's fee was $15, which seemed reasonable, since there was no fee for a yacht to transit the canal. As a parting gift, the agent gave him a prayer rug.

The transit of the Suez Canal took him three days. The first pilot came aboard *Jest* at noon. Ships couldn't pass each other in the canal, so they formed convoys and the north and south bound convoys passed each other at the lake in the middle of the canal. But *Jest* was small enough to pass the south bound ships, and the pilot liked to point out the name and nationality of each ship. In the late afternoon he tied up to a buoy at El Kabret. The same pilot returned the next morning and he proceeded up the canal, across Great Bitter Lake, to Ismailia, where he anchored in front of the yacht club. The pilot departed, saying another pilot would come out at 0600 and take Skip the rest of the way to Port Said.

Unlike the first pilot, who was Greek, the second pilot was Egyptian and didn't speak any English. At first the new pilot made a gesture with his hand, sticking his index finger out horizontally and twirling it around, which seemed to mean that he wanted Skip to go faster. But when Skip didn't go faster, the pilot seemed to lose interest in Skip and the boat. He refused all the food Skip offered him, probably because, as Skip learned later, he thought Skip might try to trick him and slip him some pork. The pilot did accept cigarettes, and Skip gave him two packs of old Lucky Strikes. Skip sensed that the pilot expected more than two packs, but Skip didn't see why he had to compete with the ships that passed through and could hand out cartons of cigarettes from their unlimited stores. As he approached Port Said, the pilot began making his hand gesture again and then tried to take the helm. Skip wouldn't give it to him. When he saw the yacht club, he dropped the anchor and backed down, mooring to the dock stern-to. An official came aboard and gave Skip a pass that he had to show at the gate when going into town. The pass gave his name, his boat's name, and his religion. Later Skip found that if he gave the guards at the gate a pack of cigarettes, he didn't have to show the pass and they wouldn't search him. That's how he got rid of all the cigarettes that Jack had stored on *Jest*.

Jo had left a letter for him at the general delivery window. It was just a note, and he could see that she had written it in a hurry. The *Oceanid* was to winter in Rhodes. He was impatient to be off, but he didn't have any charts of the Mediterranean and he couldn't buy any in Egypt. Emile, whose sloop *Aurora* was moored next to *Jest,* explained why. Nasser didn't want anyone to use their boat to slip out of the country, so charts were unavailable. As Emile said, Nasser had the sea and the desert, so he didn't need a Berlin Wall. Emile was originally from Yugoslavia but now he was an Egyptian citizen. He took Skip to the black market, where Skip could exchange 70 pounds to the dollar, instead of the 43 pounds that the bank gave. Then he took Skip to have a beer. Skip didn't really want a beer, but he changed his mind when he saw that it came with shrimp, olives, pickles, peanuts, and even oysters. Emile told him that Nasser had nationalized everything and wouldn't let anyone take money or valuables out of the country. One friend lost his shipping company and all the money he had tied up in it. Another friend was luckier, for she had a French passport, which made it possible for her to at least get her jewels out of the country. She simply wore her jewels to Zurich, had cheap copies made, and then wore the copies back to Egypt.

Emile saw Skip's impatience and guessed the reason for it. Emile was impatient himself. He wanted to sail to Beirut. There was a woman there, Simone, waiting for him. Skip guessed it was the woman with the jewels, but he didn't say so. He could see Emile's problem. No charts and he couldn't take food or other supplies on board the *Aurora* without the officials getting suspicious. Skip could easily help him with supplies, and in return Emile told him about love.

The most important thing to learn, Emile said, is that you can love badly. You can take too much, but you can also give too much. A woman wants devotion, but you must save a part of yourself, a reserve, for it is what you keep for yourself that she will love in you the most. Skip said he had never thought about the idea of loving badly. Ah, that's because you don't think about loving with your head as well as with your heart. Each love is different, but a fine love needs to be an exchange, a give and take. You need your head to figure out how to make that work, how to find a balance of desire, a reciprocity of passion.

As he waited for his charts to arrive from San Francisco, he spent a lot of time thinking about Jo and the future. She wasn't exotic. She was American, and he liked that about her because he felt a need to have something in common with her. At first he had been attracted to her, partly at least, as a way of ridding himself of his dreams of Leah. But he hadn't dreamed of Leah since Port Sudan. The Red Sea had washed him clean, and in a sense he saw that he was newly baptized, ready to pursue love, as Emile said, with his head as well as his heart. He decided that he was willing to make whatever mistakes he had to make, even the mistake of getting it all wrong. But he wouldn't be passive. He had to move forward, towards Jo. But just getting there, wherever he found her, was not enough. He had to take hold of love in the same way that he had learned to take hold of the sea. He had to take hold of Jo herself. It seemed a simple enough plan.

The night after his charts arrived, he went aboard the *Aurora* a last time and left enough food for Emile to reach Beirut. He had already supplied him with diesel, plus he had cleaned his filters for him. He also left a chart of the Eastern Mediterranean with the harbor at Beirut. It was a fair exchange for the lessons on love.

Rhodes

As he approached the island of Rhodes with the rising sun behind him, he saw the white masts of the *Oceanid* between the windmills on the seawall. The entrance to Mandraki harbor was from the north, with a narrow entrance ornamented on each side with a tall column topped with bronze deer. They say that the Colossus of Rhodes once stood astride the entrance, where the two columns now stood. The *Oceanid* was moored stern-to on the landside of the harbor. He didn't want to make himself conspicuous, so he let go his anchor on the other side of the harbor, near the windmills, and backed *Jest* next to a fishing boat with eyes painted on her bow. A fisherman helped him with his stern lines. It was a welcoming gesture that reminded him of the fellowship of the sea. He waved and the fisherman waved and then went back to beating the rocks with what looked like an old rag. Later he was to learn that the fisherman was beating an octopus, and he beat one every morning, so that Skip often woke to the sound of octopus smacking a rock. Later still he was to learn that the fisherman had a small café in the old town where he grilled the fish and octopus he had caught each morning. His name was Alexis and his café had three tables, and instead of a menu, he showed you what he had to offer. Skip liked the simple food, the grilled fish and octopus, the cucumber, tomato, and feta salad, the salted olives, the heavy bread with tzadziki, the small coffee, the retsina. The retsina was a challenge because it tasted like it had something wrong with it. But Alexis always poured him a glass and he always drank it. And much later the taste of retsina and the sound of octopus hitting a rock became one of his strongest memories of Rhodes.

Jo wasn't in Rhodes; none of the Sterlings were. In the afternoons he sat under the arches of the market building, drinking Greek coffee. He still found it relaxing to do nothing. He always had a clear view of the *Oceanid's* gangway, but except for the crew, no one arrived or departed. Then after more than a week, and a few days before New Year's, the steward of the *Oceanid* came up to him, smiled and handed him a book. *Justine.* Inside the book was a note: "Very happy that you fetched Rhodes. We return after Easter, Jo." He hadn't really expected this, to wait until Easter. The book would help him wait, but not much. He walked back around to the other side of the harbor. Once aboard *Jest,* he took up the floorboards and began to clean the bilge.

Bob showed up in Rhodes in February. He told Skip that Jo and her mother were still in Paris. When Skip said that Jo had given him a copy of *Justine,* Bob said that she was now reading the rest of Lawrence Durrell's *The Alexandria Quartet*—much to her mother's displeasure.

"Jo doesn't always do what her mother wants?"

"What her mother wants, yes. What her mother approves of, no. It would be a dull life to do only what her mother approves of."

"Could I write Jo a letter? I mean, I need her address, in Paris."

Bob had given him an idea. He assumed that if he wrote Jo, her mother would read the letter. Which meant that he could write a letter for her mother to read. Not a simple task, he knew, but he already had a plan, or at least part of one: blast Durrell's book, dismiss it with contempt and then praise some other book, some book that, even if she didn't like it, she would have to accept it because it was a classic. He needed to return to *Jest* and look at what he still thought of as "Jack's books."

Dear Jo,

... and I started to read the book you sent me, *Justine* by Lawrence Durrell. It is a strange book. In the beginning it pretends to be a story about a city, Alexandria, a city that has five of everything, including five sexes. But as I read further, it turns out to be a story of a man who feels sorry for himself because he can't afford the price of a prostitute. Maybe it gets better, but the character seems so pitiful that I find it a chore to keep reading. I know that this kind of character is fashionable today, probably because we no longer believe in heroes, but on the other hand, we still have stories of heroes. Think of the persistence and endurance of Odysseus—ten years to reach home. These are the virtues of the seafarer. Some probably think the story of Odysseus is too wondrous, such as his visit to the land of the Lotus Eaters or the visit to the Cyclops, the giants with one eye. But I have seen a Polynesian carry a pig on his back, which could be called the land where pigs ride men. And I have spent two days in an Arab village and never saw a woman, which could be called the land without women. The truth is wondrous when presented in the style of wonder . . . .

When he finally saw Jo on the *Oceanid's* gangway, going ashore, he realized that she must have arrived in Rhodes the day before. He wondered if he should wave, but then saw that she was already walking toward him. It was the first time he had seen her in a dress. In Mombasa she had worn only shorts and polo shirts.

"Skip, I just got in. Have you been waiting long?"

"Just since Christmas. But it doesn't matter now. Would you like some coffee?"

"Yes, but not here. Let's get away from the harbor." He realized that he was not only visible from the *Oceanid,* but that he had probably been making a spectacle of himself, sitting there each afternoon for months. But he would worry about that later.

They walked toward the castle. Skip wanted to show her around and so he led her to the Street of the Knights.

"I think you impressed my mother with your letter."

"I was trying to impress her."

"That impressed her, too."

"You mean she was impressed with me trying to impress her? You and your mother are always seeing right through me."

"Well, she was also impressed that you are, to quote her, more or less literate. But then she remembered that Odysseus was famous for being cunning."

When they reached the Street of the Knights she said, "This is where Durrell claims Homer got the epithet 'rosy-fingered'. He sat here in the Street of the Knights and held a glass of red wine up to the setting sun."

"The setting sun? But in the *Odyssey* it's the rosy-fingered dawn. The wrong time of day to be looking through a wineglass."

Although he wanted to show her the castle of the Knights of St. John, after all, he had been in Rhodes for over three months, she led him to the museum. She wanted to see the Marine Venus, which he hadn't heard of, but the museum was closed.

"Why do they call it the Marine Venus?"

"Because it was pulled out of the harbor here in Rhodes."

"Not that. This is Greece and Venus is a Roman name. Why isn't it called the Marine Aphrodite?"

"Probably because Rhodes was under Italian administration then, between the World Wars."

He found it difficult to impress her. He just couldn't compete with her knowledge. Then he thought of the Turkish baths in the Old Town, where he went at least twice a week, especially during the winter when it had been so cold. She hadn't heard of the baths, so he led her up Socrates Street, past the Mosque of Suleiman, to the square where the baths stood. He told her it was very relaxing inside, to sit on marble in the wet heat, with the light filtering in through high windows. And in the early afternoons it was almost always empty and quiet, except for the echo of splashing water. But he knew she would never go in, because she wouldn't go without her mother, and her mother would plead cockroaches or something.

During the two weeks before the *Oceanid* left Rhodes, they met every afternoon. Once they walked over the hill to the chapel on the other side of the island, but mostly they walked through the narrow streets of the Old Town. Then one afternoon, when he knew that Bob and Jo's mother had taken a rented car to Lindos, he asked Jo to come with him to *Jest*.

"I'll make some tzadziki."

"Will you let me see your logbook?"

"Sure. Maybe it will impress you."

"But no kissing yet."

"No kissing yet? Ok, I can wait until dark."

He chopped garlic and dill as she looked through his logbook.

"I remember this while we were coming up the Red Sea on *Oceanid:*

Wind out of the north
through Asia and Africa—
desert sand on deck.

It looks like you aren't really trying to write poetry. There's no rhyme of course, but you don't even use metaphors."

"Metaphors? Try this."

"Mmm, delicious. Metaphors, such as, 'My love is like a red, red rose.'"

"Oh, comparisons. The problem with comparisons is that they create something that isn't there. 'My love is like a red, red rose' is neither about love nor about a rose. It's about something else, a thing called a love-rose. But where's the love? Where's the rose?"

"It's odd that you write poetry, but you don't seem to be interested in the language of poetry."

"Maybe you mean the language of love poetry. I don't write love poetry."

"Have you tried? Writing love poetry would be one way to prove your love."

"The proof of love is in the kissing."

He moved up to her, but she turned away and then she asked, "Who is this in the photo?"

"That's Yvonne, the Maid of Port Sudan." He had forgotten that he used her photo to mark his place in the logbook, forgotten because he never really looked at it.

"She is very pretty."

"Pretty? She's beautiful. She has blue eyes and blond hair. She wears white dresses and golden bracelets. She would make you a wonderful bridesmaid."

"Do you think it is a good idea to praise another woman?"

"You don't really think you are the only beautiful woman in the world do you? The Maid of Port Sudan has blue eyes, the color of innocence and madness. You have brown eyes, the color of passion and something else. And your hair isn't smooth and blonde, but brown and wild. Not just wild, pagan. That's it, you have pagan hair."

"Wild and pagan. I think I see what you are leading up to."

"I'm leading up to chapter two of the Book of Love?"

"In chapter two you tell her you're never, never, never gonna part?"

"It's five nevers. In chapter two you tell her you're never, never, never, never, never gonna part."

"But I'm going back to America soon, and then I'm going to Wesleyan. And you are sailing back to San Francisco."

"That's not what 'never gonna part' means. It's not being physically apart or together that's important. It's an emotional bond, a tie of passion. As long as there is love, we will never be apart."

"Then you don't need to act so desperate, always trying to back me into a corner to kiss me."

"I don't need a corner to kiss you. I just want to tell you something. Remember what The Shirelles said."

"What?"

"It's in his kiss."

The next day they took the car to Lindos. The steward and her husband, who was the cook of the *Oceanid,* sat in the front. The cook drove. They had picked up Skip out of sight of the harbor and now he sat in the back with Jo. She wouldn't let him put his arm around her, but once in Lindos they went off by themselves. At first they wandered through the narrow streets of the town with its white houses that reflected the sun light, sometimes into their eyes. Eventually they found the path that led up to the acropolis. The steps and the fortified walls were built by the Knights, but inside were a number of older ruins, including the temple of the Lindian Athena. "It doesn't look like much now," Jo told him, "but Lindos sent nine ships to Troy. I wonder what it is like to be born, to live one's whole life among the ruins of the visible past."

"I was thinking they must be used to it. They probably don't see the ruins. But do you think they love any less today than they did in the past?"

"How could that change? If they loved any less they wouldn't be here. They wouldn't have had any children."

"So you see, it's not the gods that live forever—look at their ruins—it's love that lives forever."

"You can't kiss me up here."

"But a kiss here will make you immortal."

Naples

As soon as the *Oceanid* cleared Mandraki Harbor the next morning, Skip started his engine. He slipped his stern lines and pulled out into the harbor, cleaning the muck off his anchor chain with buckets of water as he hauled it in. When the chain was up and down, he couldn't raise the anchor. By heaving a few times on the chain he could see that the yacht moored next to him had dropped its anchor on top of his. He couldn't lift both anchors. The other yacht was called *Waltzing Matilda,* so he assumed it was Australian. He slacked off his anchor chain, put his dinghy over the side, and rowed over to the *Waltzing Matilda.* He knew that the two men on the boat had returned late the night before, as they had every night since arriving in Rhodes. He hoped they weren't too hung over to get up. First he hailed them and then he pounded on the deck. When a head finally appeared, Skip said their anchor had fouled his. Without saying anything, the head disappeared. Skip waited a little, then pounded on the deck again, as hard and as loud as he could. Then a different head appeared, turned forward to face Skip and told him to "piss off."

Skip waited two hours, but no one from the *Waltzing Matilda* appeared on deck, so he got out his skin diving gear and went over the side. He followed his chain down to his anchor but couldn't break it out. The chain from the *Waltzing Matilda* was lying across the stock of his anchor and he couldn't move it. He climbed back on *Jest,* got his marlinspike and returned to the water. It took him almost half an hour to unshackle the chain from the *Waltzing Matilda's* anchor. He climbed back on *Jest,* ate some bread with feta and olive oil, then started his engine again. He raised his anchor and headed out of the harbor, between the columns with the bronze deer on top. The chain of the *Waltzing Matilda* would hold the boat, as long as the weather remained mild and the wind came from the east. They probably wouldn't even notice their anchor was gone until they tried to raise it up.

The *Oceanid* was heading for Kos, but it was late and Skip was tired, so he decided to spend the night in Simi. He left for Kos the next morning at dawn, without having gone ashore. In the afternoon the wind came up from the southeast and he reached Kos before sundown. The entrance to the harbor was narrow and then opened out into a circular bay. The *Oceanid* wasn't there, but he stayed almost a week because his neck was swollen and he had a slight fever. He learned of a doctor who spoke some English and went to see him. It turned out that the doctor was also sick, so Skip had to sit in a chair as the doctor examined him while he was in bed. "It is the glands," the doctor said and wrote out a prescription. The pharmacist told him it was an antibiotic. Skip bought it but didn't take it.

He had to accept that he had lost the trail of the *Oceanid* for the time being. He had to take care of himself, then he had to take care of *Jest* before he continued. *Jest* had so much growth on her bottom that it was slowing her down. He needed to get her hauled out, so he could scrape and paint her bottom. After talking to another yacht, he decided on Syros, about 130 miles to the northwest. He spent two nights hove-to south of Mykonos before he reached the harbor at Ermoupolis on Syros. He went around to the boatyard to make arrangements to be hauled out, but the operator of the slipway wanted $300. Skip said no and walked away. Later that evening the operator came over to *Jest* and said he would do it for $100. Skip accepted. The operator hauled *Jest* out the next morning, doing everything himself. It took him three hours before he could get everything ready. Once *Jest* was out of the water, Skip scrubbed her bottom and put a coat of anti-fouling on the bare spots. All evening and most of the night he could hear the sound of the bouzouki from the local taverna, some times breathless, sometimes melancholic. The next morning he painted the entire bottom, and the operator came out of the taverna and put *Jest* back in the water.

As soon as he could get ready, he sailed for Vouliag-meni, just south of Athens. The *Oceanid* wasn't there. He spent the night, then sailed for Piraeus. The *Oceanid* wasn't there either, so he headed back out of Piraeus without stopping. He realized that if he tried to look in every harbor in Greece, he had a good chance of missing the *Oceanid* altogether. He had to get out in front of her and then wait for her to show up in some place where he was sure she would show up. There wasn't any such place in Greece, because now he didn't know if she had already been to Piraeus or not. But eventually she would head for Italy and he was sure she would stop in Naples. So he headed for the Corinth Canal to the west of Athens. After passing through the canal and entering the Gulf of Cor-inth, the wind was blowing so hard that he motored over to Loutraki and moored to the dock. Early in the morning he headed for Patras, on the south side of the gulf, where he spent a day getting ready for the passage to Italy.

The second day after leaving Greece he hit a storm in the Ionian Sea. He took in the jib and main, then set the storm trysail, for the first time in almost a year. The sea was short and steep, causing *Jest* to move erratically. Water seemed to pour in from everywhere: the seams, the skylight, the hatch, even the ventilators. The electric bilge pump burned out and he had to pump by hand. By the second day he was exhausted and he wondered why he was doing this. He missed the tropics, the trade winds, and the long ocean swell. Then the wind died and he slept.

He motored the rest of the way to Reggio di Calabria at the toe of Italy, where he stayed the night before continuing through the Strait of Messina. He had the current with him going through the narrows, and the name Scilla on the chart reminded him of Odysseus. He had read enough of the *Odyssey* to regret not having stopped at Ithaca after leaving the Gulf of Corinth. But he wanted to make sure he got ahead of the *Oceanid* because, as it now occurred to him, he had his own Penelope to worry about. Then again, maybe he wasn't Odysseus at all but his son, Telemachus. That would mean that Jack was Odysseus, of course, but who then was Penelope? After thinking about it for a while, he decided that it was better not to be the son in a Greek story.

The wind was from the southwest as he headed up the Tyrrhenian Sea, and two days later, after passing Campanella Point, with Capri to port and Vesuvius in the background, he entered the Bay of Naples. He moored at the Naples Yacht Club and received a very friendly welcome because, as he later learned, the second installment of his cruise in *World Traveler* was out. Anna had written the text this time, and when he noticed that she exaggerated the adventure and romance stuff, he stopped reading. He saw that Anna had used all three of his haiku. There were also a few photos he had taken, mainly of the fish he had caught, plus one photo he had taken in Kenya. It was the one of Jo with the baby elephant at the entrance to Tsavo Park. She had her hand on the elephant's head and looked amused. The elephant had raised its trunk and also looked amused. They were both laughing at some private joke.

Now he had to wait. He decided to visit Pompeii because Jo had made fun of him for not visiting the pyramids at Giza while in Egypt. The early bus to Pompeii was almost empty. He took a seat near the rear and looked out the window, waiting for the landscape to move past. His foot kicked something, and reaching down under the seat in front of him, he found a book. He placed the book on the seat next to him, but when the bus got to Pompeii, he took the book with him. The ruins of Pompeii were much more extensive than he had expected. He came first to the Forum, with the Temple of Apollo at one end and the Temple of Jupiter at the other. Then he walked through the Baths, the Theater, and the Gladiator's Barracks. He walked out to the Amphitheater, which he had to himself, so he decided to sit awhile. He opened the book he had found: Catullus, *Poems.* As he glanced through it, the word kisses caught his eye. "Give me a thousand kisses, then a hundred, then another thousand, then a second hundred. . . ." The poet went on adding a thousand and a hundred, until the number of kisses was lost, especially, he imagined, with Roman numerals. But why was the poet so worried about someone else adding up his kisses? Was his love prey to rumor and jealousy? What kind of love was that? What kind of world? But the answer to that question lay in the ruins before him.

He walked back towards the Forum, then over to the House of the Tragic Poet, with the mosaic of the dog. After the House of the Faun, he came to the House of the Vettii, with the erotic frescoes. Although the frescoes were old and stylized, they still held their erotic power in some curious way. Then he saw what it was: the men were so much darker than the women, just as he was so much darker than Jo. At that moment, another visitor came in the room behind him, paused for a moment, and then said, somewhat flatly, "Pornography." Skip didn't turn around, but he began to think about the difference between the erotic and the pornographic and decided that there was no clear line that separated them. One person's eroticism seemed to be another person's pornography, or, as Jack would say, pornography is in the eye of the beholder.

Back in Naples he liked to walk along the promenade that curved around the bay, especially in the evening, but then one evening he made the mistake of walking later than usual, when the lovers came out and occupied the benches, especially those in the shadows. He found them, perhaps in their sheer numbers, more erotic than the frescoes at Pompeii. After that night both waiting and sleeping became harder. So he began to work on *Jest*. First he cleaned her up, throwing away the deck boxes that he had used since Mexico to store fruit and vegetables in. He also got rid of the extra kerosene tank that he had carried on deck and the outboard engine that he had picked up in Singapore but had never used. From below he threw out all the half-used cans of paint and varnish, the used brushes, stiff with dried paint, the dried putty, and the sandpaper that had gotten wet and lost its sand. From under the bunks he threw out all the cans of food that had rusted or that looked like they were ready to explode. He threw out the case of strawberry juice, less one can, that he had since Mexico. He cleaned out the drawer under his chart table, throwing away last year's almanac, notepaper that was covered on both sides with calculations, and the photo of Yvonne, because she had stopped writing him. He had taken a photo of Jo in Lindos, at the acropolis. She was smiling without showing her teeth and the sun was very bright and the wind blew her hair about. He now used this photo to mark his place in the logbook.

He had painted his topsides while waiting in Rhodes, so now he began to paint his mast. He took his time, shopping each morning and cooking his lunch, usually fish or calamari fried with garlic, parsley, and potatoes. Then he climbed back into the bos'n's chair, hauled himself up the mast and continued working where he had left off. Then one day, while cleaning out his brush after putting a coat of paint on the mast, he saw the *Oceanid* arrive and tie up to the floating dock behind *Jest*. He didn't see Jo on deck, so he waited until the crew of the *Oceanid* was through adjusting the mooring lines and hooking up the water and electricity, then he went over and hailed. Jo's mother appeared on deck and told Skip she wanted him to stop following them or waiting for them or whatever it was he was doing. When he told her he just wanted to talk to Jo, she said she didn't want him and her wandering off anywhere. So he told her he just wanted to talk to Jo for a minute, on the dock.

He walked past the end of the *Oceanid* until Jo appeared. She was wearing white shorts and a light blue polo shirt, just as she had worn when he had taken her picture with the baby elephant, though of course the picture was black and white. As she came closer, he noticed that she had a fake smile, which made her face tight and her eyes dark and flat. She had something to say, so he waited.

"Mother thinks you are a boat bum."

"Boats don't have bums. They have transoms. But what do you think?"

"We have to say good-bye. Rhodes was nice and I enjoyed my time with you there, but now it's over and there's no future for us."

"There's no future for us? That's something your mother said. Why do you always do what your mother wants?"

"It's just easier."

"Easier for who? It's not easier for me, and at some point it won't be easier for you."

"How do you know so much about me?"

"Now that you ask, because of love. Love lets me know what I wouldn't otherwise know, or say, for that matter."

"Mother says it's easy to fall in love."

"Oh yes. 'It's So Easy.' Buddy Holly. You have to make up your own mind and let yourself become yourself. You can't always let your mother decide what you are."

"Do you have anything else to say?"

"Yes, a lot of things." He couldn't believe she was doing this. "I don't want you to run off with me, or anything like that. I just want you to wait and say that you won't let your mother marry you out from under me. And I want you to know that at some point you'll have to sort out your mother. This is something I know because I've had to sort out Jack. And one last thing."

"Yes?"

"This isn't easy."

He watched her walk back to the *Oceanid,* climb aboard and disappear below. She hadn't looked back. The *Oceanid* stayed only a few days in Naples, and during that time, each morning Skip watched Jo leave with her mother and return in the early afternoon. In the evening, if Bob and Jo's mother left the *Oceanid,* Jo went with them. He thought of going over and talking to Bob, but then decided against it. He didn't know what to say to Bob. On the last morning, as the crew were preparing the *Oceanid* to depart, Jo came down the dock to *Jest.*

"I liked the photo of me with the baby elephant. It came out very well. Robert says we look like twins. Do you think my nose is really that big?"

"It would be big in Bali, but here in Italy it's just average."

"I want to part friends."

Skip stepped over to the dock and stood before her. "Only if I'm parting with you and not with your mother."

"Oh, don't start that."

"Ok, but even friends need to see each other once in a while."

She took the short step toward him, reached up and kissed him. "We're going to the French Riviera." Then she turned and walked back toward the *Oceanid.*

Gibraltar

Skip let the *Oceanid* sail out of the Bay of Naples and out of sight before he got underway. Although he planned to follow them, he didn't want to make it too obvious. He didn't want to give Jo's mother any advantage. He wanted to pretend, just as Jo must be pretending, that whatever her mother thought was between them was now over, at least until he had a chance to talk to Jo again. He didn't know much about her mother—she wasn't anything like Jack—but he knew that he didn't stand much of a chance with Jo if her mother was watching. But then, when he thought of it, he never stood much of a chance of getting as far as he had, to the point where Jo wasn't ready to give him up yet, especially when her mother wanted her to.

He didn't know if they would continue up the Italian coast or cross over to Corsica and then head north. They might want to visit Rome, but then Jo's mother liked France and everything French, and he knew that Bob had planned the whole cruise to please her, so they might just skip Rome and Italy altogether and head for the closest French port. That meant southern Corsica. So he headed for Bonifacio, 250 miles to the northwest, across the Tyrrhenian Sea. Even if they continued up the Italian coast, he would still cross their path on the French Riviera, somewhere between Monaco and Toulon.

Bonifacio had a long, narrow harbor, well sheltered, with a castle and an old town built on the cliffs above. He cleared for all of France but didn't stay long. He couldn't buy anything because there wasn't any place he could change money. He reached Ajaccio farther up the west coast in one day with a good southwest wind. He stayed just long enough to change money and top off his diesel. Then he headed for Calvi at the north end of the island. At first the wind was so light that he motored, then it shifted to the southwest and blew hard. It was driving him towards the coast, and he just managed to clear the point and turn into the shelter of the bay. The gale kept him in Calvi for three days.

He left for Monaco in the afternoon. It was an overnight sail and he entered the harbor the next morning. He found a berth between two large power cruisers, the kind that have crews that wear white uniforms. He dropped his anchor and backed down between them. As he was adjusting his stern lines, a couple on the quay stopped and the woman said, "This one isn't a gin palace." Then the man addressed Skip, "What's that in your rigging? Looks like some kind of nests."

"That's baggy-wrinkle. Prevents the mainsail from chafing too much on the shrouds."

"Did you ship your boat on a freighter from San Francisco? I have a cousin who shipped his boat to Southampton, from Boston." Skip thought it odd that someone would ship a boat on a freighter, but then maybe it was a racing boat, or maybe the cousin didn't have the time to sail across the Atlantic.

"I didn't ship it. I sailed all the way."

"From San Francisco? Who do you think would believe such a thing?" And they continued on down the quay, obviously insulted. But what could he do? Some people wouldn't believe that someone would do something that they wouldn't want to do themselves. So it was either tell them a lie that they would believe or tell them a truth that they wouldn't. It was impolite to say nothing.

At the end of a week, the *Oceanid* hadn't shown up in Monaco, so Skip decided to leave and head farther west. First he went up to the Casino the evening before leaving. He had on long trousers, shoes, and a shirt that needed ironing. He bought 100 francs worth of chips and then went looking for a roulette wheel. He put 20 francs on red and lost. Then he put 30 francs on red and lost. Then he put the remaining 50 francs on red and lost that, too. Then he left. He had wanted to test his luck, but decided that gambling wasn't a true test, for it was only about money, and he wasn't that interested in money.

He left Monaco for Nice, and when he was sure that the *Oceanid* wasn't in Nice, he went on to Cannes. He realized that he should have spent the week in Cannes instead of Monaco. But he couldn't stay in Cannes because now he didn't know whether the *Oceanid* was behind him or in front of him. He left the next day for Saint Tropez. There wasn't much wind, but he wanted to save his diesel for when he really needed it. He found a French radio station that was playing American rock 'n' roll, so he brought his radio up and put it on the cabin top and let his sails flap. There were a lot of big power cruisers out. He waited for one to pass him, then he stepped aft and held on to the backstay, while he leaned over the stern. The French station was playing The Drifters, "There Goes My Baby." About half way through the song, just as he had turned to step back into the cockpit, a series of waves rolled *Jest* from gunwale to gunwale. He saw the radio slide off the cabin top, hop across the deck, bounce off the lifeline, and plop into the water. He lost his radio, a

Zenith. He didn't know if he had enough money to buy another one.

Saint Tropez was crowded, both in the harbor and in the town, so he continued on to Porquerolles on Hyeres Island. There are too many places, he realized. The *Oceanid* could be anywhere. He decided to wait in Toulon. Then, as he was approaching the harbor at Toulon, he saw a schooner coming out. He got out his binoculars to identify her: a flush deck, a dodger over the cockpit, and four portholes. It was the *Oceanid*. She was heading southwest. He changed course to follow, and he hoped that he could keep her in sight long enough to determine where she was heading, either Barcelona or Majorca. Then the wind came up from the south. He took in the jib and reefed the main. A little later he took in the main and set the storm trysail. Then he took in the staysail and hove-to.

After the gale, he looked in both Barcelona and Majorca, before continuing west along the Spanish coast. He stopped at Malaga, mainly because he was tired. It was the end of August and he knew that Jo had to leave for America to start college. Probably, he thought, she had already left with her mother from Toulon. After mooring in Malaga, he went below to write his log, but he couldn't find the photo of Jo that he used to mark his place. He looked everywhere, on the chart table, in the drawer underneath, in the locker under the drawer. He took up the floorboards and looked in the bilge, then he picked up the logbook again, holding it by its covers and letting the pages hang down. He shook it hard but it wasn't there. He had lost it.

He left Malaga for Gibraltar, and after passing the red and white Europa Point Lighthouse in the late afternoon, he anchored off the Yacht Club. Here he would buy a new radio and write Anna to meet him in the Canary Islands. He needed money because now he would have to cross the Atlantic to the Caribbean. There was a chance that he would see Jo there, if she visited the *Oceanid* during the Christmas break. Then a few hours after dark, he heard something banging against the boat. He went on deck and found Jo in the water, trying to climb aboard at the shrouds. The *Oceanid* had just anchored behind him. He helped her aboard and said, because he was a little stunned, "You swam in this filthy harbor? You smell like a sump tank." She hushed him and then said, "We can talk later."

So he led her below and helped her take off her wet shirt and shorts. There was still some warm water left from the tea he had made earlier. He poured that into a pan and got a bar of almond soap that he had never used. Then, after putting more water on, he began to wash her with a clean T-shirt. While swimming over, she had kept her head out of the water, so he started at her neck and then washed down her shoulders and arms, her hands, each finger. They did not talk. He was too absorbed in her body to say anything. Although he didn't linger at any one spot, he washed slowly and deliberately. She stood quietly in the middle of the cabin, trembling only slightly as the soapy water dripped down off her body to the deck, and then into the bilge. And although he had turned out the lights, he was sure that she had her eyes shut. He remembered the word Emile had used. Reciprocity. Five syllables. If she thought she was making him a gift, then he had to make her one in return. With the movements of his left hand, his other hand supporting her lightly, first at the shoulder and then at her lower back, he wanted to create an act that was perfect in itself. So that she felt—again he thought of Emile—that he was devoted to her, in this moment, fully and completely.

He washed her back, down to her rear, then her breasts and stomach, down to her button. Still working slowly, but even more deliberately, he washed between her thighs and then her legs below the knees. When he insisted on washing her feet and each individual toe, she had to lean her hands on the table to balance herself. When he was finished, he got clean, warm water from the kettle and started again at the top, with her neck, and rinsed away the almond scented soap that covered her. Finally he dried her with a blue and white pareu.

"I want to kiss you in three secret places."

"Which three places?"

"All on the left side. First the one at your neck, below your ear."

"Wait. What about the other two places?"

"First here."

Later he made tea and she told him that Robert and her mother were becoming impossible. They didn't actually yell at each other, or even argue; instead they bickered continually, so that sitting at the table with them was a form of torture. Plus, Robert told her that her mother had spied on them in Rhodes.

"She saw us kissing, at night in the Old Town. That's why she doesn't want me to see you. But that's not what I wanted to tell you. Until now I've thought that, as Mother said, a man has to court a woman. I see that I've left everything to you. I feel I haven't been fair and now I want to do my part."

"Like what?"

"I don't know yet. As you said in Naples, I still need to sort out Mother. You've got *Jest* and your sailing, but what have I got? Maybe it's my reading. I've always liked to read. When I was a child, Mother would take my book away and send me outside. That's when I began to hide books in the garden, in a hole at the base of a tree. Then once it rained and *The Wind in the Willows,* which was my favorite book then, was ruined. I cried and blamed Mother. I was angry with her but I wouldn't tell her why. And so she became angry with me. I remember that I found that secretly satisfying."

They slept finally, but he woke early for there wasn't enough room for two in the narrow bunk. There was light in the east, and slowly it began to filter through the skylight and fill the cabin with a yellow glow. It seemed to him that he was floating in that light, at the edge of the world, independent of everything, except Jo. The light meant something. It meant that the world had acknowledged him. It was letting him know that he had enough of what he needed and that he could let go of what he didn't need. Later he would row Jo over to the *Oceanid* and she would leave for America. But now that they had made a promise, he knew that he could wait.

When she woke, he got up and made tea. He gave her one of his T-shirts and a pair of shorts. She seemed a little self-conscious, something he had never seen in her before, so he told her she looked beautiful. She laughed at that and told him he wasn't very original. But he didn't feel the need to be original at the moment.

"Then let's talk about the Book of Love."

"Yes, I like chapter three."

"In chapter three remember the meaning of romance."

Las Palmas

He stayed in Gibraltar until the end of October, getting *Jest* ready for the passage across the Atlantic. Gibraltar had ships from all over the world, freighters mainly, but also a Malaysian gunboat and a Turkish destroyer. It was a good place to pick up stores and other ship supplies. Skip took on canned food, tuna, beans, creamed corn, peaches, and tins of crackers and biscuits. He bought a new radio, with additional batteries, extra fuel and oil filters for the engine, charts of the Caribbean, and a new almanac for the year 1965. He wrote out a clean copy of his log and then found the photo of Jo stuck between the endpaper and the back cover of his old log.

Once he cleared the Strait of Gibraltar, he had good winds and reached Las Palmas on Grand Canary in eight days of easy sailing. There were nineteen yachts anchored in the harbor, including the *Oceanid* and the *Jolly Swagman,* which he had last seen in Singapore. Walker was also there, with the *Dolphin.* Skip smiled when he saw the *Dolphin* because he knew that by going up the Red Sea instead of around Africa he had fooled them, both Walker and Jack. He wondered if Walker had been waiting for him in Las Palmas, and for how long.

When he checked at the post office for his mail, he had a letter, not from Anna as he had expected, but from Margaret, Jack's factotum, as he called her, though he knew she was more than that. It was a short letter, mainly saying that she was looking forward to seeing him again and that she had "his mother's things." What things, he wondered. And why now? He had never been really sure of Margaret, had never really trusted her. On the one hand she was always sympathetic towards him, but on the other she worked for Jack, which meant she was Jack's tool, did what Jack wanted her to do. Even now he felt that if she were trying to be helpful to him, then she would have said what things she had. But he couldn't afford to reject her offer altogether, so he wrote in turn a short note that simply said, "What things?"

He had always assumed that there was nothing for him to know about his mother, except what Jack knew, plus, of course, what Jack wanted to tell him. Now Margaret's letter suggested that there was something he could learn about his mother independently of Jack. And if Margaret knew something, then there was a good chance that Walker knew something too. He had intended to avoid Walker, but now he watched until he knew Walker was alone on the *Dolphin*, then took the bottle of Spanish brandy he had bought for the occasion and rowed over to him.

"Ah, I've been expecting you. And Fundador. That's a very good start for whatever it is you want."

He knew beforehand that there wasn't any point in pretending that he didn't want something from Walker; he just didn't want to tell Walker what it was.

"I want to know how Jack got three wives."

"You mean how did he take over a tribe in New Guinea. Well, come below and hear the story behind the story. After Jack found himself stranded in the jungles of New Guinea, the first thing he learned was that if he gave away all the equipment he had, including his uniform, he would gain considerable political power in the tribe. But what really made him king was when he learned that all the men in the tribe were afraid of copulation because they thought it would harm them if they engaged in it without magical protection. So Jack gave them magical protection. Knowing the US Army, he probably had a box of condoms with him, which was enough to make any man king in New Guinea."

"You mean the three wives had nothing to do with it? I thought it was by marrying the three most powerful women in the tribe that he became the most powerful man in the tribe. Isn't that the whole point of *King and Kinship?*"

"That came later, after he became the condom king. The wives were symbols of his power. I guess that's how he consolidated his position in the tribe, once he had given all his condoms away. Of course, from the anthropological point of view, three wives make a better story than a box of condoms, so that's what he stressed in his book. But the story of the three wives caused such a fuss that Jack was forced to defend it. But his defense, unfortunately, took the form of exaggeration, which most of his critics didn't realize, especially when he began to claim that the 'three wives complex', as he calls it, is applicable to contemporary societies."

"Applicable to contemporary societies? You mean he's planning to marry three women?"

"Not actually marry. The three wives complex is not about polygamy but about domination. The idea is quite simple. By controlling three women, a man can control other men. The problem, of course, is the three women. It's hard enough to control one woman, let alone three."

Skip couldn't get anything else of interest out of Walker, and he couldn't make any sense out of Jack's three wives complex and his own mother. He didn't know if he was the son of Cynthia Johns or a New Guinea princess, or if Jack just wanted him to keep guessing. Unless Margaret had some photos of his mother, he would probably never find out.

He received a letter from Jo. She seemed excited about college, even though she wanted to study English instead of French, as her mother wanted her to do. When they last met in Gibraltar, they hadn't had much time to talk. Now she wanted to talk about the future. She wanted to plan it out in a way he had never thought about doing. She was thinking in semesters and four-year college degrees. He was thinking in nautical miles and the next port. And he hoped she realized that however much planning she did, there were some things she couldn't plan. She couldn't plan love. No one could. Well, she planned to be in Barbados for the Christmas break. That was all the planning he needed.

He was ready to leave for Barbados anytime, but he had to wait for Anna. When she finally did arrive, she tried to take her time putting the next installment together. Skip tried to push her, without telling her why, saying she could stay in Las Palmas after he left. But she wouldn't give him the money he needed until she had everything out of him that she wanted. At first she was pleased with the photos he had taken. Those of Lindos and Pompeii made a nice change, she said, from the earlier photos they had published. But she was a little disappointed that he couldn't tell her much about what he had done since Mombasa. She complained that, except for Pompeii, it seemed as if he had just rushed through the Mediterranean without really trying to do or see anything. He tried to describe the gales he had been in, but storms in the Mediterranean didn't seem to interest her. She told him she preferred to have stories about storms when he crossed the Atlantic, and when he told her that he wouldn't meet any storms in the Atlantic that time of year, she told him not to disappoint her too much.

The day he planned to leave Las Palmas he returned from shopping in town to find a dog in his cockpit. There was a note that said, "Dear Skip, This is Charley. He will be your companion. Good Luck, *Sirius*." *Sirius* was one of the yachts that had left that day for Barbados, and Skip guessed that the *Sirius* thought they were doing him a favor by leaving their dog with him. He wondered what to do with the dog. He could take it with him to Barbados and give it back to the *Sirius,* but he didn't want to do that because he didn't want the dog on *Jest*. He couldn't throw it over the side and, after some reflection, he decided he couldn't cook it and eat it. He could ask the other yachts in the harbor if one of them wanted it, but if none did, then all of them would know he had a black cocker spaniel and all of them would wonder what he did with it. So he gave the dog some water and a can of tuna, put the dagger board in the hatchway so it couldn't get below, and thought about what to do.

After three days—three days that he would later regret—he had an answer. The first day he took the dog ashore in the evening and, when no one seemed to be about, tied it to a lamp post and walked away. But he didn't go far and he didn't stay long before he went back, untied the dog and took it back to *Jest*. The second day he took the dog out along the beach to the west, where the hotels were. When he had gone more than a mile, he took the line off the dog and walked away from the beach. The dog followed him all the way back to the harbor. The third day he took the dog and walked to the old part of town, passed the Cathedral of Santa Ana, and then farther south. The dog, as he knew by now, was well behaved. It didn't bark, it didn't jump, and it didn't slobber on him. This was important. When he came to an area where there were children on the street, he stopped and waited, sometimes squatting down to pet the dog. Eventually a boy came over to look at the dog. Skip asked him if he wanted to pet the dog. "Si." Then he asked him if he wanted to take the dog for a walk. "Si." Then he asked him if he wanted to keep the dog. "Si." So Skip gave the line he was holding to the boy, and then he gave him all the pesetas he had left—for the dog—and then he told the boy that the dog was called "Charley."

"Qué?"

"Carlito."

"Si."

Skip watched as the boy led the dog off. It was a nice dog, but he wanted to sail alone, and although some didn't count dogs when it came to being alone, Skip did.

Barbados

He sailed between Grand Canary and Tenerife. The wind was strong between the islands but by the next morning it had eased off and he could still see land astern. To reach Barbados by Christmas, he had to make about 2,800 miles in 26 days. That was about 100 miles a day, or an average of about four and a half knots an hour. With twin headsails set and poled out, he was making five knots in the northeast trades. He caught a fish that looked something like a Barracuda, which he decided was a Wahoo. After taking some photos of it, he cleaned it and filleted it. For lunch he ate some of it raw, marinated in onions, ginger, garlic, and soy sauce. He had some ice, so he was able to chill the rest of the fish. Later in the evening he fried it with ginger and soy sauce, using the last of his sesame oil.

The fifth day out of Las Palmas the wind began to shift to the southwest and ease off. *Jest* made less than 80 miles in twenty-four hours. Then it shifted back to the northwest and then the west and then it died altogether. The wind chart showed a steady northeast trade wind for the month of December. But the trade wind had simply disappeared. With the wind light and variable day after day, there wasn't much he could do. Then he remembered the big headsail in the fo'c'sle, the drifter. He had never used it because he thought it was too big for him to handle alone. It was made of Dacron and in good condition, almost new. He rigged it so that he could take it in from the cockpit. It was cut full and sheeted aft of the shrouds. When the wind fell, the drifter collapsed against the mast and when the wind rose, it snapped out again, pulling *Jest* ahead, but not enough. He began to realize that he wouldn't make Barbados even by New Year's.

On January fourth, 300 miles from Barbados, the northeast trades picked up. A few nights later he sighted the Ragged Point Lighthouse. He hove-to and waited for daylight, then sailed around South Point and up to Bridgetown. He anchored in front of the yacht club, and as soon as the port officials left *Jest,* he got his dinghy over the side and rowed over to the *Oceanid*.

"Come aboard, come on down below. There's a letter for you. Which is more than I got." The schooner looked uncared for. Gear and clothes were everywhere and the deck needed an obvious scrubbing. Bob was alone in the main cabin, drinking local rum, Mount Gay. "Go ahead and read the letter. See if there is anything in it for me."

"Jo sends her love."

"That's nice of her. You know, in the end we all fought, even Jo and I. When Jo fought with Caroline, I told Jo she had to listen to her mother, and Jo told me she didn't have to listen to me. She said she didn't have to listen to either one of us. So I broke up with Caroline, and Jo broke up with Caroline and me, though Jo and I didn't really have any kind of relationship. It must have been bad. Most of the crew left me, too. Well, I saved my boat, but I couldn't save my marriage. But what could I do about Caroline. I arrange a cruise on a yacht around the world and she says I have no imagination."

He stopped listening to Bob and started reading quickly through Jo's letter. She hadn't really sent Bob her love. She didn't mention Bob at all. But it seemed she had broken with her mother. She didn't want to stay at Wesleyan. She was leaving at the end of the semester and she had already applied for a transfer to Berkeley. She said she was still very angry with her mother but didn't want to write about it. She was also, he assumed, still too occupied with her mother to write about anything else. She was looking forward to seeing him in California, of course, but there wasn't much else in the letter. Although there was a poem on a second sheet of paper, he didn't bother to read it when he saw that Jo hadn't written it. For someone who read as much as she did, she seemed rather word-shy.

He left Bob to his rum and rowed into the harbor. He changed some money, bought a chocolate ice cream, then went to the post office. He had another letter from Margaret. She, too, was looking forward to seeing him. His mother's things, as she still called them, had been left with her. They were mostly personal things, clothes and some jewelry. But he would probably be more interested in her photos and letters. He couldn't believe it. What did she mean, "her photos?" Were they photos of his mother, or were they photos his mother had taken? It wasn't likely, it occurred to him, that his mother took photos of herself.

He left the post office to buy pen and paper. Then he went to a hotel on the beach, sat at a table on the veranda and ordered an orange squash. After all, he thought, Barbados is British. He wrote to Margaret, "Send me photos of my mother." Then he had to pause. Where did he want Margaret to send the photos? Panama? No, he'd be there too soon. He closed his eyes, and while he listened to the surf in Barbados, he imagined the west coast of America, from Panama to San Francisco. Acapulco. If he had to stop, he would stop there.

He decided to write Jo as well. He told her about the dog in Las Palmas, about the lack of wind in the Atlantic, and about Bob in Barbados. Then he took out Jo's letter again and read the poem she had sent. It was a love poem that a woman had written. The poet says that her lover kissed her the first time on the fingers, and now she can't wear a ring on that hand. Then he kissed her on the forehead, "and half missed, half falling on the hair." That was a nice touch. And finally he kissed her on the lips, the same lips that she used to declare her love. He looked at the opening lines again, more carefully this time, and then he saw it: the first time he kissed her, it was on the hand that she used to write the poem. He counted the syllables and decided to do a variation of her opening lines:

> *First time I kissed you, I but kissed the eyes*
> *That now you use to read these words of mine.*

To finish his version of the poem, he saw that he still had another twelve lines to kiss the rest of her body.

After mailing the letters, he went to the market and bought some mangos and bread. At the fish stand he hesitated, which led to him buying two flying fish fillets. When he asked how to prepare them, he got different answers: steam them with tomatoes, fry them with bread-crumbs, sauté them with peppers. All at the same time. So when he got back to *Jest,* he did what he usually did with fish: he fried them with onions and garlic.

When the sun was below the horizon, he sat in the cockpit and thought about what he needed to do next. He needed a day or two to fill his water and fuel tanks. Nothing else was holding him in Barbados. Until Jo's letter he hadn't thought about anything after Barbados, but now he had to think about San Francisco. Everyone had always expected him to return to San Francisco. But there was something in him, deep inside, that didn't want him to do what everyone expected. Anna said he had a contract with *World Traveler* and that returning to San Francisco, completing the circumnavigation, was part of it, but he hadn't signed anything. Margaret wanted him to come for "his mother's things." Why, he didn't know. Jack was probably behind it. Jack probably wanted him to return to San Francisco, to complete the circumnavigation, for some reason of his own, probably to take credit for it. But Skip had spent the last four years trying to get away from what Jack wanted, or at least what he thought Jack wanted. Now Jo expected him to return to San Francisco, but with her it was different. She wasn't thinking of the cruise of the *Jest*. She was thinking of him. For that he would return.

Acapulco

When he left Barbados, he sailed off the anchor, letting the engine idle to charge the battery. Now the northeast trades blew steadily, and by the next afternoon, *Jest*, carrying a full main and both headsails, passed between St. Vincent and St. Lucia. *Jest* was sailing near her hull speed, just over seven knots, and she began to log 160 miles from noon to noon. He sat in the cockpit, listening and watching, waiting for something to break, a sheet to snap, a seam to tear, a clew to rip out. But everything held. It was as if *Jest* had found her ideal conditions, the perfect wind and sea. She rose with each wave, then rolled to leeward as the wave slid under her, dipping her port rail in the water. The rhythm of the boat took on a life of its own, so that the days merged with one another and he began to feel the strain on the rigging as nothing more than his own urge to meet the horizon. Then on the evening of the tenth day he sighted the Toro Point Light at Panama and hove-to until morning.

In Cristóbal the canal authorities said *Jest* was too small to go through the locks alone. He would have to tie alongside a tug, and they advised him to buy some extra fenders. There weren't any pilots free to transit with a yacht just then, so while he was waiting, one of the American engineers invited him home for a chicken barbecue. The engineer and his family lived in the residential area in the Canal Zone. In the bright, tropical sun, the houses were chalk white, and although they were surrounded by palm trees, hibiscus, oleander, and over-grown grass, they still had the look of suburbia. He met the wife and daughter, Dolly, who was a few years younger than Skip. When Dolly went to get her records and her parents began to prepare the barbecue, Skip wandered through the house, looking at things: telephone, television, shower and flush toilet, washing machine. He came to a stop in the kitchen, staring at the refrigerator. General Electric. Dolly came in and asked if he wanted anything. He said he wanted to look in the freezer compartment. Inside were ice cubes, a gallon of Neapolitan ice cream, two Popsicles, a box of frozen corn, and three Swanson TV dinners.

Although they cooked outside, they ate inside. In addition to barbecued chicken, they had baked potatoes with sour cream, grilled corn on the cob, and afterwards, ice cream. As Dolly's mother said, everything came from America, including the briquettes to barbecue the chicken on. Afterwards, Dolly played some of her records for Skip. She played one he had never heard before, and when he asked who it was, she looked at him like he was crazy and said it was the Beatles and everyone was just going ape about them. But they're all singing together, he thought, like a choir.

"Aren't they just unreal. And this is a double hit. 'I Saw Her Standing There' and 'I Want to Hold Your Hand'. It's like there's no B-side."

"It's like rock 'n' roll as I know it is finished. Buddy Holly dead, Little Richard gone to religion, Elvis gone to the movies. Who's left? Fats Domino, Jerry Lee Lewis, Sam Cooke. . . ."

"Sam Cooke is dead. He was shot in a hotel in L.A."

"They shot Sam Cooke, too?"

As the engineer drove him back to the yacht club where *Jest* was moored, he began to talk about planning and decisiveness. He stressed the need for decisiveness, that it was an attribute one couldn't be taught. Skip could see that the engineer thought Skip had decisiveness, that sailing a 35-foot boat across the ocean was in some important way decisive. Then the engineer began to talk about college. Skip, the engineer said, should go to college and study engineering, it didn't matter which field. There was a need for all types of engineers. More important, America was going to need men like that, decisive men trained as engineers, for the next war. The next war, Skip asked? It'll be in Indochina. Skip leaned back then and projected a map of southeast Asia in his mind. He started with Malaysia because he had been there and was more familiar with its outline. Then he moved up the map to Burma and Thailand, then over to the right, Cambodia, Laos, and finally Vietnam, before coming to the South China Sea. It seemed an odd part of the world to be decisive about.

Early the next morning he brought *Jest* into the first lock to begin the transit of the canal. Once through the first three locks, he had to cross Gatun Lake. He wanted to transit the canal in one day, so he ran the engine as hard as he dared. It felt strange being on a flat and windless lake, with green jungle everywhere he looked. After he passed through the Gaillard Cut, he had to wait until almost dark before he could catch another tug going through the locks on the Pacific side. Once out of the last lock, he anchored off Balboa and slept, dreaming of packed refrigerators and a war in Indochina.

From Panama to Acapulco it was 1,600 miles. And there weren't any trade winds. There was very little wind at all in the Gulf of Panama, and it took three days to clear

Mala Point, plus another two days to clear Jicarón Island, before he could head northwest. When the wind came from the west, he tacked to starboard. Then it was calm and hot. When the wind came up again, it was from the north, and he tacked to port. He caught a blue and green dorado, but by then he had no ice, so he didn't eat any of it raw, but fried it instead in olive oil with parsley and onions. He followed the coast to the northwest, but he made little progress. In the Gulf of Papagayo *Jest* was knocked down on a clear and cloudless day. He hove-to under trysail, unbent his mainsail and dropped it into the cabin. For the next two days the wind blew out of the mountains, and he sat in the cabin, sewing the seams of his mainsail.

Sometimes the wind was from the south, sometimes from the west. He was close to land in the Gulf of Tehuantepec when he was hit again by a wind that came out of the mountains. He was hove-to for three days, drifting almost forty miles to the south-southwest. Seas frequently broke on deck. During the height of the gale, he discovered a school of doradoes swimming in tight circles under his transom. He hooked one, but it was too heavy for him to lift on board. When the gale blew itself out, the wind died altogether, then came up from the south-southwest. In the evening, twenty-seven days after leaving Panama, he sighted the light at La Yerbabuena, just as it switched on. When the wind died he turned on the engine and powered toward the light, and then later at night he anchored in Acapulco Bay off the yacht club, where he had anchored four years before.

Skip got up early the next morning and rowed across the harbor to town. At the market he bought two mangos and a dozen tortillas, then he went to a store and bought coffee and milk. He was back on *Jest,* drinking coffee and eating tortillas with strawberry jam when Fred rowed over from the *Omoo.* Fred had followed Skip's cruise in *World Traveler* and was very pleased to see him again. After asking Skip a few questions about what he had seen and done, Fred began to talk about his own plans. He had decided not to go to Panama after all but to cross the Pacific to the Marquesas Islands. Skip offered to return the charts that Fred had given him last time he was in Acapulco, but Fred had ordered new charts. Fred was ready to leave, except for the new battery he had ordered. Since his wife had left him, he found that he had a lot more room on the *Omoo* to make changes he had always wanted to make. The extra battery, for example. He had a battery for his engine and another one for his electricity. But he wanted a third one, as a back up, and he was building a cradle for it under the bunk where his wife had slept. As soon as the battery arrived, he'd be ready to leave. As Skip now realized, the *Omoo* had been ready to leave for the last four years. It was Fred who would never be ready.

He had three letters waiting for him at the post office. He took them out and sat on a bench in the shade of a mango tree. Jo said she was already in Berkeley. She wrote about her apartment and the classes she was going to take. She was reconciled with her mother; at least they were on speaking terms, but Jo didn't want her in Berkeley. They almost fought again about that, but in the end her mother stayed in the East. Then Jo went on to say—but he should have realized that this would happen—that she had met Anna, and through Anna, she had met Jack and Margaret. They all wanted to meet Skip when he sailed *Jest* into San Francisco. Skip put the letter down. He would have to think about that.

He opened the manila envelope from Margaret next. Inside was a photo of a young woman. It was a formal portrait. She had on a white blouse and a dark pullover. Her hair was done in a fashion he had seen in movies from the forties: it was piled above her forehead, then pulled back behind her ears, and finally let fall loosely to her shoulders. Her forehead was high, her cheeks full, and her smile included her eyes. She was about eighteen and very pretty. Skip didn't think that the woman in the photo had anything to do with him. But he would have to think about that, too.

Anna said in her letter that *World Traveler* wanted to photograph his arrival in San Francisco. They wanted Skip to bring *Jest* into Sausalito, where he had started his cruise, and anchor off the Tiburon Restaurant. They could get a good shot of him from the restaurant's sundeck. Anna also said he should call her if he needed anything. So he put the letters away, walked back to the post office, and called her. He told her he was in Acapulco and wanted to leave, but that he was having trouble with his engine. He needed his engine to get up the coast.

When the money from Anna arrived, he took *Jest* across the bay and had her hauled out of the water. He cleared out the forward locker and re-installed the head that had originally been there. He even put in a shower that used both fresh and salt water. When he was finished with the head, he scrubbed and painted the bottom of *Jest*. That was all he could do in Acapulco. The rest would have to be done later, farther up the coast. He had *Jest* put back in the water, and after saying good-bye to Fred, he sailed out of Acapulco. He had written one letter, to Jo, saying he was coming.

San Francisco

He knew what Jack wanted him to do next. Jack wanted him to return to San Francisco, so that he could greet Skip with three women. Skip could picture them all standing on the sundeck as he anchored off the Tiburon, the three women all dressed in white, with Jack looming behind, a hand on each of them, as if Jack had grown a third arm. That third arm was Jack's mistake. Jack had gone too far, using too many women to get Skip to return to San Francisco, not just Jo and Anna, but also the woman in the photo that Margaret had sent him.

He hadn't looked at that photo since sitting in the park under the mango tree in Acapulco. He stood up and checked the horizon, sweeping first to windward and then to leeward. It was clear except for the Mexican mainland, partly hidden in the haze. He went below and took out the photo that Margaret had sent him, placing it on his logbook, next to the photo of Jo. He decided that the woman in the photo had not only nothing to do with him, but also nothing to do with Jack. This idea came to him when he glanced over at the photo of Jo and saw that the woman was like Jo, too open to share in Jack's secrets. And since his mother—whoever she was—was one of Jack's secrets, Skip could see that the woman in the photo wasn't his mother. It was then that he realized he would have to decide who his mother was, that he couldn't leave that decision or secret, or whatever it was, to Jack. He closed his logbook, leaving the photo of Jo and the woman face to face. He couldn't give his mother a face, he realized, but he could give her a name. He got out his chart of New Guinea and ran his eyes over the names. So many European names, he thought. Then his eyes stopped in the highlands, at the headwaters of a river: Sari, that was her name, the name of a Papuan Princess.

He counted the miles and days, trying to make them pass as quickly as possible, as he headed up the Mexican coast, sailing as often as he could, and when he couldn't, turning on the engine and motoring. He stopped for fuel in Manzanillo and again in Cabo San Lucas, where he had to fill his fuel tank with a jerry can. Off the coast of Baja the wind blew hard from the northwest, but he refused to heave-to. Instead he set the storm trysail and staysail, letting *Jest* pound into the sea, as he stood in the cockpit, singing "Rave On."

The farther north he went, the colder it became, so that when he sighted the light at Point Loma he was wearing shoes and a jacket. But since it was toward the end of April, it warmed up enough for him to shed some of his clothes as the sun came up behind Coronado. He had been in San Diego before, on the *Astrolabe*. That was over five years ago, but he remembered the harbor, how it made a long sweep to the east around Coronado. He moored at the transient dock at the San Diego Yacht Club, his own yacht club burgee flying at his port spreader. No one was expecting him, so no one paid him any attention. As it was still early in the morning, he hoped to get everything done and leave that same day, or at the very latest, that night.

He had to go into town twice, the first time for food and the second time for clothes. He bought enough food to fill the trunk and back seat of a taxi, including some food that he had never bought before, such as maple syrup, orange marmalade, and chocolate, lots of chocolate. Then he went back into town, to a large department store. He wandered around in the woman's section until he found the right woman, and when she asked if she could help him, he read from the piece of paper he had prepared: cotton trousers, wool sweaters, cotton shorts, polo shirts, underpants, and undershirts—four of each.

"What size are you looking for?" the saleswoman asked.

He knew this could be difficult, because it could be taken the wrong way, but he didn't have a choice. So he said as tentatively as he could, "Your size?"

But the saleswoman treated his request as nothing out of the ordinary, a typical purchase of a tall, dark young man, slightly haggard, slightly anxious. He even ended up buying a few more things, including a flannel nightgown with a Tweety Bird and Sylvester the Cat motif. After he had paid for everything, the saleswoman told him that a woman wouldn't buy so many things at once.

"She would," Skip replied, "if she knew she was going to need them."

From San Diego it took him another five days before he sighted the Farallon Islands to the west of the Golden Gate. By late afternoon, with a moderate wind from the west, he passed under the bridge. He headed up Richardson Bay, and as he sailed past Hurricane Gulch, the wind gusted, as it often did at that point. He noticed he had had the flood coming in, but it was slack water now. The wind began to ease, but it didn't matter, for he was almost there. He could see the Tiburon Restaurant clearly now; then suddenly, as he drew closer, he saw that there were too many people standing on the sundeck. He couldn't moor along side, as he had planned: they would crowd aboard *Jest,* and he wouldn't be able to get them off again.

He brought *Jest* almost up to the sundeck, and then, when she was within a few yards, he released the sheets and let her fall off to starboard. With her sails flapping, *Jest* lost her momentum, came to a stop, and began to drift slowly to leeward, away from the sundeck. He knew that Jack was there, with Anna and Margaret, but his eyes were locked on Jo. There was so much noise, cheering and clapping, that he knew he couldn't make himself heard, so he mouthed his words to her, "Jump. Jump in the water."

Her first motion confused him; then he saw that she was taking off her shoes. As she straightened up, she also took off her sweater, pulling it over her head in one sweeping motion. Next she stepped deliberately to the edge of the sundeck, balanced herself on her toes, and dove into the bay. When she came up under *Jest's* stern, Skip reached down and took her hand and led her around to the lee shrouds where he could help her aboard.

"Welcome aboard. Would you like to go below?"

"What about *Jest?*"

He glanced to leeward: Belvedere, Raccoon Strait, Angel Island. "She has room to drift awhile." Once below, he tried to help her with her wet clothes, but she was too quick for him. He only had time to get towels and pull out the drawer where he stowed the clothes he had bought in San Diego. She slipped on the Tweety Bird and Sylvester the Cat nightgown and crawled into the sleeping bag that he had also remembered to buy.

"You knew I would jump." She said it as a statement, but it was meant as a question.

"I hoped you would. I didn't see how else you could get aboard."

"What would you have done if I hadn't jumped?"

"What would you have done if you hadn't jumped?"

When she stopped shivering, he asked her to sit up, so he could dry her hair some more.

"By the way, where are we heading? Half Moon Bay?"

"No, we're heading for Hawaii."

"Hawaii?" She hesitated only for a moment. "I see. I miss a semester at Berkeley, but find paradise in the islands. Well, the next time we take a trip, I'll do the planning." She let herself fall back on the bunk and snuggled down into the sleeping bag. Then she looked at him, her smile deepening. "Don't look so confused. Just remember that you aren't a single-handed sailor anymore." She rolled away from him, with her face to the hull, so he would go tend to *Jest*.

He hauled in the sheets, jibed *Jest* over to starboard, and headed for the Golden Gate. The wind gusted and *Jest* heeled over, picking up speed. The day had remained clear, and when *Jest* reached the bridge, he could still see the Farallon Islands. Soon the sun would be in his eyes, but later it would be dark. He heard Jo get up and go forward to use the head. Hearing her move around below reminded him of many things. He remembered the last chapter of the Book of Love: you break up, but you give her just one more chance. Well, he thought, they would have to rewrite that chapter. After passing Mile Rock, he remembered that somewhere, stuck in the first volume of his logbook, was a piece of paper with a latitude and longitude written on it:

Sail to position 21° 19′ N, 157° 58′ W

In his mind he could see a string of islands, lying in the tropics. It would be warmer there.

He looked astern. Tomorrow there would be nothing there to see. When the light at Mile Rock blinked on, he went below, switched on his navigation lights and put water on for tea. Jo was sleeping, so he sat at the chart table and wrote in his log:

> *Astern lies Mile Rock—*
> *ahead the sea and the sky*
> *hold another world.*

www.ingramcontent.com/pod-product-compliance
Lightning Source LLC
Chambersburg PA
CBHW031955120726
47898CB00002BA/480